J FIS   17356

Fisher

Open the doors.

"CURRIC
J. EUGE
EASTER
WILLIM
F. R. NC
Will
Will

Demco, Inc. 38-293

DATE DUE

PRINTED IN U.S.A.

Open the Doors

MARGERY FISHER

Open the Doors

17356

THE WORLD PUBLISHING COMPANY

CLEVELAND AND NEW YORK

J

3/68

Published by The World Publishing Company
2231 West 110th Street, Cleveland, Ohio 44102
First American Edition 1967
Library of Congress catalog card number: 67-13821
Text copyright © 1965 by Margery Fisher
New illustrations copyright © 1965 by Brockhampton Press, Ltd.

Printed in the United States of America. Typesetting in Great Britain
Door illustrations by Leslie Marshall, Book Designer: David Adcock

Contents

The Cottage Door

The Three Little Cats and the Three Bad Toms DIANA ROSS — 13
The Christmas Cuckoo FRANCES BROWNE — 23
Puss and Pup JOSEF ČAPEK — 45

The Door of the Great House

The Great Crumbling House BRUCE CARTER — 55
A Picnic at the Mansion ELIZABETH COATSWORTH — 61
Tom Tit Tot AMABEL WILLIAMS-ELLIS — 69
The Slaying of the Wooers ANDREW LANG — 77

The Door of the Shop

Mrs. Cumfitt's Sugar Mice URSULA HOURIHANE — 85
The Saddler's Horse MARGERY WILLIAMS BIANCO — 91
Tumble-down Shop MARY COCKETT — 99
Mrs. Pepperpot Buys Macaroni ALF PRØYSEN — 107

The Garden Gate

A Mysterious Dog LOUISA MAY ALCOTT — 115

5

Teddy Robinson's Night Out JOAN G. ROBINSON 127
Miss Lark's Andrew P. L. TRAVERS 137

The Door of the Train

A Trip by Train HELEN CLARE 149
Riding in the Cars LAURA INGALLS WILDER 159

The Kitchen Door

Dick and the Beanstalk WALTER DE LA MARE 169
Bunchy and the Pastry Dough JOYCE LANKESTER
 BRISLEY 179
Betsy Goes to School DOROTHY CANFIELD 187
The Scarecrow of Scatterbrook BARBARA EUPHAN TODD 193

Trapdoor to the Roof

Galldora and the Little Cat MODWENA SEDGWICK 205
The Wheel on the School MEINDERT DEJONG 217
*The Story of the Elephant Who Pretended to be a
 Mosquito* CLAUDE AVELINE 223

The Door of the School

The China Spaniel RICHARD HUGHES 229
Counting the Class WILLIAM MAYNE 233
Ginger on the Fire Escape ELEANOR ESTES 237

The Bedroom Door

My First Frock and Trousers RICHARD HENGIST
 HORNE ("MRS. FAIRSTAR") 249
The Little Sweep CHARLES KINGSLEY 257

The Gate of the Sports' Field

Football Boots H. E. TODD   267
Marmaduke at the Races ELIZABETH CHAPMAN   275
Jennings Arrives Late ANTHONY BUCKERIDGE   281

Miniature Doors

Maria Makes Friends T. H. WHITE   293
Conversation with a Salmon MARGARET J. MILLER   301

The Stable Door

Brownie's Ride DINAH CRAIK   311
The Roundup KATE SEREDY   327
Rosina Copper KITTY BARNE   337

Field Gates

Slipper-Slopper ALISON UTTLEY   347
The Fire Engine Runs Away LEILA BERG   355
Little Boy Pie ELEANOR FARJEON   367
Mary Plants the Hose-in-Hose JULIANA EWING   373

Guide to Further Reading   383

Index   395

ACKNOWLEDGMENTS

The editor and The World Publishing Company herewith render thanks to the following authors, publishers, and agents whose interest, co-operation, and permission to reprint have made possible the preparation of *Open the Doors*.

Alison Uttley and Faber & Faber Ltd., for "Slipper-Slopper" from *The Adventures of No Ordinary Rabbit*, copyright 1937 by Alison Uttley. Reprinted by permission of Faber & Faber Ltd.
Amabel Williams-Ellis, for "Tom Tit Tot" from *Fairies and Enchanters*, copyright 1934 by Amabel Williams-Ellis. Reprinted by permission of Amabel Williams-Ellis.
Anthony Buckeridge, for "Jennings Arrives Late" from *Jennings Goes to School*, copyright 1950 by Anthony Buckeridge. Reprinted by permission of Anthony Buckeridge.
Astor-Honor, Inc., for "Mrs. Pepperpot Buys Macaroni" from *Little Old Mrs. Pepperpot* by Alf Prøysen, copyright 1956 by Alf Prøysen. An Astor Book, reprinted by permission of Astor-Honor, Inc.
A. Watkins, Inc., for "The China Spaniel" from *The Spider's Palace* by Richard Hughes, copyright 1932 by Richard Hughes. Reprinted by permission of A. Watkins, Inc.
Barbara Euphan Todd, for "The Scarecrow of Scatterbrook" from *Worzel Gummidge*, copyright 1936 by Barbara Euphan Todd. Reprinted by permission of Barbara Euphan Todd.
Bruce Carter and Hamish Hamilton Ltd., for "The Great Crumbling House" from *Tricycle Tim*, copyright 1957 by Bruce Carter. Reprinted by permission of Hamish Hamilton Ltd.
Claude Aveline and George G. Harrap & Co. Ltd., for "The Story of the Elephant Who Pretended to be a Mosquito" from *The Bird that Flew into the Sea and Other Stories*, copyright 1961 by Claude Aveline. Reprinted by permission of George G. Harrap & Co. Ltd.
Diana Ross and Faber & Faber Ltd., for "The Three Little Cats and the Three Bad Toms" from *The Golden Hen*, copyright 1942 by Diana Ross. Reprinted by permission of Faber & Faber Ltd.
Elizabeth Chapman and Brockhampton Press Ltd., for "Marmaduke at the Races" from *Marmaduke and His Friends*, copyright 1958 by Elizabeth Chapman. Reprinted by permission of Brockhampton Press Ltd.
Evans Brothers Ltd., for "Rosina Copper" from *Rosina Copper* by Kitty

Acknowledgments

Barne, copyright 1954 by Kitty Barne. Reprinted by permission of Evans Brothers Ltd.

Francesco M. Bianco, for "The Saddler's Horse" from *A Street of Little Shops* by Margery Williams Bianco, copyright 1932 by Margery Williams Bianco. Renewal, 1960, by Francesco M. Bianco. Reprinted by permission of Francesco M. Bianco, Assignee of the Estate of Margery Williams Bianco.

G. P. Putnam's Sons, for "Maria Makes Friends" from *Mistress Masham's Repose* by T. H. White, copyright 1946 by T. H. White; Capricorn Edition. Reprinted by permission of G. P. Putnam's Sons.

Harcourt, Brace & World, Inc., for "Ginger on the Fire Escape" from *Ginger Pye* by Eleanor Estes, copyright 1951 by Eleanor Estes. Reprinted by permission of Harcourt, Brace & World, Inc.; for "Miss Lark's Andrew" from *Mary Poppins* by P. L. Travers, copyright 1934 by Harcourt, Brace, Inc. Renewal, 1962, by P. L. Travers. Reprinted by permission of Harcourt, Brace & World, Inc.

Harold Ober Associates, Inc., for "Little Boy Pie" from *Jim at the Corner* by Eleanor Farjeon, copyright 1934 by Eleanor Farjeon. Reprinted by permission of Harold Ober Associates, Inc.

Harper & Row, Publishers, Inc., for "Riding in the Cars" from *By the Shores of Silver Lake* by Laura Ingalls Wilder, copyright 1939 by Harper & Row, Publishers, Inc.; for "The Wheel on the School" from *The Wheel on the School* by Meindert DeJong, copyright 1954 by Meindert DeJong. Reprinted by permission of Harper & Row, Publishers, Inc.

Helen Clare, for "A Trip by Train" from *Five Dolls in the Snow*, copyright 1957 by Helen Clare. Reprinted by permission of Helen Clare.

H. E. Todd and Brockhampton Press Ltd, for "Football Boots" from *Bobby Brewster's Shadow*, copyright 1956 by H. E. Todd. Reprinted by permission of Brockhampton Press Ltd.

Holt, Rinehart and Winston, Inc., for "Betsy Goes to School" from *Understood Betsy* by Dorothy Canfield, copyright 1916, 1917 by The Century Company. Copyright 1916, 1917 by Holt, Rinehart and Winston, Inc. Copyright 1944, 1945 by Dorothy Canfield Fisher. Copyright 1946 by Holt, Rinehart and Winston, Inc. Reprinted by permission of Holt, Rinehart and Winston, Inc.

Joan G. Robinson and George G. Harrap & Co. Ltd, for "Teddy Robinson's Night Out" from *Teddy Robinson*, copyright 1953 by Joan G. Robinson. Reprinted by permission of George G. Harrap & Co. Ltd.

Joyce Lankester Brisley and George G. Harrap & Co. Ltd., for "Bunchy and the Pastry Dough" from *Bunchy*, copyright 1937 by Joyce Lankester Brisley. Reprinted by permission of George G. Harrap & Co. Ltd.

9

Acknowledgments

Leila Berg and Brockhampton Press Ltd., for "The Fire Engine Runs Away" from *Fire Engine By Mistake*, copyright 1955 by Leila Berg. Reprinted by permission of Brockhampton Press Ltd.

Modwena Sedgwick, for "Galldora and the Little Cat" from *Adventures of Galldora*, copyright 1960 by Modwena Sedgwick. Reprinted by permission of Modwena Sedgwick.

Margaret J. Miller and Brockhampton Press Ltd, for "Conversation with a Salmon" from *Doctor Boomer*, copyright 1964 by Margaret J. Miller. Reprinted by permission of Brockhampton Press Ltd.

Mary Cockett and George G. Harrap & Co. Ltd., for "Tumble-down Shop" from *Out With Felicity and Jonathan*, copyright 1962 by Mary Cockett. Reprinted by permission of George G. Harrap & Co. Ltd.

The Literary Trustees of Walter de la Mare and the Society of Authors, for "Dick and the Beanstalk" from *Collected Stories for Children* by Walter de la Mare, copyright 1947 by Walter de la Mare. Reprinted by permission of The Literary Trustees of Walter de la Mare.

The Macmillan Company, for "A Picnic at the Mansion" from *Alice-All-By-Herself* by Elizabeth Coatsworth, copyright 1937 by The Macmillan Company. Renewal, 1965, by Elizabeth Coatsworth Beston. Reprinted by permission of the Macmillan Company.

The Viking Press, Inc., for "The Roundup" from *The Good Master* by Kate Seredy, copyright 1935 by Kate Seredy. Renewal, 1963, by Kate Seredy. Reprinted by permission of The Viking Press, Inc.

Ursula Hourihane and Methuen & Co. Ltd., for "Mrs. Cumfitt's Sugar Mice" from *Sugar and Spice*, copyright 1956 by Ursula Hourihane. Reprinted by permission of Methuen & Co. Ltd.

William Mayne and Hamish Hamilton Ltd, for "Counting the Class" from *The Fishing Party*, copyright 1960 by William Mayne. Reprinted by permission of Hamish Hamilton Ltd.

W. W. Norton & Company, Inc., for "Puss and Pup" from *Harum-Scarum* by Josef Čapek, copyright 1959 by Josef Čapek. English translation copyright 1963 by Methuen & Company, Ltd. Reprinted by permission of W. W. Norton & Company, Ltd.

The
Cottage Door

Diana Ross's stories open the door to worlds that are partly remem-
bered and partly imagined. The Little Red Engine of her picture story
books trundles through a very English landscape, and in a cottage that
could come straight out of an English village, gentle Miss Pussy tries
to reform Mr. Jackanapes. The story I have chosen here belongs to the
stories of Miss Pussy, and was one of the first that Diana Ross wrote.
At the time she was moving from place to place with her soldier husband
and "wherever we went we took basic furniture and tried to create a
decent home, so the story was very much based on the struggle one al-
ways has, of chaos against order." All her stories, she says, are rooted
in reality: every setting is a known place and generally the stories start
from a real experience. Because cats were always prominent members
of her family, they were the "alternative people" for her when she was a
child—which may explain why the cats in this story are extremely
feline and yet human in the way they behave.

DIANA ROSS

The Three Little Cats and the Three Bad Toms

ONCE upon a time there were three little cats who lived in a little house set back from the road, with a garden in front where they grew flowers, and a big garden behind where they had apple trees and a vegetable patch.

And what good little creatures they were!

Every day they turned out every single room; every day they changed and washed and mended their clothes; and they would never dream of going to sleep without first putting clean sheets on the bed, all smelling sweet of lavender fresh from the airing cupboard.

And how the silver shone! And what a polish on the furniture!

Some people might have thought them too particular, but since they had the time and the will, I, for one, cannot think them mistaken.

Their names were Miss Tabitha, Miss Malkin and Miss Agatha, and so dearly did they love each other they never were apart. If they went into market, or out on a picnic, where one went the other went, and from year's end to year's end not a cross word between them.

Now one day, RAT TAT TAT! Someone at the door.

13

Miss Tabby ran with her duster in her hand and was the first to open it.

But, oh dear! what a sight she saw.

On the clean white threshold stood a big Tom cat, big and black and ugly. One of his eyes was completely closed, his ears were only two stumps crumpled on his head; his fur was matted, and torn from his sides; his nose was scratched and bleeding, and as he stood there he held one leg in the air, and it looked as if it must be broken from the way it hung.

But this was not the worst, for behind him was a big ugly ginger cat, and if one was villainous to look at, this other was no less so.

And behind him again was a third, who might have been white, only it was hard to tell, the mud and dust and blood so matted his coat. Miss Tabby had never seen such bedraggled, filthy, smelly creatures in all her life.

Standing there not knowing what to do, she hardly could decide whether to pity them most or be most disgusted.

But little Miss Agatha, running by at that moment, cried, "Heaven help us! Whatever has happened? Bring them in and let us revive them. I never saw such miserable creatures in all my life!"

"Miserable yourself," snarled the big black Tom.

"Creature to you!" hissed the Ginger.

"We mean to come in, for that is what we came for," said the last, and the three strange Toms staggered into the little room.

Miss Malkin, who by now had run in from the garden, busied herself with getting chairs, and Miss Agatha ran for a bowl of warm water and their biggest brush and a comb, and Tabitha hurried to the kitchen to see what the larder contained most likely to revive the strangers.

When they all returned, the Toms were sprawling about

with such savage looks in their solitary eyes that the three little cats hardly knew how to introduce the subject of washing.

"Excuse us," said Tabby, "the water will not be a moment now."

"Water!" said the Black. "And what shall I do with water?"

"Water is good for drowning," sneered the Ginger.

"Kittens," added the White, with a laugh that quite put the sisters in a tremble.

"Well, here is a brush and here is the comb," said Agatha shyly.

"I've never used a brush or comb."

"I never want to use one," said the second.

"I am what I am, and that's good enough for me," said the third.

"And that's that!" added the Black.

Never had the three sisters heard such language in their house and they hurried into the kitchen, where the stew was heating up nicely, to discuss this sudden invasion and decide what to do about it.

"Whoever can they be?" said Tabitha.

"Wherever have they come from?" said Malkin.

"Whatever do they want?" wondered Agatha.

"However shall we get rid of them?" said Tabitha.

"Poor things, their sufferings make them savage," said Malkin.

"Let's feed them first and question them after," said Agatha. And since the stew was now ready they carried it in on a tray with three little bowls to serve it in.

In the few moments they had been gone, what had happened to their room! The Toms seemed to have tried every chair there was and left a stain on each. The cushions were thrown about the floor and the Black was lounging on the sofa and the other two were sitting on the table.

No sooner did they see the food than they each of them made a rush at the tray and tipped it up so that much of the stew was spilled upon the floor.

Miss Tabitha said,

"Just a moment. I will serve you and that will make it easier." And the others ran out to get a cloth to wipe up the mess.

When the cats had been served they began to eat.

"Too hot," said the Black, and spilled it out on the carpet.

"Too cold," said the Ginger, and threw it out of the window.

"Not enough," said the White, with his mouth full, and held out his dish for more.

Miss Malkin brought them some milk.

"Watered," said the Black.

"Sour," said the Ginger.

"Not enough," said the White, and they poured their milk into the fireplace.

"Excuse me," said Miss Tabitha. "Who are you and what do you come for?"

"I'm Tom," said the Black.

"I'm Tom Trotter," said the Ginger.

"I'm Tom Tricer," said the White.

"And we've come to marry you," said Tom.

"Don't you wish you may?" sneered Tom Trotter.

"But now we are tired and must go to bed," said Tom Tricer.

"And hurry up about it," said Tom.

The three little cats were too astonished to speak. They led the strangers upstairs to their bedroom, where three little beds were set side by side opposite the window.

All filthy as they were the three Toms fell immediately into bed and shouted at the sisters to be quick and draw the blinds; and were asleep and snoring horribly before the little cats were well out of the room.

"Did you ever hear the like?" said Tabitha.

"Did you ever see the like?" said Malkin.

"And as for their asking to marry us, I don't know whether to laugh or cry," said Agatha.

And they began to talk it over this way and that and couldn't reach the end of it.

"As politely as we can without hurting their feelings we must certainly tell them we cannot possibly marry them," said Agatha.

"Indeed," said Malkin. "It's a pity to disappoint them, for it seems to me that they are the kind of people for whom everything goes wrong. But all the same we really couldn't marry them."

"I hope we shall not break their hearts," said Tabitha. "Everything else about them seems broken."

And then they went hurrying about the house trying to get it to rights again, and it was past their bedtime before they had done so.

As the strangers were sleeping in their beds the three sisters had to make do with the hearth rug and the sofa.

In the morning they got up rather nervously, and tiptoed up to knock on the strangers' door.

"Let us be," cried Tom.

"Bring us our breakfast," cried Trotter.

"Can't you see we are ill?" screamed Tricer. Which was an unreasonable remark, because the sisters were still outside the door and could therefore see nothing.

But now they timidly opened the door, and sure enough the three Toms looked pretty bad, but whether from disease or dirt or temper it would have been hard to decide.

"If you are ill we will call the doctor," said Tabitha.

"If you call the doctor he will need one himself," cried Tom.

"And plaster!" said Trotter.

17

"And bandages!" said Tricer.

But the sisters had already gone off to fetch him; at least Agatha had gone because she could run the fastest, and the other two were busy getting the breakfast.

When the doctor came and they took him upstairs he only showed his nose round the door and such a screaming, cater-wauling, yowling and screeching, the doctor ran downstairs again as fast as he could.

"Rest and quiet, rest and quiet," he said. "And that will be ten dollars, please," and he hurried down the garden path without even waiting for his bill to be settled.

Well, the three little sisters didn't know what to do, but since the strangers upstairs really seemed to be ill they decided each to nurse one until they should be better.

"I will look after Tom," said Tabitha. "I think that I can manage him."

"I will look after Tom Trotter. He doesn't seem to be quite so rude to me," said Malkin, with a sigh.

"And I will take care of Tom Tricer. And when they are better and are gone we shall have to have a spring cleaning."

So then what a life began!

They cooked delicate and tempting dishes and the Toms wouldn't eat them, but spilled them all over the bed.

They tried to comb their matted hair and dress their wounds, but the Toms screamed and scratched so, the sisters were no match for them.

They tried to tidy the room, and the Toms threw things at their heads; they were glad to get out alive.

But if for a moment they left the invalids alone, there'd be cries of,

"Come here!" "Is this the way you care for the sick?" "Are we to be left to die alone?" and all sorts of cruel and unkind things.

In this way a week passed by and the three little cats were worn to a shadow. And with it all, the Toms seemed to grow worse.

One day, when they went up in the morning, the room seemed strangely quiet, and on going in, the sisters found the Toms not sleeping as they had supposed, but lying with their eyes open, too weak to misbehave, and obviously at the point of death.

Each little cat ran to the bed of her patient and when they saw how matters stood they could not help it, but began to cry.

"Alas," cried Tabitha. "I hoped he would get better and perhaps grow tamer after all."

"Poor Trotter," cried Malkin. "Now you will never be able to learn how nice it can be to be clean."

"Oh! Tricer," wept Agatha, "what a miserable life yours must have been, and now you will never know a better."

And their tears overflowed onto the pillow and wetted the cheeks of the three sick Toms.

And then! Whatever has happened?

The dying Toms jumped up from their beds! But changed! You cannot imagine it!

Sleek and fat with a smooth and shining coat, whiskers quivering with delight, ears no longer crumpled, tails held proudly and each with two bright eyes shining and winking at the sisters.

"Mercy on us!" cried Agatha. "Whatever has happened?"

"Your tears have made us whole," said Tom with a gracious bow, and in such a voice, summer honey from the south could not have been more sweet.

"Had your tears not touched us we must have died," said Tom Trotter, in a quiet and gentle yowl.

"And never have resumed our proper shape," said Tricer, jumping lightly from the bed and stretching from the tips of his toes to the quivering tip of his tail.

"Tell them our story," said Trotter.

And Tom turned politely to the sisters.

"We were cursed," he said, "and a terrible curse it was. One day we saw a cat as villainous and miserable as we appeared but now. In our foolishness and pride we mocked it, condemned it, and never thought to inquire into the circumstances which had led it into such a condition.

"For this unkindness we were condemned to appear the frightful, brutal, horrifying creatures we have been till now, and we should not be released until a tear should fall upon us, shed in pity and not in anger."

"Tears we have caused in plenty," said Trotter.

"But never before of pity."

And now you can believe it, if the sisters shed tears they were tears of joy! And the three Tom cats came elegantly downstairs and behaved in such a way the sisters were sure they could only have grown up at court.

And the very next day they went to the church and were

married, and three such charming and graceful couples you never did see before or since.

And they lived all together in their pretty little house until a growing family of kittens obliged them to move into a larger.

And of them all it would be hard to tell who were the neater, the most thoughtful or the most particular, Tabitha, Malkin, and Agatha, or Tom, Tom Trotter, and Tom Tricer.

From THE GOLDEN HEN
Illustrated by Gri

"The Christmas Cuckoo' has the form and atmosphere of a fairy tale and the affectionate wisdom and simplicity that belong to Frances Browne. The daughter of a postmaster in a small Irish village, she was born blind, but her imagination created people and places entirely real to her. The stories that were read to her she told again to younger brothers and sisters, and added others of her own in the same vein. In 1857 a collection of her stories was published under the title "Granny's Wonderful Chair". As a linking device for the stories, she described a little girl, Snowflower, living with a grandmother who gave her for company, when she had to go away for a time, a chair with the power of storytelling. Snowflower is summoned by the king of the country to a court full of self-seeking and greed, and, as each story is told, its lesson of humility and simple goodness goes home to the hearts of the courtiers. Frances Browne has an assured place with Juliana Ewing and Mary Molesworth for the charming way she uses fairy tale to convey lessons of behavior to the nursery.

FRANCES BROWNE

The Christmas Cuckoo

ONCE upon a time there stood in the midst of a bleak moor, in the north country, a certain village. All its inhabitants were poor, for their fields were barren and they had little trade; but the poorest of them all were two brothers called Scrub and Spare, who followed the cobbler's craft and had but one stall between them. It was a hut built of clay and wattles. The door was low and always open by day, for there was no window. The roof did not entirely keep out the rain and the only thing comfortable about it was a wide hearth, for which the brothers could never find wood enough to make a sufficient fire. There they worked in most brotherly friendship, though with little encouragement.

The people of that village were not extravagant in shoes, and better cobblers than Scrub and Spare might be found. Spiteful people said there were no shoes so bad that they would not be worse for their mending. Nevertheless Scrub and Spare managed to live between their own trade, a small barley field and a cottage garden, till one unlucky day when a new cobbler arrived in the village. He had lived in the capital city of the kingdom, and by his own account cobbled for the queen and the princesses. His awls were sharp, his lasts were new; he set up his stall in a neat cottage with two windows. The villagers soon found out that one patch of his would wear two of the brothers'. In short, all the mending left Scrub and Spare and went to the new cobbler. The season had been wet and cold, their barley did not ripen well and the cabbages never half closed in the garden. So the brothers were poor that winter, and when Christmas came they had nothing to feast on but a barley loaf, a piece of rusty bacon and some small beer of their own brewing. Worse than that, the snow was very deep and they could get no firewood. Their hut stood at the end of the village and beyond it spread the bleak moor, now all white and silent; but that moor had once been a forest and great roots of old trees were still to be found in it, loosened from the soil and laid bare by the winds and rains—one of these, a rough, gnarled log, lay hard by their door, the half of it above the snow, and Spare said to his brother:

"Shall we sit here cold on Christmas while the great root lies yonder? Let us chop it up for firewood; the work will make us warm."

"No," said Scrub;"it's not right to chop wood on Christmas; besides, that root is too hard to be broken with any hatchet."

"Hard or not, we must have a fire," replied Spare. "Come, brother, help me in with it. Poor as we are, there is nobody in the village will have such a yule log as ours."

Scrub liked a little grandeur, and in hopes of having a fine yule log both brothers strained and strove with all their might till, between pulling and pushing, the great old root was safe on the hearth and beginning to crackle and blaze with the red embers. In high glee the cobblers sat down to their beer and bacon. The door was shut, for there was nothing but cold moonlight and snow outside; but the hut, strewn with fir boughs, and ornamented with holly, looked cheerful as the ruddy blaze flared up and rejoiced their hearts.

"Long life and good fortune to ourselves, brother!" said Spare. "I hope you will drink that toast, and may we never have a worse fire on Christmas—but what is that?"

Spare set down the drinking horn, and the brothers listened astonished, for out of the blazing root they heard, "Cuckoo! cuckoo!" as plain as ever the spring bird's voice came over the moor on a May morning.

"It is something bad," said Scrub, terribly frightened.

"Maybe not," said Spare; and out of the deep hole at the side which the fire had not reached flew a large gray cuckoo, and lit on the table before them. Much as the cobblers had been surprised, they were still more so when it said:

"Good gentlemen, what season is this?"

"It's Christmas," said Spare.

"Then a merry Christmas to you!" said the cuckoo. "I went to sleep in the hollow of that old root one evening last summer and never woke till the heat of your fire made me think it was summer again; but now, since you have burned my lodging, let me stay in your hut till the spring comes 'round—I only want a hole to sleep in, and when I go on my travels next summer be assured I will bring you some present for your trouble."

"Stay, and welcome," said Spare, while Scrub sat wondering if it were something bad or not; "I'll make you a good warm hole in the thatch. But you must be hungry after that long sleep. Here is a slice of barley bread. Come, help us to keep Christmas!"

The cuckoo ate up the slice, drank water from the brown jug, for he would take no beer, and flew into a snug hole which Spare scooped for him in the thatch of the hut.

Scrub said he was afraid it wouldn't be lucky; but as it slept on and the days passed he forgot his fears. So the snow melted, the heavy rains came, the cold grew less, the days lengthened, and one sunny morning the brothers were awakened by the cuckoo shouting its own cry to let them know the spring had come.

"Now I'm going on my travels," said the bird, "over the world to tell men of the spring. There is no country where trees bud or flowers bloom that I will not cry in before the year goes 'round. Give me another slice of barley bread to keep me on my journey and tell me what present I shall bring you at the twelvemonth's end."

Scrub would have been angry with his brother for cutting so large a slice, their store of barley meal being low; but his mind was occupied with what present would be most prudent to ask; at length a lucky thought struck him.

"Good master cuckoo," said he, "if a great traveler who

26

sees all the world like you, could know of any place where diamonds or pearls were to be found, one of a tolerable size brought in your beak would help such poor men as my brother and I to provide something better than barley bread for your next entertainment."

"I know nothing of diamonds or pearls," said the cuckoo; "they are in the hearts of rocks and the sands of rivers. My knowledge is only of that which grows on the earth. But there are two trees hard by the well that lies at the world's end: one of them is called the golden tree, for its leaves are all of beaten gold; every winter they fall into the well with a sound like scattered coin, and I know not what becomes of them. As for the other, it is always green like a laurel. Some call it the wise, and some the merry tree. Its leaves never fall, but they that get one of them keep a blithe heart in spite of all misfortunes and can make themselves as merry in a hut as in a palace."

"Good master cuckoo, bring me a leaf off that tree!" cried Spare.

"Now, brother, don't be a fool!" said Scrub. "Think of the leaves of beaten gold! Dear master cuckoo, bring me one of them!"

Before another word could be spoken, the cuckoo had flown out of the open door, and was shouting its spring cry over moor and meadow. The brothers were poorer than ever that year; nobody would send them a single shoe to mend. The new cobbler said in scorn they should come to be his apprentices; and Scrub and Spare would have left the village but for their barley field, their cabbage garden and a certain maid called Fairfeather, whom both the cobblers had courted for seven years without even knowing which she meant to favor.

Sometimes Fairfeather seemed inclined to Scrub, sometimes she smiled on Spare; but the brothers never disputed for

27

that. They sowed their barley, planted their cabbage and, now that their trade was gone, worked in the rich villagers' fields to make out a scanty living. So the seasons came and passed: spring, summer, harvest and winter followed each other as they have done from the beginning. At the end of the last, Scrub and Spare had grown so poor and ragged that Fairfeather thought them beneath her notice. Old neighbors forgot to invite them to wedding feasts or merrymaking; and they thought the cuckoo had forgotten them too, when at daybreak, on the first of April, they heard a hard beak knocking at their door and a voice crying:

"Cuckoo! cuckoo! Let me in with my presents."

Spare ran to open the door, and in came the cuckoo, carrying in one side of his bill a golden leaf larger than that of any tree in the north country; and in the other, one like that of the common laurel, only it had a fresher green.

"Here," it said, giving the gold to Scrub and the green to Spare, "it is a long way from the world's end. Give me a slice of barley bread, for I must tell the north country that the spring has come."

Scrub did not grudge the thickness of that slice, though it was cut from their last loaf. So much gold had never been in the cobbler's hands before and he could not help exulting over his brother.

"See the wisdom of my choice!" he said, holding up the large leaf of gold. "As for yours, as good might be plucked from any hedge. I wonder a sensible bird would carry the like so far."

"Good master cobbler," cried the cuckoo, finishing the slice, "your conclusions are more hasty than courteous. If your brother be disappointed this time, I go on the same journey every year, and for your hospitable entertainment will think it no trouble to bring each of you whichever leaf you desire."

"Darling cuckoo," cried Scrub, "bring me a golden one";

and Spare, looking up from the green leaf on which he gazed as though it were a crown jewel, said:

"Be sure to bring me one from the merry tree," and away flew the cuckoo.

"This is the Feast of All Fools, and it ought to be your birthday," said Scrub. "Did ever man fling away such an opportunity of getting rich! Much good your merry leaves will do in the midst of rags and poverty!" So he went on, but Spare laughed at him and answered with quaint old proverbs concerning the cares that come with gold, till Scrub, at length getting angry, vowed his brother was not fit to live with a respectable man; and taking his lasts, his awls and his golden leaf, he left the wattle hut and went to tell the villagers.

They were astonished at the folly of Spare and charmed with Scrub's good sense, particularly when he showed them the golden leaf, and told that the cuckoo would bring him one every spring. The new cobbler immediately took him into partnership, the greatest people sent him their shoes to mend, Fairfeather smiled graciously upon him and in the course of that summer they were married, with a grand wedding feast, at which the whole village danced, except Spare, who was not invited, because the bride could not bear his low-mindedness, and his brother thought him a disgrace to the family.

Indeed all who heard the story concluded that Spare must be mad, and nobody would associate with him but a lame tinker, a beggar boy and a poor woman reputed to be a witch because she was old and ugly. As for Scrub, he established himself with Fairfeather in a cottage close by that of the new cobbler, and quite as fine. There he mended shoes to everybody's satisfaction, had a scarlet coat for holidays and a fat goose for dinner every wedding day. Fairfeather, too, had a crimson gown and fine blue ribands; but neither she nor Scrub were content, for to buy this grandeur the golden leaf had to be broken and parted with piece by piece, so the last morsel was gone before the cuckoo came with another.

Spare lived on in the old hut, and worked in the cabbage garden. (Scrub had got the barley field because he was the elder.) Every day his coat grew more ragged, and the hut more weather-beaten; but people remarked that he never looked sad nor sour; and the wonder was that, from the time they began to keep his company, the tinker grew kinder to the poor ass with which he traveled the country, the beggar boy kept out of mischief and the old woman was never cross to her cat or angry with the children.

Every first of April the cuckoo came tapping at their doors with the golden leaf to Scrub and the green to Spare. Fairfeather would have entertained him nobly with wheaten bread and honey, for she had some notion of persuading him to bring two gold leaves instead of one; but the cuckoo flew away to eat barley bread with Spare, saying he was not fit company for fine people, and liked the old hut where he slept so snugly from Christmas till spring.

Scrub spent the golden leaves, and Spare kept the merry ones; and I know not how many years passed in this manner, when a certain great lord who owned that village came to the neighborhood. His castle stood on the moor. It was ancient and strong, with high towers and a deep moat. All the country, as far as one could see from the highest turret, belonged to its lord; but he had not been there for twenty years, and would not have come then, only he was melancholy. The cause of his grief was that he had been prime minister at court and in high favor, till somebody told the crown prince that he had spoken disrespectfully concerning the turning out of his royal highness's toes, and of the king that he did not lay on taxes enough, whereon the north country lord was turned out of office and banished to his own estate. There he lived for some weeks in very bad temper. The servants said nothing would please him, and the villagers put on their worst clothes lest he should raise their rents; but one day in the harvest time his lordship chanced to meet Spare gathering watercress at a meadow stream, and fell into talk with the cobbler.

How it was nobody could tell, but from the hour of that discourse the great lord cast away his melancholy; he forgot his lost office and his court enemies, the king's taxes and the crown prince's toes, and went about with a noble train, hunting, fishing and making merry in his hall, where all travelers were entertained and all the poor were welcome. This strange story spread through the north country, and great company came to the cobbler's hut—rich men who had lost their money, poor men who had lost their friends, beauties who had grown old, wits who had gone out of fashion— all came to talk with Spare, and whatever their troubles had been, all went home merry. The rich gave him presents, the poor gave him thanks. Spare's coat ceased to be ragged, he had bacon with his cabbage and the villagers began to think there was some sense in him.

By this time his fame had reached the capital city, and even the court. There were a great many discontented people there besides the king, who had lately fallen into ill-humor because a neighboring princess, with seven islands for her dowry, would not marry his eldest son. So a royal messenger was sent to Spare, with a velvet mantle, a diamond ring and a command that he should repair to court immediately.

"Tomorrow is the first of April," said Spare, "and I will go with you two hours after sunrise."

The messenger lodged all night at the castle, and the cuckoo came at sunrise with the merry leaf.

"Court is a fine place," he said, when the cobbler told him he was going, "but I cannot come there, they would lay snares and catch me; so be careful of the leaves I have brought you, and give me a farewell slice of barley bread."

Spare was sorry to part with the cuckoo, little as he had of his company, but he gave him a slice which would have broken Scrub's heart in former times—it was so thick and large—and, having sewed up the leaves in the lining of his leathern doublet, he set out with the messenger on his way to court.

His coming caused great surprise there. Everybody wondered what the king could see in such a common looking man; but scarce had his majesty conversed with him half an hour, when the princess and her seven islands were forgotten, and orders given that a feast for all comers should be spread in the banquet hall. The princes of the blood, the great lords and ladies, ministers of state and judges of the land, after that, discoursed with Spare, and the more they talked the lighter grew their hearts, so that such changes had never been seen at court. The lords forgot their spites and the ladies their envies, the princes and ministers made friends among themselves, and the judges showed no favor.

As for Spare, he had a chamber assigned him in the palace and a seat at the king's table; one sent him rich robes and another costly jewels; but in the midst of all his grandeur he still wore the leathern doublet, which the palace servants thought remarkably shabby. One day, the king's attention being drawn to it by the chief page, his majesty inquired why Spare didn't give it to a beggar? But the cobbler answered:

"High and mighty monarch, this doublet was with me before silk and velvet came—I find it easier to wear than the court cut; moreover it serves to keep me humble, by recalling the days when it was my holiday garment."

32

The king thought this a wise speech, and commanded that no one should find fault with the leathern doublet. So things went, till tidings of his brother's good fortune reached Scrub in the moorland cottage on another first of April, when the cuckoo came with two golden leaves, because he had none to carry for Spare.

"Think of that!" said Fairfeather. "Here we are spending our lives in this humdrum place, and Spare making his fortune at court with two or three paltry green leaves! What would they say to our golden ones? Let us pack up and make our way to the king's palace; I'm sure he will make you a lord and me a lady of honor, not to speak of all the fine clothes and presents we shall have."

Scrub thought this excellent reasoning, and their packing up began; but it was soon found that the cottage contained few things fit for carrying to court. Fairfeather could not think of her wooden bowls, spoons and trenchers being seen there. Scrub considered his lasts and awls better left behind as without them, he concluded, no one would suspect him of being a cobbler. So putting on their holiday clothes, Fairfeather took her looking glass and Scrub his drinking horn, which happened to have a very thin rim of silver, and each carrying a golden leaf carefully wrapped up that none might see it till they reached the palace, the pair set out in great expectation.

How far Scrub and Fairfeather journeyed I cannot say, but when the sun was high and warm at noon, they came into a wood, both tired and hungry.

"If I had known it was so far to court," said Scrub, "I would have brought the end of that barley loaf which we left in the cupboard."

"Husband," said Fairfeather, "you shouldn't have such base thoughts: how could one eat barley bread on the way to a palace? Let us rest ourselves under this tree, and look at our golden leaves to see if they are safe." In looking at the leaves, and talking of their fine prospects, Scrub and Fairfeather did not perceive that a very thin old woman had slipped from behind the tree, with a long staff in her hand and a great knapsack by her side.

"Noble lord and lady," she said, "for I know you are such by your voices, though my eyes are dim and my hearing none of the sharpest, will you condescend to tell me where I may find some water to mix a bottle of mead which I carry in my knapsack, because it is too strong for me?"

As the old woman spoke, she pulled out a large wooden bottle such as shepherds used in the ancient times, corked with leaves rolled together and having a small wooden cup hanging from its handle.

"Perhaps you will do me the favor to taste," she said. "It is only made of the best honey. I have also cream cheese and a wheaten loaf here, if such honorable persons as you would eat the like."

Scrub and Fairfeather became very condescending after this speech. They were now sure that there must be some appearance of nobility about them; besides, they were very hungry, and having hastily wrapped up the golden leaves, they assured the old woman they were not at all proud, notwithstanding the lands and castles they had left behind them in the north country, and would willingly help to lighten the knapsack. The old woman could scarcely be persuaded to sit down for pure humility, but at length she did, and before the knapsack was half empty Scrub and Fairfeather firmly believed that there must be something remarkably noble-looking about them. This was not entirely owing to her ingenious discourse. The old woman was a wood witch; her name was Buttertongue; and all her time was spent in making mead, which, being boiled with curious herbs and spells, had the power of making all who drank it fall asleep and dream with their eyes open. She had two dwarfs of sons; one was named Spy and the other Pounce. Wherever their mother went they were not far behind; and whoever tasted her mead was sure to be robbed by the dwarfs.

Scrub and Fairfeather sat leaning against the old tree. The cobbler had a lump of cheese in his hand; his wife held fast a chunk of bread. Their eyes and mouths were both open, but they were dreaming of great grandeur at court, when the old woman raised her shrill voice:

"What ho, my sons, come here and carry home the harvest!"

No sooner had she spoken than the two little dwarfs darted out of the neighboring thicket.

"Idle boys!" cried the mother. "What have you done today to help our living?"

"I have been to the city," said Spy, "and could see nothing. These are hard times for us—everybody minds his business so contentedly since that cobbler came; but here is a leathern doublet which his page threw out of the window; it's of no use, but I brought it to let you see I was not idle." And he tossed down Spare's doublet, with the merry leaves in it, which he had carried like a bundle on his little back.

To explain how Spy came by it, I must tell you that the forest was not far from the great city where Spare lived in such high esteem. All things had gone well with the cobbler till the king thought it was quite unbecoming to see such a worthy man without a servant. His majesty, therefore, to let all men understand his royal favor towards Spare, appointed one of his own pages to wait upon him. The name of this youth was Tinseltoes, and though he was the seventh of the king's pages nobody in all the court had grander notions. Nothing could please him that had not gold or silver about it, and his grandmother feared he would hang himself for being appointed page to a cobbler. As for Spare, if anything could have troubled him, this token of his majesty's kindness would have done it.

The honest man had been so used to serving himself that the page was always in the way, but his merry leaves came to his assistance; and, to the great surprise of his grandmother, Tinseltoes took wonderfully to the new service. Some said it was because Spare gave him nothing to do but play at bowls all day on the palace green. Yet one thing grieved the heart of Tinseltoes, and that was his master's leathern doublet; but for it, he was persuaded, people would never remember that Spare had been a cobbler, and the page took great pains to let him see how unfashionable it was at court; but Spare answered Tinseltoes as he had done the king, and at last, finding nothing better would do, the page got up one fine morning earlier than his master, and tossed the leathern doublet out of the back window into a certain lane where Spy found it, and brought it to his mother.

"That nasty thing!" said the old woman. "Where is the good in it?"

By this time Pounce had taken everything of value from Scrub and Fairfeather—the looking glass, the silver-rimmed horn, the husband's scarlet coat, the wife's gay mantle, and above all the golden leaves, which so rejoiced old Buttertongue and her sons that they threw the leathern doublet over the sleeping cobbler for a jest, and went off to their hut in the heart of the forest.

The sun was going down when Scrub and Fairfeather awoke from dreaming that they had been made a lord and a lady and sat clothed in silk and velvet, feasting with the king in his palace hall. It was a great disappointment to find their golden leaves and all their best things gone. Scrub tore his hair and vowed to take the old woman's life, while Fairfeather

37

lamented sore; but Scrub, feeling cold for want of his coat, put on the leathern doublet without asking or caring whence it came.

Scarcely was it buttoned on when a change came over him; he addressed such merry discourse to Fairfeather, that, instead of lamentations, she made the wood ring with laughter. Both busied themselves in getting up a hut of boughs, in which Scrub kindled a fire with a flint and steel, which, together with his pipe, he had brought unknown to Fairfeather, who had told him the like was never heard of at court. Then they found a pheasant's nest at the root of an old oak, made a meal of roasted eggs, and went to sleep on a heap of long green grass which they had gathered, with nightingales singing all night long in the old trees about them. So it happened that Scrub and Fairfeather stayed day after day in the forest, making their hut larger and more comfortable against the winter, living on wild birds' eggs and berries and never thinking of their lost golden leaves, or their journey to court.

In the meantime, Spare had got up and missed his doublet. Tinseltoes, of course, said he knew nothing about it. The whole palace was searched, and every servant questioned, till all the court wondered why such a fuss was made about an old leathern doublet. That very day things came back to their old fashion. Quarrels began among the lords, and jealousies among the ladies. The king said his subjects did not pay him half enough taxes, the queen wanted more jewels, the servants took to their old bickerings and got up some new ones. Spare found himself getting wonderfully dull, and very much out of place; nobles began to ask what business a cobbler had at the king's table, and his majesty ordered the palace chronicles to be searched for a precedent. The cobbler was too wise to tell all he had lost with that doublet, but being by this time somewhat familiar with court customs, he proclaimed a reward of fifty gold pieces to any who would bring him news concerning it.

Scarcely was this made known in the city when the gates and outer courts of the palace were filled by men, women and children, some bringing leathern doublets of every cut and color—some with tales of what they had heard and seen in their walks about the neighborhood. And so much news concerning all sorts of great people came out of these stories that lords and ladies ran to the king with complaints of Spare as a speaker of slander; and his majesty, being now satisfied that there was no example in all the palace records of such a retainer, issued a decree banishing the cobbler forever from court and confiscating all his goods in favor of Tinseltoes.

That royal edict was scarcely published before the page was in full possession of his rich chamber, his costly garments and all the presents the courtiers had given him; while Spare, having no longer the fifty pieces of gold to give, was glad to make his escape out of the back window, for fear of the nobles, who vowed to be revenged on him, and the crowd, who were prepared to stone him for cheating them about his doublet.

The window from which Spare let himself down with a strong rope was that from which Tinseltoes had tossed the doublet, and as the cobbler came down late in the twilight, a poor woodman with a heavy load of faggots stopped and stared at him in great astonishment.

"What's the matter, friend?" said Spare. "Did you never see a man coming down from a back window before?"

"Why," said the woodman, "the last morning I passed here a leathern doublet came out of that very window, and I'll be bound you are the owner of it."

"That I am, friend," said the cobbler. "Can you tell me which way that doublet went?"

"As I walked on," said the woodman, "a dwarf, called Spy, bundled it up and ran off to his mother in the forest."

"Honest friend," said Spare, taking off the last of his fine clothes (a grass-green mantle edged with gold), "I'll give you this if you will follow the dwarf and bring me back my doublet."

"It would not be good to carry faggots in," said the woodman. "But if you want back your doublet, the road to the forest lies at the end of this lane," and he trudged away.

Determined to find his doublet, and sure that neither crowd nor courtiers could catch him in the forest, Spare went on his way, and was soon among the tall trees; but neither hut nor dwarf could he see. Moreover the night came on; the wood was dark and tangled, but here and there the moon shone through its alleys, the great owls flitted about, and the nightingales sang. So he went on, hoping to find some place of shelter. At last the red light of a fire, gleaming through a thicket, led him to the door of a low hut. It stood half open, as if there was nothing to fear, and within he saw his brother Scrub snoring loudly on a bed of grass, at the foot of which lay his own leathern doublet; while Fairfeather, in a dress made of plaited rushes, sat roasting pheasants' eggs by the fire.

"Good evening, mistress," said Spare, stepping in.

The blaze shone on him, but so changed was her brother-in-law with his court life, that Fairfeather did not know him, and she answered far more courteously than was her wont.

"Good evening, master. Whence come ye so late? But speak low, for my good man has sorely tired himself cleaving wood, and is taking a sleep, as you see, before supper."

"A good rest to him," said Spare, perceiving he was not known. "I come from the court for a day's hunting, and have lost my way in the forest."

"Sit down and have a share of our supper," said Fairfeather. "I will put some more eggs in the ashes; and tell me the news of court—I used to think of it long ago when I was young and foolish."

"Did you never go there?" said the cobbler. "So fair a dame as you would make the ladies marvel."

"You are pleased to flatter," said Fairfeather; "but my husband has a brother there, and we left our moorland village to try our fortune also. An old woman enticed us with fair words and strong drink at the entrance of this forest, where we fell asleep and dreamed of great things; but when we woke, everything had been robbed from us—my looking

41

glass, my scarlet cloak, my husband's Sunday coat; and, in place of all, the robbers left him that old leathern doublet, which he has worn ever since, and never was so merry in all his life, though we live in this poor hut."

"It is a shabby doublet, that," said Spare, taking up the garment, and seeing that it was his own, for the merry leaves were still sewed in its lining. "It would be good for hunting in, however—your husband would be glad to part with it, I dare say, in exchange for this handsome cloak"; and he pulled off the green mantle and buttoned on the doublet, much to Fairfeather's delight, who ran and shook Scrub, crying:

"Husband! husband! rise and see what a good bargain I have made!"

Scrub gave one closing snore, and muttered something about the root being hard; but he rubbed his eyes, gazed up at his brother, and said:

"Spare, is that really you? How did you like the court, and have you made your fortune?"

"That I have, brother," said Spare, "in getting back my own good leathern doublet. Come, let us eat eggs and rest ourselves here this night. In the morning we will return to our own old hut, at the end of the moorland village where the Christmas Cuckoo will come and bring us leaves."

Scrub and Fairfeather agreed. So in the morning they all returned, and found the old hut the worse for wear and weather. The neighbors came about them to ask the news of court, and see if they had made their fortune. Everybody was astonished to find the three poorer than ever, but somehow they liked to go back to the hut. Spare brought out the lasts and awls he had hidden in a corner; Scrub and he began their old trade, and the whole north country found out that there never were such cobblers.

They mended the shoes of lords and ladies as well as the common people; everybody was satisfied. Their business increased from day to day, and all that were disappointed, discontented or unlucky came to the hut as in old times before Spare went to court.

The rich brought them presents, the poor did them service. The hut itself changed, no one knew how. Flowering honeysuckle grew over its roof; red and white roses grew thick about its door. Moreover the Christmas Cuckoo always came on the first of April, bringing three leaves of the merry tree—for Scrub and Fairfeather would have no more golden ones. So it was with them when I last heard the news of the north country.

From GRANNY'S WONDERFUL CHAIR
Illustrated here by George Adamson

*This comes from a collection of eight stories about a dog and a cat
who talk like humans and belong to the world of cheerful nonsense.
Josef and Karel Čapek, born in northeast Bohemia, are probably
best known for "The Insect Play," that grim warning of totalitarian
government which they wrote in collaboration in 1921. The brothers
were actively anti-Nazi, and Josef was one of the first Czechs to be
arrested when his country was invaded. He died in Belsen in 1945.
By profession he was a painter and art critic, and children enjoy his
eccentric illustrations for his brother's book of fairy tales. The Čapeks
obviously liked and understood cats and dogs, and Karel Čapek's
stories of their family pets show that Puss and Pup, who live in a
cottage straight out of nursery rhyme, are drawn from life.*

JOSEF ČAPEK

Puss and Pup

ONCE upon a time Puss and Pup kept house together. They had their own little cottage in the wood. Here they lived together and tried to do everything just like real grown-up people. But somehow they couldn't always manage this. You see, they had small clumsy paws, without any fingers like people have, only little soft pads with claws on them. So they couldn't do everything just like real grown-ups. And they didn't go to school, because school is not meant for animals.

Of course it isn't. School is only for children.

Their home was not always as tidy as it might have been. Some things they did well, and others not so well. And sometimes there was rather a mess.

One day they noticed that the cottage floor was very dirty.

"I say, Pup," said Puss, "our floor's horribly dirty. Don't you think so?"

"Yes, I do. It really is rather dirty," said Pup. "Just look how grubby it's made my paws."

"They're filthy," said Puss. "Ugh, you ought to be ashamed of yourself! We must scrub the floor. People don't have dirty floors. They scrub them."

"All right," replied Pup. "But how are we going to do it?"

"Oh, it's easy," said Puss. "You go and fetch some water, and I'll see to the rest."

Pup took a pail and went for water. Meanwhile Puss took a piece of soap out of her bag and put it on the table. Then she went off to the attic for something; I expect she kept a piece of smoked mouse there.

While she was away Pup came back with the water and saw something lying on the table. He unwrapped it. It was pink.

"Ha, ha! This looks good," said Pup to himself. And because it made him feel hungry, he pushed the whole piece into his mouth and started chewing it.

But it didn't taste so good. Soon Puss came in and heard Pup making all sorts of funny spluttering noises. She saw that Pup's mouth was full of foam and his eyes were streaming with tears.

"Goodness me!" cried Puss. "Whatever's happened to you, Pup? You must be ill. There's foam dripping from your mouth. Whatever's the matter?"

"Well," said Pup, "I found something lying on the table. I thought it might be some cheese, or a piece of cake, so I ate it. But it stings horribly and makes my mouth all full of foam."

"What a silly you are!" scolded Puss. "That was soap! Soap's for washing with, not eating."

"Oh," said Pup. "So that's why it hurts so much. Ow, ow, it stings! Ow, it stings!"

"Have a good drink of water," suggested Puss; "that'll stop it smarting."

Pup drank away until he had finished up all the water. It had stopped smarting by now, but there was still plenty of foam. So he went and wiped his muzzle on the grass outside. Then he had to go and fetch some more water because he had drunk it all and there was none left. Luckily Puss had a dime, and she went off to buy some more soap.

"I won't eat that again," said Pup, when Puss returned with the soap. "But, Puss, how are we going to manage without a scrubbing brush?"

"I've already thought about that," said Puss. "You've got a rough, bristly coat, just like a brush. We can scrub the floor with you."

"Right ho!" said Pup. And Puss took the soap and the pail of water, and knelt down on the floor. Then she scrubbed the whole floor with Pup.

By now the floor was all wet, and it wasn't any too clean either.

"We ought to rub it over with something dry," said Puss.

"I'll tell you what," said Pup. "I'm sopping wet, but you're dry, and your fur is nice and soft. It'll make a lovely floor cloth. I'll dry the floor with you."

48

So he took hold of Puss and dried the whole floor with her.

The floor was now washed and dried, but Puss and Pup were all wet and terribly dirty from having been used to wash the floor.

"Well, we do look a sight!" they both said, looking at each other. "We've got the floor clean all right, but now look at us! We can't possibly stay like this. Everybody will laugh. We'll have to be sent to the wash."

"Let's wash each other, like they do at the laundry," said Pup. "You wash me, and when I'm done, I'll wash you."

"Very well," said Puss.

They filled the tub of water and took a scrubbing board. Pup got into the tub and Puss washed him. She rubbed him so much on the scrubbing board that Pup begged her not to press so hard, as his legs were getting all tangled up.

When Pup was finished, Puss got into the tub and Pup scrubbed and squeezed her so much that she begged him not to press her so hard on the scrubbing board in case he made a hole in her fur.

Then they wrung each other out.

"Now we'll hang ourselves out to dry," said Puss. So they put out the clothes line.

"First you hang me up on the line, and when I'm up, I'll get down and hang you up," Pup told Puss.

So Pup took hold of Puss and hung her up, just like washing. They didn't need any pegs, because they could hold on to the line with their claws. Once Puss was on the line, she jumped down and hung up Pup.

By now the two of them were hanging nicely and the sun was shining brightly.

"The sun's shining on us," cried Pup. "We'll soon be dry."

No sooner had he said this than it began to rain.

"Oh, dear, it's raining!" shouted Puss and Pup. "The washing will get wet. Let's take it down!"

They jumped down quickly and ran to the cottage for shelter.

"Is it still raining?" asked Puss.

"It's stopped," said Pup, and sure enough the sun was out again.

"Let's hang the washing out again, then," said Puss.

So they hung themselves on the line a second time. First Pup put Puss up, and as soon as she was hanging up she jumped down and put up Pup. So they both hung on the line, just like washing, and were very pleased at the way the sun shone and made such a good drying day.

But then it began to rain again.

"It's raining! Our washing will get wet!" cried Puss and Pup. And they ran for shelter. Soon the sun came out again, and again they hung each other up on the clothes line. Then it started raining, and off they scampered. Then the sun

50

came out again and they hung themselves up again, and so it went on till the evening. By that time they were both quite dry.

"Our washing's dry,' they said."Let's put it in the basket."

So they clambered into the basket. But then they felt so sleepy that they both fell asleep. And they slept in the basket right through until the next morning.

From HARUM-SCARUM
Illustrated by the author

The Door
of
the Great House

A small boy sets out one morning on his tricycle to find that person whose name has always puzzled him—Mr. Nobody. He finds a Mr. Boddy, who has turned a rambling old house into a playground for all the neighborhood children. The author of this story writes: "Between the age of four and seven years I seem to have spent most of the time when I was not sleeping or eating on a very old tricycle. This had belonged to my brother, who had also used it a great deal. By the time I had it, there was only a little bit of rubber and a wormy bit of spring that had once been the inside of the tire on the front wheel. This soon went, and for the rest of its life, I rode my tricycle on its wheel rims. It was therefore very noisy. The pedal operated directly on to the front wheel hubs, but as the wheel was a big one, I could go quite fast. The main point about tricycling is to go fast, like Tricycle Tim. The best speed on my tricycle could be obtained by squatting on the rear axle tube, with the saddle in your chest, and the rear wheels slicing through the air within inches of your ears. I once tricycled a mile, up and down the veranda of our house, in a figure-of-eight pattern, in twelve minutes. This meant nearly two hundred corners, flat out, with the iron wheels screaming on the tiles."

BRUCE CARTER

The Great Crumbling House

THE man with the red beard took hold of the rusty iron handle of the front door of the house and half pushed and half lifted the door open.

"Come on in, Tim," he called behind him.

Tim could hardly hear him for the noise from inside the house.

Tim stood beside the man, with one hand on the handlebars of his tricycle, looking about him in wonder.

He was standing in the old hall of the house, a huge room stretching right up to the roof that was no longer there. Far above he could see the sky through the remains of the rafters.

Once there had been a wide staircase. But now instead of stairs there were smooth boards that made a gentle curving hill leading to a wide landing, and then up again to the next landing, up and up to all the rooms above.

And coming down this hill at a great speed, shouting and ringing their bells, were many boys on many tricycles.

One after another the boys braked at the bottom of the hill, some turning left across the hall, waving and grinning at Tim and the man, while others turned the other way and disappeared through a doorway into another room.

55

Before they had gone, more boys on more tricycles appeared, shooting out from the doors all around the hall, whooping and swooping, charging and shouting, pedaling at a great speed across the smooth wooden floors of the house, rushing up and down the stairs, in and out of the rooms above, in and out of the rooms below.

Tim had never seen such tricycling and he had never heard such a noise.

"Hullo, Mr. Boddy," shouted a boy in a Red Indian costume as he raced past, chasing another boy dressed as a cowboy.

There were girls there, too, tricycling just as fast and shouting just as loudly as the boys. Wherever Tim looked there were tricycles: black, green, blue tricycles, red tricycles like Tim's, big old tricycles with pedals on the front wheels, little new tricycles with chains, tricycles with hooters, tricycles with saddlebags, tricycles towing trailers with boys in them.

And they were all rushing wildly at a great speed round and round this broken-down great house, in and out of the rooms, up and down the stairs.

"Well, what are you waiting for, Tim?" asked the man. "Off you go."

Still wondering, still uncertain, half thrilled and half afraid, Tim got on his tricycle.

"Bob," the man called to a passing boy with black hair on a black tricycle. "Here's Tim. He's a new member. Take him around, will you?"

"All right," said the boy, slowing down just for a moment. "Come on then."

Tim followed the boy called Bob across the smooth boards of the hall, getting up speed quickly. It was just as well Tim was such a good tricyclist for Bob went very fast.

They dodged in and out of other tricycles, racing through doorways, in and out of rooms with cracked pillars and glassless windows and chipping walls.

They came at last to a long room packed with whirling, braking, racing tricycles.

"This is super," said Bob. "I'll do it first, then you do it."

Tim watched Bob making for a huge tilted plank in the middle of the room. Up it went Bob, slowing down halfway as the plank rose up one side and fell down the other. It was a tricycle seesaw. Down the other side raced Bob, tricycling off the plank just as it struck the floor with a great crash.

Tim did it next. He had never before done anything so exciting.

"What'll we do now?" asked Tim, hot and panting but not at all tired.

"Mr. Boddy's Whirligig," said Bob. He grinned at Tim. "That's super."

"Is the man with the beard Mr. Nobody?" asked Tim.

"No, Mr. Boddy. He's super. We all like Mr. Boddy. B.T.C.," he said, pointing at Tim's red badge. "Boddy's Tricycle Club. See?"

"Oh," said Tim. "I thought he was Mr. Nobody."

So he had still not found the poor old lonely man. But he was too excited to be disappointed.

"And what's the Whirligig?"

"You'll see," said Bob. "Come on."

And away he raced, with Tim racing behind.

Tim and Bob did not tricycle quite so fast to the Whirligig. Sometimes they stopped and talked to other children. They were all happy and friendly. They had a race with a boy called Jim, which they won, and Bob had a short fight, but only a friendly one, with a boy called Ted.

They went up the stairs, up and up, to the very top floor. In and out of the roofless bedrooms and bathrooms they went, then at a terrific speed down some long steep stairs, with planks over them like the big stairs, at the back of the house.

They tricycled through the great old kitchen, with its rusting iron range and old stoves, copper boilers and toppling cupboards. Then they tricycled out of the back of the house.

The Whirligig was in the old kitchen yard. It was like a fun house slide, but instead of whirling down on mats, you came down on tricycles.

"We go up like this," said Bob.

He led Tim through a hole at the bottom of the Whirligig, then he showed Tim how to hook his tricycle on a rope.

"When you get to the top of the ladder, you pull it up and drop the rope for the next person," said Bob.

You could see for miles from the top of the Whirligig. Tim stood for a moment, looking at the great old crumbling house that was used only for tricycling, looking down at the boys and girls below, tricycling in and out of the house, racing round the yard, shouting and screaming, talking and laughing.

"This is the best place in the world," thought Tricycle Tim.

From TRICYCLE TIM
Illustrated by Prudence Seward

"The author's first impulse," Elizabeth Coatsworth once wrote,"is to say, Look!" and again,"Let an author enjoy his own book and it is probable that there will be children who will enjoy it too." Her stories draw their living quality from her love and observation of New England towns and people, in her own day and in the remembered past. One of her best books,"Away Goes Sally", was suggested when she found, in the grounds of the farm she and her husband had bought in Maine, a small house with a stove in it, fastened to runners, which had been used by woodcutters in winter. "Thief Island" grew out of one rowboat journey when she saw an island with deserted houses on the shore."Most often I begin with place," she says, and this is the secret of her skill, that she creates a complete world for her characters to live in, and her readers too. "Alice-all-by-herself" is about an observant child going about in the little town on the Damariscotta river, half a century ago, and seeing round her the signs of a far older world—oxen still used for ploughing, an old goose born in 1873, and a parrot still older, Mr. Parsons making figureheads for ships and Miss Abbey tending her herb garden, Simeon Hall's junk shop with its trading beads and treaty blankets and old carved mantels. But it was in the deserted mansion, built in the eighteenth century, that Alice found what was to be her greatest treasure.

ELIZABETH COATSWORTH

A Picnic at the Mansion

EVERY fine Saturday morning Olga put up a picnic lunch for three, neatly packed away in the old covered basket that Alice's grandmother had bought from the Indians, who in those days sold their work from door to door. Alice loved to watch the bright blue beetleware cups and plates, the curious knobby parcels done up in wax paper, and the salad bowl with the nasturtiums on it tucked each into its place by Olga's quick fingers. Olga never forgot anything, not even salt, nor the fresh-picked sprigs of marjoram for the top of the salad. She kept her mind on what she was doing; not like Alice, whose mind half the time seemed to be on something else.

When the picnic basket was all packed, Olga went out and rang the ship's bell that hung near the kitchen door, and then Alice's father got up from his knees beside the herb garden where he had been doing some late weeding, and Alice's mother at her desk hastily finished a letter and addressed its envelope, and Alice very carefully carried the big basket and the thermos bottles out to the car, and they were off for another day of exploration.

. . . On this August Saturday the men were out cutting the hay on the sloping fields that stretched down to the river, and Alice and her father and mother waved to them all and every one waved back good-naturedly to them. But there was an air of hurry in the fields, for the day which had begun so sunnily was growing overcast, and the big white clouds had somehow turned black and stood up like a dark wall in the northwest, against which the woods and fields shone bright emerald. A little thunder began like the rattle and rumble of a haywagon over a bridge.

Alice's mother, who never cared for storms, suggested that perhaps they had better be going home, but her father shook his head.

"We shan't be able to make it," he said, "it's coming fast. Hear the leaves rustle already. Perhaps we'd better try to go on to the Mansion."

"It may pass over," said Alice's mother hopefully.

But the storm had no intention of passing over. Fast as they drove, they had just reached the big square empty house with its sagging verandas when the leaves began to rustle and whisper, "Rain, rain, rain," and then the sun suddenly disappeared and the first slow drops began to fall, and then came a flash of lightning and a clap of nearby thunder and the rain began to fall faster and faster.

It certainly seemed a very bad day for a picnic.

'Perhaps we'd better eat our lunch on the veranda," Alice's father suggested. "There's going to be a regular downpour, I'm afraid." So while there was still time they each seized something and ran towards the house.

But the rain fell more and more heavily and splashed into the open veranda, and the thunder and lightning crashed and flared above them, and Alice and her father and mother looked as dismal as three cats on a doorstep in a shower. Her father had begun poking and prying at the windows of the old house and all of a sudden he shouted, "Hurrah! Here's

an open one!" and held it up while Alice and her mother and
the picnic basket and the thermos bottles were all lifted in, and
then he came in, too.

They had climbed into the kitchen: the stove was there,

and broken dishes in the sink, and an old calendar of many years ago hung on the wall. The house smelled unused. They tiptoed into the next room. There was no furniture in it, except a clock that had lost its pendulum. But the parlor still had its rose-flowered carpet tacked on the floor, and there were still steel engravings of a congress of American authors and of St. Cecilia and a Landseer stag. Someone had tumbled most of the books out of the shelves on one side of the fireplace, but there was a haircloth sofa and chairs with grape ornaments, and in the corner between the windows stood a little flat-topped organ, with old music still on its rack.

The rest of the house was almost empty except for big beds too heavy to carry away and pictures that nobody wanted, but it had an air of dignity, and its old wallpapers had been there since before the Civil War, Alice's father said.

Outside, the lightning and thunder had increased and the rain turned the windowpanes gray with streams of water running down the glass. Alice went into the kitchen and came back with some old wooden boxes she had found.

"Let's make a fire, Father," she said.

"Would it be right?" asked her mother, looking very cold in her damp summer dress.

Alice's father made up his mind quickly. "I can't see that it would do any harm," he said. "The chimneys seem sound."

In five minutes the parlor of the Mansion had become a real refuge against the storm. A small fire crackled and spat out sparks from the old fireplace (Alice put them out when they fell on the carpet) and the books were put back on the shelves, and while her mother laid the marble-topped table with the checked red and white tablecloth from the picnic basket, her father played Scotch songs on the little sweet-voiced organ, which Alice liked better than any piano she

had ever seen or heard, even though it was somewhat out of tune.

"Luncheon is served," said her mother, and they all pulled up chairs and began eating hungrily.

"It's like being someone else," remarked Alice dreamily. "It's all so *secret*, like an enchanted house. I wonder who lived here?"

But they never knew.

After lunch they explored the sheds that opened out from the kitchen and found a broom made from a single piece of birch, with its end sliced into hundreds of splinters and tied together, so that broom and handle were all one.

"An Indian broom," Alice's father said. "I've heard that the squaws used to sell one for ten cents, though they took a long time to make."

There were cheese-making things, too, and a spinning-wheel and loom, and a cobbler's bench with wooden lasts hanging on the wall near by so that the traveling shoemaker could use them for fitting shoes for the whole family during the days he lived at the house, once or twice a year. One of the pairs of lasts was the size of Alice's feet, but whether they had been a little boy's or a little girl's was another of the things she never knew.

By this time the storm had lifted and there was a rainbow over the pines and the leaves were dripping with drops that caught in the new sunlight.

Alice's father carefully put out the fire and then took the paper bag that had had three peaches in it and wrote a note on it to whomever the house belonged to, explaining who they were and how they had happened to break in where only spiders were at home. But what else he wrote in the note Alice never knew until Christmas morning when she woke up to hear "O Little Town of Bethlehem" being played very sweetly and softly in her own playroom, and so went flying out of bed without her slippers or bathrobe, with her brown hair unbraided and her eyes half blind with sleep, to throw her arms about her father and welcome the little organ from the Mansion, which had come to be her very own, all in tune now, with her name on an ivory heart set into the wood just above the old keys.

From ALICE-ALL-BY-HERSELF
Illustrated here by Ionicus

Here is the East Anglian version of "Rumpelstiltskin", slightly edited from the story written down by the folklorist Joseph Jacobs in the nineteenth century. Everyone who reads fairy tales is free to imagine a palace just as he wishes, but in "Tom Tit Tot" the king is as homely as his subjects. This is also the way Eleanor Farjeon imagined him when she wrote "The Silver Curlew", a charming tale based on this old and well-known one.

AMABEL
WILLIAMS-ELLIS

Tom Tit Tot

WELL, once upon a time there were a woman, and she baked
five pies. And when they come out of the oven they was that
overbaked the crust were too hard to eat. So she says to her
daughter: "Darter," says she, "put you them there pies on the
shelf an' leave 'em there a little, an' they'll come agin."

She meant, you know, the crust would get soft.

But the girl, she says to herself, "Well, if they'll come
agin, I'll eat 'em now." And she set to work and ate 'em all,
first and last.

Well, come suppertime, the woman she said:

"Goo you and git one o' them there pies. I daresay they've
come agin now."

The girl she went an' she looked, and there warn't nothin'
but the dishes. So back she come and says she:

"Noo, they ain't come agin."

"Not none on 'em?" says the mother.

"Not none of 'em," says she.

"Well, come agin or not come agin," says the woman, "I'll
have one for supper."

"But you can't, if they ain't come," says the girl.

"But I can," says she. "Goo you and bring the best of 'em."

"Best or worst," says the girl, "I've ate 'em all, and you can't have one till that's come agin."

Well, the woman was done, and she took her spinning to the door to spin, and as she span she sang:

> *My darter ha' ate five, five pies today,*
> *My darter ha' ate five, five pies today.*

The king he were a-coming down the street and he heard her sing, but what she sang he couldn't hear, so he stopped and said:"What were that you was a-singing of, my good woman? '

The woman, she were ashamed to let him hear what her daughter had been doing, so she sang instid of that:

> *My darter ha' spun five, five skeins today,*
> *My darter ha' spun five, five skeins today.*

"Stars o'mine!" said the king, "I never heard tell of any one as could do that."

Then he said,"Look you here, I want a wife, and I'll marry your daughter. But look you here," says he, "eleven months out of the year she shall have all the vittles she likes to eat, and all the gowns she likes to git, and all the company she likes to have; but the last month of the year she'll ha' to spin five skeins every day. If she don't, I shall kill her."

"All right," says the woman. For she thought what a grand marriage that was. And as for them five skeins, when the time came there'd be plenty of ways of getting out of it, and likeliest he'd ha' forgotten about it.

Well, so they were married. And for eleven months the girl had all the vittles she liked to eat, and all the gowns she liked to get, and all the company she liked to keep.

But when the time was gettin' over, she began to think about them there skeins, an' to wonder if he had 'em in mind. But not one word did he say about 'em, and she wholly thought he'd forgot 'em.

Howsoiver, the last day of the last month, he takes her to

a room she'd never set eyes on afore. There weren't nothing in it but a spinning wheel and a stool. An' says he:"Now, my dear, here you'll be shut in tomorrow with some vittles and some flax, and if you haven't spun five skeins by the night, your head'll go off."

An' away he went about his business.

Well, she were that frightened! She'd allus been such a gatless girl, that she didn't so much as know how to spin, and what were she to do tomorrow, with no one to come nigh her to help her? She sat down on a stool in the kitchen, and lork! how she did cry!

All on a sudden she heard a sort of a knockin' low down on the door. She upped and oped it, an' what should she see but a small little black thing with a long tail. That looked up at her right curious, an' that said:"What are you a-cryin' for?"

"What's that to you?" says she.

"Never you mind," that said,"but tell me what you're a-cryin' for."

"That wouldn't do me no good if I do," says she.

"You don't know that," that said, an' twirled that's tail round.

"Well," says she,"that wouldn't do no harm if that don't do no good." And she upped and told about the pies, an' the skeins, an' everything.

"This is what I'll do," says the little black thing:"I'll come to your window every morning and take the flax and bring it spun at night."

"What's your pay?" says she.

That looked out o' the corners o' that's eyes an' that said: "I'll give you three guesses every night to guess my name, an' if you haven't guessed it afore the month's up, you shall be mine."

Well, she thought she'd be sure to guess that's name afore the month was up. "All right," says she."I agree."

71

"All right!" that says, an lork! how that twirled that's tail.

Well, the next day, her husband he took her into the room, an' there was the flax an' the day's vittles.

"Now, there's the flax," says he, "an' if that ain't spun up this night, off goes your head." An' then he went out an' locked the door.

He'd hardly gone, when there was a knocking agin the window.

She upped and she oped it, and there, sure enough, was the little old thing a-sittin' on the ledge.

"Where's the flax?" says that.

"Here it be," says she. And she gave it to that.

Well, come the evenin', a knockin' came agin the window. She upped and she oped it, and there was the little old thing, with five skeins of flax on that's arm.

"Here it be," says that, and gave it to her. "Now, what's my name?" says that.

"What, is it Bill?" says she.

"No, that ain't," says that. An' that twirled that's tail.

"Is that Ned?" says she.

"No, that ain't," says that. An' that twirled that's tail harder.

"Is that Mark?" says she.

"No, that ain't," says that. And that twirled that's tail still harder, and away that flew.

Well, when her husband he came in, there was the five skeins ready for him.

"I see I shan't have to kill you tonight, me dear," says he. "You'll have your vittles and your flax in the morning," says he, and away he goes.

Well, every day the flax and the vittles they were brought, and every day that there little black impet used to come mornings and evenings. An' all the day the girl she set a-tryin' to think of names to say to that when that came at

night. But she never got on the right one. And as it got towards the end of the month the impet began for to look so maliceful, an' that twirled that's tail faster an' faster each time she gave a guess.

At last it came to the last day but one. The impet come at night along of the five skeins, and that said:"What, haven't you got my name yet?"

"Is that Nicodemus?" says she.

"No, t'ain't," that says.

"Is that Sammle?" says she.

"No, t'ain't," that says.

"A-well, is that Methusalem?" says she.

"No, t'ain't that neither," says that.

Then that looks at her with that's eyes like a coal of fire, an' that says, "Woman, there's only tomorrow night, and then you'll be mine!" An' away that flew.

Well, she felt that horrid! Howsomedever, she heard the king a-coming along the passage. In he came, and when he sees the five skeins, he says, says he:"Well, me dear, I don't see but what you'll have your skeins ready tomorrow night as well, an' as I reckon I shan't have to kill you, I'll have supper in here tonight."

So they brought supper, an' another stool for him, and down the two sat.

Well, he hadn't eat but a mouthful or so, when he stops and begins to laugh.

"What is it?" says she.

"A-why," says he, "I was out a-hunting today, an' I got away to a place in the wood I'd never seen afore. An' there was an old chalk pit. An' I heard a sort of a hummin', kind o'. So I got off my hobby, and I went right quiet to the pit, an' I looked down. Well, what should there be but the funniest little black thing you ever set eyes on. An' what was that a-doing on, but that had a little spinning wheel, an' that

74

were a-spinnin' wonderful fast, an' a-twirlin' that's tail. An' as that span, that sang:

> *Nimmy nimmy not,*
> *My name's Tom Tit Tot.*

Well, when the girl heard this, she felt as if she could have jumped out of her skin for joy, but she didn't say a word.

Next day, that there little thing looked so maliceful when it came for the flax! And when night came, she heard that a-knocking agin the windowpanes. She oped the window, and that came right in on the ledge. That was grinning from ear to ear, an' O! that's tail was twirlin' round so fast.

"What's my name?" that says, as that gave her the skeins.

"Is that Solomon?" she says, pretendin' to be afeard.

"No, t'ain't," that says, an' that came farther into the room.

"Well, is that Zebedee?" says she again.

"No, t'ain't," says the impet. An' then that laughed and twirled that's tail till you couldn't hardly see it.

"Take time, woman," that says; "next guess an' you're mine!" An' that stretched out that's black hands at her.

Well, she backed a step or two, an' she looked at it, and then she laughed out, an', says she, a-pointing her finger at it:

> *Nimmy nimmy not,*
> *Your name's Tom Tit Tot.*

Well, when that heard her, that shrieked awful an' away that flew into the dark, and she never saw it no more.

From FAIRIES AND ENCHANTERS
Illustrated here by George Adamson

From earliest childhood Andrew Lang's mind was filled with myth and fairy tale, and classical learning never made him academic. "Tales of Troy and Greece" was intended as an extra volume in his series of Fairy Books, and he wrote as familiarly and naturally about Odysseus as if he had been a fairy tale hero. Odysseus, returned from his travels after many years, drives the suitors from a great hall that is at once grand and simple, part of a life where princesses washed linen that queens had spun, while men might have to fight giants and fabulous monsters. In this book children may happily make a first acquaintance with Hector and Paris, Jason and Theseus, and many other legendary heroes whose stories are part of everyone's reading life.

ANDREW LANG

The Slaying of the Wooers

ULYSSES let all his rags fall down, and with one leap he reached the high threshold, the door being behind him, and he dropped the arrows from the quiver at his feet. "Now!" he said, "I will strike another mark that no man yet has stricken!" He aimed the arrow at Antinous, who was drinking out of a golden cup. The arrow passed clean through the throat of Antinous; he fell, the cup rang on the ground, and the wooers leaped up, looking round the walls for shields and spears, but the walls were bare.

"Thou shalt die, and vultures shall devour thee," they shouted, thinking the beggar had let the arrow fly by mischance.

"Dogs!" he answered, "ye said that never should I come home from Troy; ye wasted my goods, and insulted my wife, and had no fear of the Gods, but now the day of death has come upon you! Fight or flee, if you may, but some shall not escape!"

"Draw your blades!" cried Eurymachus to the others; "draw your blades, and hold up the tables as shields against this man's arrows. Have at him, and drive him from the doorway." He drew his own sword, and leaped on Ulysses with a cry, but the swift arrow pierced his breast, and he fell and died. Then Amphinomus rushed towards Ulysses, but Telemachus sent his spear from behind through his shoulders. He could not draw forth the spear, but he ran to his father, and said, "Let me bring shields, spears, and helmets from the inner chamber, for us, and for the swineherd and cowherd." "Go!" said Ulysses, and Telemachus ran through a narrow doorway, down a gallery to the secret chamber, and brought four shields, four helmets, and eight spears, and the men armed themselves, while Ulysses kept shooting down the wooers. When his arrows were spent he armed himself, protected by the other three. But the goatherd, Melanthius, knew a way of reaching the armory, and he climbed up, and brought twelve helmets, spears, and shields to the wooers.

Ulysses thought that one of the women was showering down the weapons into the hall, but the swineherd and cow-

herd went to the armory, through the doorway, as Telemachus had gone, and there they caught Melanthius, and bound him like a bundle, with a rope, and, throwing the rope over a rafter, dragged him up, and fastened him there, and left him swinging. Then they ran back to Ulysses, four men keeping the doorway against all the wooers that were not yet slain. But the Goddess Athene appeared to Ulysses, in the form of Mentor, and gave him courage. He needed it, for the wooers, having spears, threw them in volleys, six at a time, at the four. They missed, but the spears of the four slew each his man. Again the wooers threw, and dealt two or three slight wounds, but the spears of the four were winged with death. They charged, striking with spear and sword, into the crowd, who lost heart, and flew here and there, crying for mercy and falling at every blow. Ulysses slew the prophet, Leiodes, but Phemius, the minstrel, he spared, for he had done no wrong, and Medon, a slave, crept out from beneath an ox hide, where he had been lying, and asked Telemachus to pity him, and Ulysses sent him and the minstrel into the courtyard, where they sat trembling. All the rest of the wooers lay dead in heaps, like heaps of fish on the seashore, when they had been netted, and drawn to land.

Then Ulysses sent Telemachus to bring Eurycleia, who, when she came and saw the wooers dead, raised a scream of joy, but Ulysses said "it is an unholy thing to boast over dead men." He bade Telemachus and the servants carry the corpses into the courtyard, and he made the women wash and clean the hall, and the seats, and tables, and the pillars. When all was clean, they took Melanthius and slew him, and then they washed themselves, and the maidens who were faithful to Penelope came out of their rooms, with torches in their hands, for it was now night, and they kissed Ulysses with tears of joy. These were not young women, for Ulysses remembered all of them.

Meanwhile old Eurycleia ran to tell Penelope all the good news: up the stairs to her chamber she ran, tripping, and falling, and rising, and laughing for joy. In she came, and awakened Penelope, saying:

"Come and see what you have long desired: Ulysses in his own house, and all the wicked wooers slain by the sword." "Surely you are mad, dear nurse," said Penelope, "to waken me with such a wild story. Never have I slept so soundly since Ulysses went to that ill Ilios, never to be named. Angry would I have been with any of the girls that awakened me with such a silly story; but you are old: go back to the women's working room." The good nurse answered: "Indeed, I tell you no silly tale. Indeed, he is in the hall; he is that poor guest whom all men struck and insulted, but Telemachus knew his father."

Then Penelope leaped up gladly, and kissed the nurse, but yet she was not sure that her husband had come, she feared it might be some god disguised as a man, or some evil man pretending to be Ulysses. "Surely Ulysses has met his death far away," she said, and though Eurycleia vowed that she herself had seen the scar dealt by the boar, long ago, she would not be convinced. "None the less," she said, "let us go and see my son, and the wooers lying dead, and the man who slew them." So they went down the stairs and along the gallery on the ground floor that led into the courtyard, and so entered the door of the hall, and crossed the high stone threshold on which Ulysses stood when he shot down Antinous. Penelope went up to the hearth and sat opposite Ulysses, who was leaning against one of the four tall pillars that supported the roof; there she sat and gazed at him, still wearing his rags, and still not cleansed from the blood of battle. She did not know him, and was silent, though Telemachus called her hard of belief and cold of heart.

"My child," she said, "I am bewildered, and can hardly speak, but if this man is Ulysses, he knows things unknown to any except him and me." Then Ulysses bade Telemachus go to the baths and wash, and put on fresh garments, and bade the maidens bring the minstrel to play music, while they danced in the hall. In the town the friends and kinsfolk of the wooers did not know that they were dead, and when they heard the music they would not guess that anything strange had happened. It was necessary that nobody should know, for, if the kinsfolk of the dead men learned the truth, they would seek to take revenge, and might burn down the house. Indeed, Ulysses was still in great danger, for the law was that the brothers and cousins of slain men must slay their slayers, and the dead were many, and had many clansmen.

Now Eurynome bathed Ulysses himself, and anointed him with oil, and clad him in new raiment, so that he looked like himself again, full of strength and beauty. He sat down on his own high seat beside the fire, and said,"Lady, you are the fairest and most cruel Queen alive. No other woman would harden her heart against her husband, come home through many dangers after so many years. Nurse," he cried to Eurycleia,"strew me a bed to lie alone, for her heart is hard as iron."

Now Penelope put him to a trial. "Eurycleia," she said, "strew a bed for him outside the bridal chamber that he built for himself, and bring the good bedstead out of that room for him."

"How can any man bring out that bedstead?" said Ulysses, "Did I not make it with my own hands, with a standing tree for the bedpost? No man could move that bed unless he first cut down the tree trunk."

Then at last Penelope ran to Ulysses and threw her arms round his neck, kissing him, and said: "Do not be angry, for always I have feared that some strange man of cunning would come and deceive me, pretending to be my lord. But now you have told me the secret of the bed, which no mortal has ever seen or knows but you and I, and my maiden whom I brought from my own home, and who kept the doors of our chamber." Then they embraced, and it seemed as if her white arms would never quite leave their hold on his neck.

Ulysses told her many things, all the story of his wanderings, and how he must wander again, on land, not on the sea, till he came to the country of men who had never seen salt. "The Gods will defend you and bring you home to your rest in the end," said Penelope, and then they went to their own chamber, and Eurynome went before them with lighted torches in her hands, for the Gods had brought them to the haven where they would be.

From TALES OF TROY AND GREECE
Illustrated by Edward Bawden

The
Door of the Shop

Ursula Hourihane, like the authors of the three pieces which follow hers, is describing the kind of shop that belongs to the past—trying, in fact, to put into words the charm and oddity of a past that is half imagined. When she pictured Mrs. Cumfitt's shop, she may have remembered childhood days in Manchester, England, when "the shops were all village type and personal in service," or the little shops in the Welsh seaside town where she went to school. Much experience with children has gone into her stories, for she worked in nursery schools for many years, and did not begin to write until her daughter went to school. She is a born storyteller, and many of her stories have been heard on the British radio. She uses many of the devices that belong to the oral tradition—as, in this story, the pattern of three mice, three happenings. She now runs a children's bookshop in Cirencester, England, and so keeps in touch with what children like to read.

URSULA HOURIHANE

Mrs. Cumfitt's Sugar Mice

MRS. CUMFITT'S shop stood halfway down the village street. It was really a nice little cottage with a small square of garden in front and a little green gate that went *click* whenever anyone opened or shut it.

The shop part of Mrs. Cumfitt's cottage was in the front room and she had a neat little counter across the back of the room and lots and lots of shelves behind where she kept all the things she had for sale. Mrs. Cumfitt sold reels of cotton and candles and packets of tea and biscuits and pens and pencils and notebooks and almost everything else you can think of. And, of course, she sold sweets. She sold all sorts of sweets—fat, stripy peppermints, jelly babies, toffees, fruit drops, chocolate drops, wine gums, barley sugar sticks, and—best of all—pink and white sugar mice with shiny eyes and string tails. No wonder Mrs. Cumfitt was a busy person and no wonder her green gate was always going *click! click! click!*

Of course Mrs. Cumfitt was very glad to have so many customers to buy all the nice things in her shop, but sometimes she got very, very tired.

"Dearie me," she would say when she heard the gate click yet again, "Dearie me, shall I ever get even a cup of tea in peace?" And then one day she had a really splendid idea. "I know what I'll do," she said to herself. "I'll shut up my shop for a whole week and go away to the sea for a holiday. That will give me a nice rest and when I come back I'll be as fresh as a daisy again."

So Mrs. Cumfitt wrote out a notice and stuck it on her green gate. The notice said, THIS SHOP WILL BE SHUT FOR ALL NEXT WEEK. PLEASE BUY EVERYTHING YOU WANT QUICKLY.

Well, the people in the village were surprised. They came hurrying along to the shop and they bought tea and biscuits and cotton and matches and candles and soap and all the things they could remember, so that they would be sure to have enough of everything in their houses while Mrs. Cumfitt was away on her holiday.

Very soon the shelves began to look nearly empty. By Friday afternoon there were no peppermints left, no fruit drops, no wine gums, no jelly babies. And at last the only sweets Mrs. Cumfitt had to sell were three sugar mice—two pink and one white.

"I'd better put a notice on the gate to say I've sold out," she said to herself. "It's not worth keeping open just for those three sugar mice."

She went into her back parlor and got out some paper and a fat blue pencil and began to write. She was just crossing the T of O.U.T. for OUT when she heard the gate go *click!*

"Botheration me!" she cried. "There's someone there again. I wonder what they'll be wanting." And she hurried into the shop. A little girl stood by the counter. She had a blue plastic handbag in her hand.

"Well, my dear," said Mrs. Cumfitt kindly, "and what can I do for you?" The little girl poked about in her blue handbag and said, "Have you any sweets for this much money?" She

showed Mrs. Cumfitt two pennies.

"Let me see," said Mrs. Cumfitt. "Well, I haven't any packets of sweets left, I'm afraid, but I could let you have a sugar mouse for two cents, if you'd like that?"

The little girl went quite pink with delight. "Can I really have a sugar mouse for this money?" she said. "That would be much better than sweets. I shall call it Whiskers and I shall keep it forever."

Mrs. Cumfitt laughed. "I'm afraid it might melt after a bit," she said. "Which color will you choose?"

The little girl chose a pink mouse. She put it in her hand-bag, said "Thank you" and "Good-by" to Mrs. Cumfitt, and went off down the garden path. Mrs. Cumfitt hurried into her back parlor and began to write the next bit of her notice.

"SOLD OUT. Signed, Mrs.——" she was writing when, *click!* there was that gate again!

"Botheration me!" cried Mrs. Cumfitt putting down the blue pencil again. "Now who in the world can it be this time?" There was a little boy in the shop. He looked thin and brown-faced and rather anxious.

"A little gipsy, I don't doubt," said Mrs. Cumfitt to herself. "What do you want, young man?"

The little boy held up a penny. "Have you anything I can buy for a penny? A lady gave it to me for weeding her path."

Mrs. Cumfitt shook her head. "A penny won't buy much, I'm afraid," she said. "And I've sold out of all my sweets really. I've only got these two sugar mice left. They're two cents apiece. I'm sorry."

The little boy looked sadder than ever. Mrs. Cumfitt felt quite unhappy too.

"I know," she said. "I've got a good idea. Would you like to weed my path for me and get another penny and then you can buy a sugar mouse, can't you?"

The gipsy boy gave a big smile and his teeth looked strong and white against his brown face.

"Oh, that would be fine," he said, and he hurried into the garden and set to work at once.

In next to no time his thin brown fingers had pulled up every bit of grass and weed in the little path. Mrs. Cumfitt was delighted.

"Now then, which mouse are you going to choose?" she said. The gipsy boy chose the white sugar mouse.

"It's much too nice to eat!" he said. "I've never had a sugar mouse before. I shall call it Frisky and I shall keep it forever."

Mrs. Cumfitt laughed. "I'm afraid it will melt after a bit," she said. "Here you are, then. And here's a glass of milk and a biscuit because you made such a good job of my path."

Mrs. Cumfitt's Sugar Mice

The gipsy boy said, "Thank you, ma'm." And he drank the milk and munched the biscuit. Then he said, "Good-by" and went off down the tidy garden path.

Mrs. Cumfitt hurried into her back parlor and finished her notice. "SOLD OUT. Signed, Mrs. Cumfitt," she wrote. Then she took the notice and pinned it on the green gate. She ran into the house and shut the door.

"Now I must get my packing done, ready for my holiday," she said.

She worked away till it was quite late and she was so tired that she fell fast asleep the moment she lay down in bed. And while Mrs. Cumfitt lay dreaming of the lovely holiday she was going to have, a very strange thing happened.

Down below in the shop there was a scratching and a scrabbling and a lot of excited squeaking and scuffling. And, would you believe it? A family of mice that lived under the stairs went up into Mrs. Cumfitt's shop and took away the last sugar mouse!—the pink one. They pulled and tugged and pushed and rolled that pink sugar mouse all the way down from the counter, over the shop floor, through the door and across the passage to their hole under the stairs.

When Mrs. Cumfitt looked for it the next morning to take with her, she couldn't imagine what had become of it.

"Oh, well, it doesn't matter," she said to herself cheerfully. "I've sandwiches and biscuits and a bag of apples, and that's more than enough surely."

From SUGAR AND SPICE
Illustrated here by Edward Ardizzone

Margery Williams Bianco, who died in 1944, was born in London and was taken to America when she was nine. Early memories of the Thames Embankment at Chelsea merged with those of New York's Central Park, then partly wild, of a Pennsylvanian farm and school in Philadelphia, interspersed with visits to England. During her married life, in Paris and then in Italy, she put aside the writing which had so far been for adults, but was suddenly moved by seeing her children's toys in a heap, to write a story, "The Velveteen Rabbit"; the first of many tales for children. In an article called "Our Youngest Critics," she once wrote, "What appeals to children is not so much adventure in its widest sense as the possibility of adventure in everyday surroundings and among everyday things—something that might, by a happy chance, conceivably happen in their own lives . . . not for nothing has the harlequinade, one of the oldest of all magic plays, been staged invariably outside a prosaic grocer shop in a most prosaic street." But "A Street of Little Shops" is not wholly prosaic, for it reflects an American small town of a past era; and the humor of "The Saddler's Horse" belongs absolutely to its setting.

MARGERY WILLIAMS BIANCO

The Saddler's Horse

I WONDER how many of you who read this story have ever seen a cigarette shop Indian?

I don't mean in pictures, or in someone's collection of old-fashioned curiosities, but a real one, all carved and painted and standing just where he should stand, on the pavement outside a cigarette shop door. Not so many years ago a cigarette shop Indian used to be quite an everyday sight, almost as common as a barber's pole. And as for saddlers' horses, many a town that really was a town used to have one, and very proud they were of him.

I don't know where all these Indians have gone to. Perhaps they are still living somewhere, here and there, in private families. Perhaps they have all migrated in a body to the great open spaces, or wherever it is that Wooden Indians do go. Certainly one does not see them any more on the pavement, kindly offering one a cigarette or a pinch of snuff, as they used to do.

But I do know of one place where there is still a Saddler's Horse.

He is very big and tall, painted all over a pleasant varnishy dapple gray, and he stands outside what is still the saddler's shop—though it sells other things as well nowadays—in the open space near the railway station, just two minutes' walk from Mr. Murdle's shop. All day long he stands there and dreams.

He dreams of the old days when there were no airplanes and no cars and no gasoline pumps; when the railway station was very much smaller and the big hotel had not yet been built, nor the concrete roadway; when it took country folk a whole day, instead of an hour, to get to town and back, and they drove in pony traps and farm wagons, and instead of parked cars by the pavement edge there were horses, long rows of them, tied in the shade to hitching posts under the big elm trees.

In those days the feed shop and the hardware shop and the saddler's were quite the most important shops in town. And the Saddler's Horse, standing out there with the very newest style of shiny harness buckled on his back for every passer-by to admire, would gaze down his nose at the country horses switching their tails under the elms, and feel that he was very, very superior.

But times have changed. There are gasoline pumps now instead of hitching posts. Cars and trucks go up and down the street; very few teams pass by, and the Saddler's Horse rarely sees a pony trap at all. But still he stands there, all day long, watching the traffic go past, and at six o'clock, when the train whistle blows, the saddler wheels him indoors and puts him to bed for the night.

Just across the street is an antique shop. It happened that one day, not very long ago, the shopkeeper came across a Wooden Indian. I don't know where he found him, but he brought him home, together with a grandfather clock and an old bureau and a print of a little girl hugging a kitten, and he stood him out on the pavement just beside the shop door.

As soon as the Wooden Indian saw the Saddler's Horse, and as soon as the Saddler's Horse caught sight of the Wooden Indian, they began to shout to one another across the street. The Saddler's Horse was very pleased. He hadn't seen a Wooden Indian for years and years. It was just like old times come back again.

"Hello," cried the Indian. "What are you doing there? I haven't seen a horse like you for ages!"

"Oh, I live here," said the Saddler's Horse. "I'm the oldest person in this town! I've been here longer than the Town Hall itself."

"Well, well," said the Wooden Indian. "Times have surely changed, haven't they? None of these nasty cars about when *we* were young! I don't like them, and I don't like the gasoline pumps, either. Things used to be much better. You and I are losing our jobs now. I've lost mine already. Antiques, that's what they call us nowadays! Still, I've spent the last five years in a barn, and it feels good to stand out on the pavement again and see the folks passing. I've always been used to an outdoor life, and I like it. But tomorrow I suppose someone will come along and buy me, and then there'll be an end of it all——"

Just then a big truck passed by. It made so much noise that neither of them could hear the other speaking.

"*That's* what I complain of!" said the Saddler's Horse, when it had passed. "All that noise, and it shakes one to pieces! Yes, the old times were much better."

"Tell you what," cried the Wooden Indian as soon as he could make himself heard once more. "Suppose you and I take a trip together? We might never get the chance again! Everyone should have a good gallop once in his life. They think we are back numbers here, but we'll show them! Come along!"

He hopped across the street, right between the cars, and

93

made one spring to the back of the Saddler's Horse. The Saddler's Horse had no time even to think; he just threw up his head and snorted, and off they went! Out ran the antique dealer, out ran the saddler, waving his arms and shouting, but it was too late. The Saddler's Horse and the Wooden Indian were off together, and nothing could stop them!

First they galloped by the railway station, dodging in and out among the buses and parked cars; then up the hill, 'round the corner by the Post Office and into Main Street. Everyone turned and stared. Little boys yelled, shopkeepers ran to their doorways, old ladies dropped their parcels and screamed. People shouted:

"It's a circus parade!"

"It's a new advertisement!"

"It's a wild Indian gone crazy!"

And among all the shouting and excitement the saddler and the antique dealer ran puffing and panting along, shouting: "Stop them! Stop them!"

But no one could stop them.

Down Main Street they galloped, right through all the traffic. The policeman ran out and blew his whistle at them, but they dashed straight by him. Past the cinema, past the bank and Town Hall, and when they came to the tall Stop and Go sign on the corner the Saddler's Horse jumped clear over it. Then his great hoofs thundered over the bridge, and they were gone.

The townsfolk were left staring.

"Did you ever hear of such a thing!" they gasped. The old gentlemen mopped their foreheads, and the old ladies picked up their parcels again. "The idea of tearing along like that!" they cried indignantly. "Something ought to be done about it!" As for the traffic cop, he was as red in the face as a beet, and he shouted and waved at the cars as if it were all their fault.

The little boys craned their necks down the street. They were still hoping to see the rest of the circus parade.

Before long the news had gone out over the whole countryside. Startled motorists pulled up at wayside gas stations, telling of great hoofs that had thundered behind them along the highway, of a huge grey horse that had flashed by in a cloud of dust and disappeared. Up and down the roads, far and wide, motorcycle cops went whizzing past, looking everywhere for a crazy Indian on a big gray horse.

Meantime, many miles away in a green meadow by the roadside, the Wooden Indian and the Saddler's Horse had stopped to rest.

"That was a grand ride!" said the Wooden Indian as he slid off.

"It was!" panted the Saddler's Horse.

95

"Didn't we give them a scare?" said the Wooden Indian.

"We did!" puffed the Saddler's Horse.

To tell the truth, he was beginning to feel a bit tired, and was quite glad to stop galloping for a while and just rest quietly in the deep grass. It had been grand while it lasted, but now, all at once, his wooden limbs began to tremble and his wooden back began to ache. Tomorrow, he knew, he would be terribly stiff in all his joints. After all, when one is as old as the Saddler's Horse, and has never galloped before in one's life, one is bound to feel it!

Just then, somewhere in the distance, a train whistle blew; a long, plaintive note. The Saddler's Horse gave a start. He thought all at once of the pavement and the trees and the railway station, the familiar street that he had gazed on for so many years. Six o'clock . . . at this very moment, perhaps, the saddler was stepping out of the doorway in his apron, ready to wheel him back into the cool, dark shop to sleep.

"Don't you think," said the Saddler's Horse in a rather shaky voice, "that we ought to be turning back now?"

"Back?" said the Wooden Indian. "I'm not going back! You can go if you want to. I shall stay here for the rest of my life and live in the woods!"

The Saddler's Horse looked doubtfully at the meadows, at the tall dark woods behind, and the sky already deepening to sunset.

"Well . . . good-by!" he said at last.

"Good-by!" said the Wooden Indian.

Slowly and stiffly the Saddler's Horse began to limp back along the dusty highroad towards town. Every once in a while he turned his head to gaze back. There in the middle of the field, grown each moment smaller and smaller, he could see the Wooden Indian standing, waving his arms, clear and distinct against the sunset.

The Saddler's Horse

The saddler felt not at all cheerful that evening as he stood in his doorway, staring across the street. For one thing, he was afraid that at any moment the policeman might come and arrest him, on account of all the disturbance that had occurred. He had talked it over with the antique dealer and they had both decided that the wisest thing was to say nothing about it. Still, one never knew.

Besides, he really did miss the Horse. He was proud of him, and they had lived together so long that he was like an old friend. All these years the saddler had wheeled him out every morning, and wheeled him in every night, and now goodness alone knew where he was or what had happened to him!

When the six o'clock whistle blew, the saddler had all he could do to keep from bursting into tears.

But the next morning, when he opened the shop door, his heart gave a great jump.

"Bless me!" cried the saddler.

For there in his old place on the pavement stood the Saddler's Horse, gazing down his nose at the cars just as usual. He looked a little dusty and perhaps a bit shaky on his legs, and of all strange things, there was a burdock caught in his long tail! But otherwise he was none the worse. There he stood, and there he stands to this day, perfectly contented, for he has never tried to run away again. You may see him yourself, any time between eight and six, if you happen to be passing by.

As for the Wooden Indian, no one has ever set eyes on him again.

From A STREET OF LITTLE SHOPS
Illustrated by Grace Paull

Mary Cockett remembers and uses the past as often as she uses her day to day observation. What she sees clearest of all, perhaps, is the way children enjoy themselves—a little boy having a junk sale in the back garden, two boys racing caterpillars on a box by a market stall, a child running hot water from a steamroller to wash his hands. She has always tried out her stories on her own children, and they read as if they were being told. This story is made up of many things; a narrow tumble-down street in Chiswick, England, where a cobbler's shop displayed a notice like the one in the story; another cobbler's in the village where she spent her childhood, where "I used to linger to smell the new leather and watch the cobbler at work and warm myself by the stove"; a remark overheard once, "I've all the time in the world," which filled her with wonder for she was hardpressed then and had no time at all. Like all her stories, this one builds up with minute details a vivid whole.

MARY COCKETT

Tumble-down Shop

NOT very far from Felicity and Jonathan's house there was a small, narrow tumble-down street, hardly to be called a street at all. They were surprised when they found it. Even the way to it was not an ordinary way. It was through an alleyway, with high walls on either side. There were doors in the wall, doors that were always closed. They led into gardens, but to Felicity and Jonathan they were just doorways to hide in. The walls were old, and mossy there, and tiny ferns grew from them.

"It's like a secret place," said Felicity.

"I wish this alleyway belonged to us," said Jonathan.

His sister said, "Well, in a way it does. We can use it whenever we like. I wish we'd known about it long ago."

It was the old man next door who had said to their mummy, "The cobbler in that street through the alleyway has a very poor sort of shop, but he mends shoes better than anyone else I know. His name is Bryony."

After that Felicity and Jonathan took their shoes to Bryony's, and they were able to go by themselves.

On the way there one morning Jonathan said, "I like going to his shop. His eyes are twinkly, and I think he likes me."

"It isn't only you," said his sister. "Mummy says he seems to like most small things: small shops, small shoes, small animals, and small children."

"He's small himself," said Jonathan. "His head only just peeps over the counter."

"He's the right size for the shop," said Felicity. "A big fat man would look silly in it."

Indeed it was a small shop, old and shabby, altogether tumble-down. It was one room, and that was dark at the back, but it was the sort of shop one grew fond of all the same.

When Bryony the cobbler saw Jonathan that morning he said, "Oh, it's you. I'm afraid your shoes aren't ready. I've had such a lot to do. I've finished one, but that isn't much good to you by itself."

"No," said Jonathan, laughing. "I can't hop very far."

"I'm just working on the other. Would you like to sit on those two stools and wait?"

Gladly they climbed onto the stools by the counter.

There was a small glass case next to Jonathan. It held shoelaces, black and white and brown. It held tins of polish and tubes of shoe cream and brushes of various sizes.

They weren't what Jonathan was looking at. He was looking at a notice which was pasted on the side of the glass case.

"Well," said Bryony, "can you read it?"

Jonathan could only read a few of the words, but he nodded his head and smiled. Felicity hopped off her stool and stood beside the notice.

She said to Jonathan, "What does it say, then?"

Jonathan giggled and said, "It says:

> *Cobbler, cobbler, mend my shoe,*
> *Get it done by half past two.*"

"Oh, Jonathan, you are silly. It doesn't say that at all."

100

"Read it out, then," said Jonathan. That was what he had wanted all along.

So Felicity read aloud, "Boots and shoes not collected after three months will be . . . disposed of."

Jonathan said nothing. He was disappointed. He thought it sounded dull. Felicity said nothing either. After a little pause she read out the notice again, thoughtfully.

"Boots and shoes not collected after three months will be disposed of."

She could read the words, but she sounded puzzled.

Bryony said, "You don't quite understand it, do you?"

She shook her head.

"It means if people don't collect their shoes within three months after they are mended I get rid of them."

"Get rid of people's shoes?" said Felicity, and she looked shocked.

"Well, they can't want them much if they haven't collected them after all that time. I'm short of space. I can't keep shoes forever in a shop this size. As a matter of fact, I do keep them quite a bit longer than three months, just in case their owners turn up to collect them."

"I don't really understand now," said Felicity. "Do you mean that some people bring shoes to be mended and then never come to fetch them?"

"That's right," said Bryony, "that's just what I mean, and they're a trouble to me, that's what they are."

Jonathan said, "*Why* don't they come?"

He could not understand it at all, and neither could Felicity.

"I don't know," said Bryony. "I wish I did. Perhaps they forget at which cobbler's they've left their shoes for repair, or maybe they change their minds and think the shoes weren't worth bothering with after all. Perhaps they are ill and then forget about their shoes. Perhaps they move out of the district and forget to collect them before they go."

"Grown-up people?" said Felicity.

Bryony nodded.

She said, "I thought it was only children who forgot things."

"Oh, dear, no," said Bryony. "Most children are better to deal with than grown-ups. I'm put to a lot of trouble, a lot of waste. You see, I've had to pay for the leather or rubber that is used on their shoes, and I've spent my time doing the mending."

"Poor you!" said Felicity. "What a shame!"

Bryony went to the back of the shop and switched on a very poor light. There in a jumble in the corner of the shop were dozens of shoes.

"All those not collected?" said Felicity.

"All those! I've had them for nearly six months, most of them, so if I can get a little money for them I think I have a right to it."

"Of course you have," said Felicity.

"I hope you'll get a lot," said Jonathan.

Bryony said, "No chance of that."

He went on mending Jonathan's shoe.

Before long the door opened, and a tramp came in, a man in ragged clothes.

"Good morning, Mr. Bryony," said the tramp.

"Good morning, sir," said Bryony. (That word 'sir' pleased the tramp very much. Nobody else ever called him sir.) "What can I do for you this morning?"

"Well," said the tramp, "that last pair of boots you sold me from the back there has lasted very well. They're just about worn out now, though. Have you another pair of left-over boots in size 10?"

"I'll just look and see," said Bryony, and he went over to the back of the shop.

Jonathan stood on his stool to get a better view. Bryony poked about a little, and then picked up a large boot for a left foot.

"I think this will be size 10," he said, bringing it to the counter.

Jonathan got down from standing on his stool and just sat on it.

"Thank you," said the tramp. "A good boot, that. I hope it fits."

Felicity gave him her stool to sit on.

He bent down and took off his left boot. The laces were made of string, Jonathan noticed. There was an enormous hole in his sock. He laughed, and wiggled his big toe through it.

"It's very particular about having a bit of fresh air," he said, and the children smiled shyly. "Now, let's see if this

boot fits . . . There, isn't that a bit of luck? Just right! I'll
have this pair if they're going cheap, Mr. Bryony."

"You can have them for seventy-five cents, if that suits you.
It's less than the mending cost, but it's better than nothing—
for me."

"They're a proper bargain," said the tramp, "if the other
one's as comfortable as this."

"I'll look for it in just a minute," said Bryony. "I'd like to
finish this child's shoe repair first, if you don't mind. He's
been waiting for some time. You're not in a hurry, are you?"

"Me?" said the tramp, and he smiled, and there were gaps
in three places where there should have been teeth. "In a
hurry? No, I leave that to other folks. I've all the time in
the world."

Felicity had never heard anyone say that.

Jonathan said, "Let me look for the right boot to match
the other one."

"And me," said Felicity.

"With pleasure," said Bryony, and he lifted the counter
flap and let them through.

It was not as easy as you might think to find the other
boot. The light was poor, and the boots and shoes were in
an awful muddle. But soon Jonathan shouted that he had
found it.

Then both he and Felicity said, "O-o-oh!" and they stepped
back from the boot.

"What's the matter?" Bryony asked, moving towards them.

"It has straw inside!" said Felicity.

"And lots of tiny bits of paper!" added Jonathan.

Bryony picked up the boot and took it where the light was
better.

"It's been a nest for mice," he said.

"No doubt of it," said the tramp, "but they don't live there
any more."

104

He reached over for the boot, and turned it upside down into a rubbish tin. He removed every scrap of straw and paper, and then took the boot to the door to have a really good look inside.

"It doesn't seem to have come to any harm," he said.

He wiped it out with a bit of rag that was as black as the boot, looking over it at Jonathan and Felicity meanwhile.

"Just making sure there's nothing inside to nibble my toe," he said.

They giggled, and they watched him while he tried it on.

"Fine," he said, holding out his right leg. "Fine."

Jonathan said, "I was thinking it must feel funny to have your foot in a mouse's house."

"Well, I'm bothered," said the tramp. "It's the mouse who should have felt funny to be making a house out of a man's boot."

Then he paid for his boots, and Bryony gave him a new pair of laces to keep until he needed them. He went out into the morning, whistling.

When he had gone Felicity read out the notice once again: "Boots and shoes not collected after three months will be disposed of."

"I see what it means now," said Jonathan.

From OUT WITH FELICITY AND JONATHAN
Illustrated by Richard G. Robinson

*The Norwegian stories about Mrs. Pepperpot depend on one fact—
that this sharp-tongued housewife is apt, now and then, to go small,
to the size of a pepperpot. She can never predict this and the odd
situations she and her husband are caught in seem all the more odd
because the village shop, and the little house with brass bedstead and
potted plants and cat, are all the time perfectly ordinary and everyday.*

ALF PRØYSEN

Mrs. Pepperpot Buys Macaroni

"It's a very long time since we've had macaroni for supper," said Mr. Pepperpot one day.

"Then you shall have it today, my love," said his wife. "But I shall have to go to the grocer for some. So first of all you'll have to find me."

"Find you?" said Mr. Pepperpot. "What sort of nonsense is that?" But when he looked round for her he couldn't see her anywhere. "Don't be silly, wife," he said, "if you're hiding in the cupboard you must come out this minute. We're too big to play hide-and-seek."

"*I'm* not too big, I'm just the right size for 'hunt-the-pepperpot'," laughed Mrs. Pepperpot. "Find me if you can!"

"I'm not going to charge around my own bedroom looking for my wife," he said crossly.

"Now, now! I'll help you; I'll tell you when you're warm. Just now you're very cold." For Mr. Pepperpot was peering out of the window, thinking she might have jumped out. As he searched around the room she called out "Warm!," "Colder!," "Getting hotter!" until he was quite dizzy.

At last she shouted, "You'll burn the top of your bald head if you don't look up!" And there she was, sitting on the bed-

post, swinging her legs and laughing at him.

Her husband pulled a very long face when he saw her. "This is a bad business—a very bad business," he said, stroking her cheek with his little finger.

"I don't think it's a bad business," said Mrs. Pepperpot.

"I shall have a terrible time. The whole town will laugh when they see I have a wife the size of a pepperpot."

"Who cares?" she answered. "That doesn't matter a bit. Now put me down on the floor so that I can get ready to go to the grocer and buy your macaroni."

But her husband wouldn't hear of her going; he would go to the grocer himself.

"That'll be a lot of use!" she said. "When you get home you'll have forgotten to buy the macaroni. I'm sure even if I wrote 'macaroni' right across your forehead you'd bring back cinnamon and salt herrings instead."

"But how are you going to walk all that way with those tiny legs?"

"Put me in your coat pocket; then I won't need to walk."

There was no help for it, so Mr. Pepperpot put his wife in his pocket and set off for the shop.

Soon she started talking: "My goodness me, what a lot of strange things you have in your pocket—screws and nails, tobacco and matches—there's even a fishhook! You'll have to take that out at once; I might get it caught in my skirt."

"Don't talk so loud," said her husband as he took out the fishhook. "We're going into the shop now."

It was an old-fashioned village store where they sold everything from prunes to coffee cups. The grocer was particularly proud of the coffee cups and held one up for Mr. Pepperpot to see. This made his wife curious and she popped her head out of his pocket.

"You stay where you are!" whispered Mr. Pepperpot.

"I beg your pardon, did you say anything?" asked the grocer.

"No, no, I was just humming a little tune," said Mr. Pepperpot. "Tra-la-la!"

"What color are the cups?" whispered his wife. And her husband sang:

The cups are blue
With gold edge too,
But they cost too much
So that won't do!

After that Mrs. Pepperpot kept quiet—but not for long. When her husband pulled out his tobacco tin she couldn't resist hanging onto the lid. Neither her husband nor anyone else in the shop noticed her slipping onto the counter and hiding behind a flour bag. From there she darted silently across to the scales, crawled under them, past a pair of kippers wrapped in newspaper, and found herself next to the coffee cups.

"Aren't they pretty!" she whispered, and took a step backwards to get a better view. Whoops! She fell right into the macaroni drawer which had been left open. She hastily covered herself up with macaroni, but the grocer heard the scratching noise and quickly banged the drawer shut. You see, it did sometimes happen that mice got in the drawers, and that's not the sort of thing you want people to know about,

so the grocer pretended nothing had happened and went on serving.

There was Mrs. Pepperpot all in the dark; she could hear the grocer serving her husband now. "That's good," she thought. "When he orders macaroni I'll get my chance to slip into the bag with it."

But it was just as she had feared; her husband forgot what he had come to buy. Mrs. Pepperpot shouted at the top of her voice, "MACARONI!"; but it was impossible to get him to hear.

"A quarter of a pound of coffee, please," said her husband.

"Anything else?" asked the grocer.

"MACARONI!" shouted Mrs. Pepperpot.

"Two pounds of sugar," said her husband.

"Anything more?"

"MACARONI!" shouted Mrs. Pepperpot.

But at last her husband remembered the macaroni of his own accord. The grocer hurriedly filled a bag. He thought he felt something move, but he didn't say a word.

"That's all, thank you," said Mr. Pepperpot. When he got outside the door he was just about to make sure his wife was still in his pocket when a truck drew up and offered to give him a lift all the way home. Once there, he took off his knapsack with all the shopping in it and put his hand in his pocket to lift out his wife.

The pocket was empty.

Now he was really frightened. First he thought she was teasing him, but when he had called three times and still no wife appeared, he put on his hat again and hurried back to the shop.

The grocer saw him coming. "He's probably going to complain about the mouse in the macaroni," he thought.

"Have you forgotten anything, Mr. Pepperpot?" he asked, and smiled as pleasantly as he could.

111

Mr. Pepperpot was looking all around. "Yes," he said.

"I would be very grateful, Mr. Pepperpot, if you would keep it to yourself about the mouse being in the macaroni. I'll let you have these fine blue coffee cups if you'll say no more about it."

"Mouse?" Mr. Pepperpot looked puzzled.

"Shh!" said the grocer, and hurriedly started wrapping up the cups.

Then Mr. Pepperpot realized that the grocer had mistaken his wife for a mouse. So he took the cups and rushed home as fast as he could. By the time he got there he was in a sweat of fear that his wife might have been squeezed to death in the macaroni bag.

"Oh, my dear wife," he muttered to himself. "My poor darling wife. I'll never again be ashamed of you being the size of a pepperpot—as long as you're still alive!"

When he opened the door she was standing by the cooking-stove, dishing up the macaroni—as large as life; in fact, as large as you or I.

From LITTLE OLD MRS. PEPPERPOT
Illustrated by Bjorn Berg

The
Garden Gate

When Louisa May Alcott began to write to help family funds she studied magazines to find out what was popular in the Boston of the 1850s; poems, tales of flower fairies and sensational melodramas came from her ready pen. When a publisher suggested a story for girls, she replied that she did not understand girls; but she was persuaded to try. The result was "Little Women" and those other books of hers, none of which will ever date because they are based on the essentials of family life. "Under the Lilacs" is among her most delightful books. From the quiet beginning, which introduces two small girls and their mother (caretaker at the Great House), it broadens into a tale of a circus boy and his lost father, which is full of color and variety; but the quiet secure home is always in the background.

LOUISA MAY ALCOTT

A Mysterious Dog

THE elm-tree avenue was all overgrown, the great gate was never unlocked, and the old house had been shut up for several years. Yet voices were heard about the place, the lilacs nodded over the high wall as if they said, "We could tell fine secrets if we chose," and the mullein outside the gate made haste to reach the keyhole, that it might peep in and see what was going on.

If it had suddenly grown up like a magic beanstalk, and looked in on a certain June day, it would have seen a droll but pleasant sight, for somebody evidently was going to have a party.

From the gate to the porch went a wide walk, paved with smooth slabs of dark stone, and bordered with the tall bushes which met overhead, making a green roof. All sorts of neglected flowers and wild weeds grew between their stems, covering the walls of this summer parlor with the prettiest tapestry. A board, propped on two blocks of wood, stood in the middle of the walk, covered with a little plaid shawl much the worse for wear, and on it a miniature tea service was set forth with great elegance. To be sure, the teapot had lost its spout, the cream jug its handle, the sugar bowl its cover, and the cups and plates were all more or less cracked or nicked; but polite persons would not take notice of these trifling deficiencies, and none but polite persons were invited to this party.

On either side of the porch was a seat, and here a somewhat remarkable sight would have been revealed to any inquisitive eye peering through the aforesaid keyhole. Upon the left-hand seat lay seven dolls, upon the right-hand seat lay six; and so varied were the expressions of their countenances, owing to fractures, dirt, age, and other afflictions, that one would very naturally have thought this a doll's hospital, and these the patients waiting for their tea. This, however, would have been a sad mistake; for if the wind had lifted the coverings laid over them, it would have disclosed the fact that all were in full dress, and merely reposing before the feast should begin.

There was another interesting feature of the scene which would have puzzled any but those well acquainted with the manners and customs of dolls. A fourteenth rag baby, with a china head, hung by her neck from the rusty knocker in the middle of the door. A sprig of white and one of purple lilac nodded over her, a dress of yellow calico, richly trimmed with red-flannel scallops, shrouded her slender form, a garland of small flowers crowned her glossy curls, and a pair of blue boots touched toes in the friendliest, if not the most graceful, manner. An emotion of grief, as well as of surprise, might well have thrilled any youthful breast at such a spectacle; for why, oh! why, was this resplendent dolly hung up there to be stared at by thirteen of her kindred? Was she a criminal, the sight of whose execution threw them flat upon their backs in speechless horror? Or was she an idol, to be adored in that humble posture? Neither, my friends. She was blonde Belinda, set, or rather hung, aloft, in the place of honor, for this was her seventh birthday, and a superb ball was about to celebrate the great event.

All were evidently awaiting a summons to the festive

116

board; but such was the perfect breeding of these dolls, that not a single eye out of the whole twenty-seven (Dutch Hans had lost one of the black beads from his worsted countenance) turned for a moment toward the table, or so much as winked, as they lay in decorous rows, gazing with mute admiration at Belinda. She, unable to repress the joy and pride which swelled her sawdust bosom till the seams gaped, gave an occasional bounce as the wind waved her yellow skirts, or made the blue boots dance a sort of jig upon the door. Hanging was evidently not a painful operation, for she smiled contentedly, and looked as if the red ribbon around her neck was not uncomfortably tight; therefore, if slow suffocation suited *her*, who else had any right to complain? So a pleasing silence

117

reigned, not even broken by a snore from Dinah, the top of whose turban alone was visible above the coverlet, or a cry from baby Jane, though her bare feet stuck out in a way that would have produced shrieks from a less well-trained infant.

Presently voices were heard approaching, and through the arch which led to a side path came two little girls, one carrying a small pitcher, the other proudly bearing a basket covered with a napkin. They looked like twins, but were not, for Bab was a year older than Betty, though only an inch taller. Both had on brown calico frocks, much the worse for a week's wear; but clean pink pinatores, in honor of the occasion, made up for that, as well as the gray stockings and thick boots. Both had round, rosy faces rather sunburned, pug noses somewhat freckled, merry blue eyes, and braided tails of hair hanging down their backs like those of the dear little Kenwigses.

"Don't they look sweet?" cried Bab, gazing with maternal pride upon the left-hand row of dolls, who might appropriately have sung in chorus, "We are seven."

"Very nice; but my Belinda beats them all. I do think she is the splendidest child that ever was!" And Betty set down the basket to run and embrace the suspended darling, just then kicking up her heels with joyful abandon.

"The cake can be cooling while we fix the children. It does smell perfectly delicious!" said Bab, lifting the napkin to hang over the basket, fondly regarding the little round loaf that lay inside.

"Leave some smell for me!" commanded Betty, rushing back to get her fair share of the spicy fragrance.

The pug noses sniffed it up luxuriously, and the bright eyes feasted upon the loveliness of the cake, so brown and shiny, with a tipsy-looking B in pie crust, staggering down one side, instead of sitting properly atop.

"Ma let me put it on the very last minute, and it baked so hard I couldn't pick it off. We can give Belinda that piece, so it's just as well," observed Betty, taking the lead as her child was queen of the revel.

"Let's set them around, so they can see too," proposed Bab, going, with a hop, skip, and jump, to collect her young family.

Betty agreed, and for several minutes both were absorbed in seating their dolls about the table; for some of the dear things were so limp they wouldn't sit up, and others so stiff they wouldn't sit down, and all sorts of seats had to be contrived to suit the peculiarities of their spines. This arduous task accomplished, the fond mammas stepped back to enjoy the spectacle, which, I assure you, was an impressive one. Belinda sat with great dignity at the head, her hands genteelly holding a pink cambric pocket handkerchief in her lap. Josephus, her cousin, took the foot, elegantly arrayed in a new suit of purple and green gingham, with his speaking countenance much obscured by a straw hat several sizes too large for him; while on either side sat guests of every size, complexion, and costume, producing a very gay and varied effect, as all were dressed with a noble disregard of fashion.

"They will like to see us get tea. Did you forget the buns?" inquired Betty anxiously.

"No, got them in my pocket." And Bab produced from that chaotic cupboard two rather stale and crumbly ones, saved from lunch for the fête. These were cut up and arranged in plates, forming a graceful circle around the cake, still in its basket.

"Ma couldn't spare much milk, so we must mix water with it. Strong tea isn't good for children, she says." And Bab contentedly surveyed the gill of skim milk which was to satisfy the thirst of the company.

"While the tea draws and the cake cools, let's sit down and rest; I'm so tired!" sighed Betty, dropping down on the doorstep and stretching out the stout little legs which had been on the go all day; for Saturday had its tasks as well as its fun, and much business had preceded this unusual pleasure.

Bab went and sat beside her, looking idly down the walk toward the gate, where a fine cobweb shone in the afternoon sun.

"Ma says she is going over the house in a day or two, now it is warm and dry after the storm, and we may go with her. You know she wouldn't take us in the fall, 'cause we had whooping cough, and it was damp there. Now we shall see all the nice things; won't it be fun?" observed Bab, after a pause.

"Yes, indeed! Ma says there's lots of books in one room, and I can look at 'em while she goes around. Maybe I'll have time to read some, and then I can tell you," answered Betty, who dearly loved stories, and seldom got any new ones.

"I'd rather see the old spinning wheel up in the garret, and the big pictures, and the queer clothes in the blue chest. It makes me mad to have them all shut up there, when we might have such fun with them. I'd just like to bang that old door down!" And Bab twisted 'round to give it a thump with her boots. "You needn't laugh; you know you'd like it as much as me," she added, twisting back again, rather ashamed of her impatience.

"I didn't laugh."

"You did! Don't you suppose I know what laughing is?"

"I guess I know I didn't."

"You did laugh! How dare you tell such a fib?"

"If you say that again I'll take Belinda and go right home; then what will you do?"

"I'll eat up the cake."

"No, you won't! It's mine, Ma said so; and you are only company, so you'd better behave or I won't have any party at all, so now."

This awful threat calmed Bab's anger at once, and she hastened to introduce a safer subject.

"Never mind; don't let's fight before the children. Do you know, Ma says she will let us play in the coach house next time it rains, and keep the key if we want to."

"Oh, goody! that's because we told her how we found the little window under the woodbine, and didn't try to go in, though we might have just as easy as not," cried Betty, appeased at once, for, after a ten years' acquaintance, she had grown used to Bab's peppery temper.

"I suppose the coach will be all dust and rats and spiders, but I don't care. You and the dolls can be the passengers, and I shall sit up in front and drive."

"You always do. I shall like riding better than being horse all the time, with that old wooden bit in my mouth, and you jerking my arms off," said poor Betty, who was tired of being horse continually.

"I guess we'd better go and get the water now," suggested Bab, feeling that it was not safe to encourage her sister in such complaints.

"It is not many people who would dare to leave their children all alone with such a lovely cake, and know they wouldn't pick at it," said Betty proudly, as they trotted away to the spring, each with a little tin pail in her hand.

Alas, for the faith of these too confiding mammas! They were gone about five minutes, and when they returned a sight met their astonished eyes which produced a simultaneous shriek of horror. Flat upon their faces lay the fourteen dolls, and the cake, the cherished cake, was gone!

For an instant the little girls could only stand motionless,

121

gazing at the dreadful scene. Then Bab cast her water pail wildly away, and, doubling up her fist, cried out fiercely:

"It was that Sally! She said she'd pay me for slapping her when she pinched little Mary Ann, and now she has. I'll give it to her! You run that way. I'll run this. Quick! quick!"

Away they went, Bab racing straight on, and bewildered Betty turning obediently around to trot in the opposite direction as fast as she could, with the water splashing all over her as she ran, for she had forgotten to put down her pail. Around the house they went, and met with a crash at the back door, but no sign of the thief appeared.

"In the lane!" shouted Bab,

"Down by the spring!" panted Betty; and off they went again, one to scramble up a pile of stones and look over the wall into the avenue, the other to scamper to the spot they had just left. Still, nothing appeared but the dandelions' innocent faces looking up at Bab, and a brown bird scared from his bath in the spring by Betty's hasty approach.

Back they rushed, but only to meet a new scare, which made them both cry "Ow!" and fly into the porch for refuge.

A strange dog was sitting calmly among the ruins of the feast, licking his lips after basely eating up the last poor bits of bun, when he had bolted the cake, basket and all, apparently.

"Oh, the horrid thing!" cried Bab, longing to give battle, but afraid, for the dog was a peculiar as well as a dishonest animal.

"He looks like our china poodle, doesn't he?" whispered Betty, making herself as small as possible behind her more valiant sister.

He certainly did; for, though much larger and dirtier than the well-washed china dog, this live one had the same tassel at the end of his tail, ruffles of hair around his ankles,

122

and a body shaven behind and curly before. His eyes,
however, were yellow, instead of glassy black, like the
other's; his red nose worked as he cocked it up, as if smelling
for more cakes, in the most impudent manner; and never,
during the three years he had stood on the parlor mantelpiece, had the china poodle done the surprising feats with
which this mysterious dog now proceeded to astonish the
little girls almost out of their wits.

First he sat up, put his forepaws together, and begged
prettily; then he suddenly flung his hind legs into the air,
and walked about with great ease. Hardly had they re-

covered from this shock, when the hind legs came down, the forelegs went up, and he paraded in a soldierly manner to and fro, like a sentinel on guard. But the crowning performance was when he took his tail in his mouth and waltzed down the walk, over the prostrate dolls, to the gate and back again, barely escaping a general upset of the ravaged table.

Bab and Betty could only hold each other tight and squeal with delight, for never had they seen anything so funny; but, when the gymnastics ended, and the dizzy dog came and stood on the step before them barking loudly, with that pink nose of his sniffing at their feet, and his queer eyes fixed sharply upon them, their amusement turned to fear again, and they dared not stir.

"Whish, go away!" commanded Bab.

"Scat!" meekly quavered Betty.

To their great relief, the poodle gave several more inquiring barks, and then vanished as suddenly as he appeared. With one impulse, the children ran to see what became of him, and, after a brisk scamper through the orchard, saw the tasseled tail disappear under the fence at the far end.

"Where *do* you s'pose he came from?" asked Betty, stopping to rest on a big stone.

"I'd like to know where he's gone, too, and give him a good beating, old thief!" scolded Bab, remembering their wrongs.

"Oh, dear, yes! I hope the cake burned him dreadfully if he did eat it," groaned Betty, sadly remembering the dozen good raisins she chopped up, and the "lots of 'lasses" Mother put into the dear lost loaf.

"The party's all spoiled, so we may as well go home," and Bab mournfully led the way back.

Betty puckered up her face to cry, but burst out laughing in spite of her woe. "It was *so* funny to see him spin around and walk on his head! I wish he'd do it all over again; don't you?"

"Yes; but I hate him just the same. I wonder what Ma will say when—Why! Why!" and Bab stopped short in the arch, with her eyes as round and almost as large as the blue saucers on the tea tray.

"What is it? Oh, what is it?" cried Betty, all ready to run away if any new terror appeared.

"Look! There! It's come back!" said Bab in an awe-stricken whisper, pointing to the table.

Betty did look, and her eyes opened even wider —as well they might —for there, just where they first put it, was the lost cake, unhurt, unchanged, except that the big B had coasted a little further down the gingerbread hill.

From UNDER THE LILACS
Illustrated here by Robin Jacques

When Deborah Robinson's teacher came on a visit to the house she asked how "Teddy Robinson" was, and it seemed a good title for a volume of stories; this was the start of a series still in progress, always fresh and entertaining. Mrs. Robinson says, "My chief concern was to produce little adventures that might happen to any teddy bear. Unlike many others, he is kept strictly limited to what could happen. This has meant a great deal of juggling to keep him apparently active when in fact he was just sitting or lying around. Consequently he's rather a subjective kind of chap." This is clearly shown in the story given here, the first of all the Teddy Robinson stories. Although they are written about Mrs. Robinson's daughter and her bear, and the very real relationship that existed between them, they were not told to Deborah first, when she was a small child, but were written carefully, with many drafts, and only then read to their heroine.

JOAN G. ROBINSON

Teddy Robinson's Night Out

TEDDY ROBINSON was a nice, big, comfortable, friendly teddy bear. He had light brown fur and kind brown eyes, and he belonged to a little girl called Deborah. He was Deborah's favorite teddy bear, and Deborah was Teddy Robinson's favorite little girl, so they got on very well together, and wherever one of them went the other one usually went too.

One Saturday afternoon Teddy Robinson and Deborah looked out of the window and saw that the sun was shining and the almond tree in the garden was covered with pink blossoms.

"That's nice," said Deborah. "We can play out there. We will make our house under the little pink tree, and you can get brown in the sun, Teddy Robinson."

So she took out a little tray with the dolls' tea set on it, and a blanket to sit on, and the toy telephone in case anyone called them up, and she laid all the things out on the grass under the tree. Then she fetched a coloring book and some chalks for herself, and a book of nursery rhymes for Teddy Robinson.

Deborah lay on her tummy and colored the whole of an elephant and half a Noah's ark, and Teddy Robinson stared hard at a picture of Humpty-Dumpty and tried to remember

the words. He couldn't really read, but he loved pretending to.

"Hump, hump, humpety-hump," he said to himself over and over again; and then, "Hump, hump, humpety-hump, Deborah's drawing an elephump."

"Oh, Teddy Robinson," said Deborah, "don't think so loud— I can't hear myself chalking." Then, seeing him still bending over his book, she said, "Poor boy, I expect you're tired. It's time for your rest now." And she laid him down flat on his back so that he could look up into the sky.

At that moment there was a loud *rat-tat* on the front door and a long ring on the doorbell. Deborah jumped up and ran indoors to see who it could be, and Teddy Robinson lay back and began to count the number of blossoms he could see in the almond tree. He couldn't count more than four because he only had two arms and two legs to count on, so he counted up to four a great many times over, and then he began counting backward, and the wrong way 'round, and any way 'round that he could think of, and sometimes he put words in between his counting, so that in the end it went something like this:

> *One, two, three, four,*
> *someone knocking at the door.*
> *One, four, three, two,*
> *open the door and how d'you do?*
> *Four, two, three, one,*
> *isn't it nice to lie in the sun?*
> *One, two, four, three,*
> *underneath the almond tree.*

And he was very happy counting and singing to himself for quite a long time.

Then Teddy Robinson noticed that the sun was going down and there were long shadows in the garden. It looked as if it must be getting near bedtime.

Deborah will come and fetch me soon, he thought; and he watched the birds flying home to their nests in the trees above him.

A blackbird flew quite close to him and whistled and chirped, "Good night, teddy bear."

"Good night, bird," said Teddy Robinson and waved an arm at him.

Then a snail came crawling past.

"Are you sleeping out tonight? That will be nice for you," he said. "Good night, teddy bear."

"Good night, snail," said Teddy Robinson, and he watched it crawl slowly away into the long grass.

She will come and fetch me soon, he thought. It must be getting quite late.

But Deborah didn't come and fetch him. Do you know why? She was fast asleep in bed!

This is what had happened. When she had run to see who was knocking at the front door, Deborah had found Uncle Michael standing on the doorstep. He had come in his new car, and he said there was just time to take her out for a ride if she came quickly, but she must hurry because he had to get into the town before teatime. There was only just time for Mummy to get Deborah's coat on and wave good-by before they were off. They had come home ever so much later than they meant to because they had tea out in a shop, and then on the way home the new car had suddenly stopped and it took Uncle Michael a long time to find out what was wrong with it.

By the time they reached home Deborah was half asleep, and Mummy had bundled her into bed before she had time to really wake up again and remember about Teddy Robinson still being in the garden.

He didn't know all this, of course, but he guessed something unusual must have happened to make Deborah forget about him.

Soon a little wind blew across the garden, and down fluttered some blossoms from the almond tree. They fell right in the middle of Teddy Robinson's tummy.

"Thank you," he said, "I like pink flowers for a blanket."

So the almond tree shook its branches again, and more and more blossoms came tumbling down.

The garden tortoise came tramping slowly past.

"Hallo, teddy bear," he said. "Are you sleeping out? I hope you won't be cold. I felt a little breeze blowing up just now. I'm glad I've got my house with me."

"But I have a fur coat," said Teddy Robinson, "and pink blossoms for a blanket."

"So you have," said the tortoise. "That's lucky. Well, good night," and he drew his head into his shell and went to sleep close by.

The next-door kitten came padding softly through the grass and rubbed against him gently.

"You *are* out late," she said.

"Yes, I think I'm sleeping out tonight," said Teddy Robinson.

"Are you?" said the kitten. "You'll love that. I did it once. I'm going to do it a lot oftener when I'm older. Perhaps I'll stay out tonight."

But just then a window opened in the house next door and a voice called, "Puss! Puss! Puss! Come and have your fish! Fish! Fish!" and the kitten scampered off as fast as she could go.

Teddy Robinson heard the window shut down and then everything was quiet again.

The sky grew darker and darker blue, and soon the stars come out. Teddy Robinson lay and stared at them without blinking, and they twinkled and shone and winked at him as if they were surprised to see a teddy bear lying in the garden.

And after a while they began to sing to him, a very soft and sweet and far-away little song, to the tune of *Rock-a-Bye Baby*, and it went something like this:

> *Rock-a-bye Teddy, go to sleep soon.*
> *We will be watching, so will the moon.*
> *When you awake with dew on your paws*
> *Down will come Debbie and take you indoors.*

Teddy Robinson thought that was a lovely song, so when it was finished he sang one back to them. He sang it in a grunty voice because he was rather shy, and it went something like this:

> *This is me*
> *under the tree,*
> *the bravest bear you ever did see.*
> *All alone,*
> *so brave I've grown,*
> *I'm camping out on my very own.*

The stars nodded and winked and twinkled to show that they liked Teddy Robinson's song, and then they sang *Rock-a-bye Teddy* all over again, and he stared and stared at them until he fell asleep.

Very early in the morning a blackbird whistled, then another blackbird answered, and then all the birds in the garden opened their beaks and twittered and cheeped and sang. And Teddy Robinson woke up.

One of the blackbirds hopped up with a worm in his beak.

"Good morning, teddy bear," he said. "Would you like a worm for your breakfast?"

"Oh, no, thank you," said Teddy Robinson. "I don't usually bother about breakfast. Do eat it yourself."

"Thank you, I will," said the blackbird, and he gobbled it up and hopped off to find some more.

Then the snail came slipping past.

"Good morning, teddy bear," he said. "Did you sleep well?"

"Oh, yes, thank you," said Teddy Robinson.

The next-door kitten came scampering up, purring.

"You lucky pur-r-son," she said as she rubbed against Teddy Robinson. "Your fur-r is damp but it was a pur-r-fect night for staying out. I didn't want to miss my fish supper last night, otherwise I'd have stayed with you. Pur-r-haps I will another night. Did you enjoy it?"

"Oh, yes," said Teddy Robinson. "You were quite right about sleeping out. It was lovely."

The tortoise poked his head out and blinked.

133

"Hallo," he said. "There's a lot of talking going on for so early in the morning. What is it all about? Oh, good morning, bear. I'd forgotten you were here. I hope you had a comfortable night." And before Teddy Robinson could answer he had popped back inside his shell.

Then a moment later Teddy Robinson heard a little shuffling noise in the grass behind him, and there was Deborah out in the garden with bare feet, and in her pyjamas!

She picked him up and hugged him and kissed him and whispered to him very quietly, and then she ran through the wet grass and in at the kitchen door and up the stairs into her own room. A minute later she and Teddy Robinson were snuggled down in her warm little bed.

"You poor, poor boy," she whispered as she stroked his damp fur. "I never meant to leave you out all night. Oh, you poor, poor boy."

But Teddy Robinson whispered back, "I aren't a poor boy at all. I was camping out, and it was lovely." And then he tried to tell her all about the blackbird, and the snail, and the tortoise, and the kitten, and the stars. But because it was really so very early in the morning, and Deborah's bed was really so very warm and cosy, they both got drowsy; and before he had even got to the part about the stars singing their song to him both Teddy Robinson and Deborah were fast asleep.

And that is the end of the story about how Teddy Robinson stayed out all night.

From TEDDY ROBINSON
Illustrated by the author

135

When Mary Poppins came to the Banks family as nannie, in the London suburb that belongs to thirty years ago, she was incisive, down to earth and, to mischievous Jane and Michael and the pram-bound twins, a little alarming. It was not long before the children found that she had powers beyond those of a nursery disciplinarian. Pamela Travers believes that children will always need to enrich their imagination with the wonders of folklore and fairy tale. When Mary Poppins pushes out her pram it is from an orthodox establish-ment, precisely described, where the gardener sweeps up leaves, and meals and bedtime have their proper hours; when the author lets in the poetry of fairy tale, essential to her from her own childhood, what happens is just as precisely described. Mary Poppins is one of the most triumphantly real of all fantasy characters, and the books about her belong to everyone—from the imaginative adult or child, to that reader who starts by thinking that only here and now are real and who is, in the end, swept into the rich and strange world Pamela Travers has created.

P. L. TRAVERS

Miss Lark's Andrew

MISS LARK lived Next Door.

But before we go any further I must tell you what Next Door looked like. It was a very grand house, by far the grandest in Cherry Tree Lane. Even Admiral Boom had been known to envy Miss Lark her wonderful house, though his own had ship's funnels instead of chimneys and a flagstaff in the front garden. Over and over again the inhabitants of the Lane heard him say, as he rolled past Miss Lark's mansion: "Blast my gizzard! What does *she* want with a house like that?"

And the reason of Admiral Boom's jealousy was that Miss Lark had two gates. One was for Miss Lark's friends and relations, and the other for the Butcher and the Baker and the Milkman.

Once the Baker made a mistake and came in through the gate reserved for the friends and relations, and Miss Lark was so angry that she said she wouldn't have any more bread ever.

But in the end she had to forgive the Baker because he was the only one in the neighborhood who made those little flat rolls with the curly twists of crust on the top. She never really liked him very much after that, however, and when he came he pulled his hat far down over his eyes so that Miss Lark might think he was somebody else. But she never did.

Jane and Michael always knew when Miss Lark was in the garden or coming along the Lane, because she wore so many brooches and necklaces and earrings that she jingled and jangled just like a brass band. And whenever she met them, she always said the same thing:

"Good morning!" (or "Good afternoon!" if it happened to be after luncheon), "and how are *we* today?"

And Jane and Michael were never quite sure whether Miss Lark was asking how *they* were, or how she and Andrew were.

So they just replied: "Good afternoon!" (or, of course, "Good morning!" if it was before luncheon).

All day long, no matter where the children were, they could hear Miss Lark calling, in a very loud voice, things like:

"Andrew, where are you?" or

"Andrew, you mustn't go out without your overcoat!" or

"Andrew, come to Mother!"

And, if you didn't know, you would think that Andrew must be a little boy. Indeed, Jane thought that Miss Lark thought that Andrew *was* a little boy. But Andrew wasn't. He was a dog—one of those small, silky, fluffy dogs that look like a fur necklet, until they begin to bark. But, of course, when they do that you *know* that they're dogs. No fur necklet ever made a noise like that.

Now, Andrew led such a luxurious life that you might have thought he was the Shah of Persia in disguise. He slept on a silk pillow in Miss Lark's room; he went by car to the Hairdresser's twice a week to be shampooed; he had cream for every meal and sometimes oysters, and he possessed four overcoats with checks and stripes in different colors. Andrew's ordinary days were filled with the kind of things most people have only on birthdays. And when Andrew himself had a birthday he had *two* candles on his cake for every year, instead of only one.

The effect of all this was to make Andrew very much disliked in the neighborhood. People used to laugh heartily when they saw Andrew sitting up in the back seat of Miss Lark's car on the way to the Hairdresser's, with the fur rug over his knees and his best coat on. And on the day when Miss Lark bought him two pairs of small leather boots so that he could go out in the Park wet or fine, everybody in the Lane came down to their front gates to watch him go by and to smile secretly behind their hands.

"Pooh!" said Michael, as they were watching Andrew one day through the fence that separated Number Seventeen from Next Door. "Pooh, he's a ninkypoop!"

"How do you know?" asked Jane, very interested.

"I know because I heard Daddy call him one this morning!" said Michael, and he laughed at Andrew very rudely.

"He is *not* a nincompoop," said Mary Poppins. "And that is that."

And Mary Poppins was right. Andrew wasn't a nincompoop, as you will very soon see.

You must not think he did not respect Miss Lark. He did. He was even fond of her in a mild sort of way. He couldn't help having a kindly feeling for somebody who had been so good to him ever since he was a puppy, even if she *did* kiss him rather too often. But there was no doubt about it that the life Andrew led bored him to distraction. He would have given half his fortune, if he had one, for a nice piece of raw, red meat, instead of the usual breast of chicken or scrambled eggs with asparagus.

For in his secret, innermost heart, Andrew longed to be a common dog. He never passed his pedigree (which hung on the wall in Miss Lark's drawing room) without a shudder of shame. And many a time he wished he'd never had a father, nor a grandfather, nor a great-grandfather, if Miss Lark was going to make such a fuss of it.

It was this desire of his to *be* a common dog that made Andrew choose common dogs for his friends. And whenever he got the chance, he would run down to the front gate and sit there watching for them, so that he could exchange a few common remarks. But Miss Lark, when she discovered him, would be sure to call out:

"Andrew, Andrew, come in, my darling! Come away from those dreadful street arabs!"

And of course Andrew would *have* to come in, or Miss Lark would shame him by coming out and *bringing* him in. And Andrew would blush and hurry up the steps so that his friends should not hear her calling him her Precious, her Joy, her Little Lump of Sugar.

Andrew's most special friend was more than common, he was a Byword. He was half an Airedale and half a Retriever and the worst half of both. Whenever there was a fight in the road he would be sure to be in the thick of it; he was always getting into trouble with the Postman or the Policeman, and there was nothing he loved better than sniffing about in drains or garbage tins. He was, in fact, the talk of the whole street, and more than one person had been heard to say thankfully that they were glad he was not *their* dog.

But Andrew loved him and was continually on the watch for him. Sometimes they had only time to exchange a sniff in the Park, but on luckier occasions—though these were very rare—they would have long talks at the gate. From his friend, Andrew heard all the town gossip, and you could see by the rude way in which the other dog laughed as he told it, that it wasn't very complimentary.

Then, suddenly, Miss Lark's voice would be heard calling from a window, and the other dog would get up, loll out his tongue at Miss Lark, wink at Andrew and wander off, waving his hind quarters as he went just to show that *he* didn't care.

Andrew, of course, was never allowed outside the gate

unless he went with Miss Lark for a walk in the Park, or with one of the maids to have his toes manicured.

Imagine, then, the surprise of Jane and Michael when they saw Andrew, all alone, careering past them through the Park, with his ears back and his tail up as though he were on the track of a tiger.

Mary Poppins pulled the perambulator up with a jerk, in case Andrew, in his wild flight, should upset it and the Twins. And Jane and Michael screamed at him as he passed.

"Hi, Andrew! Where's your overcoat?" cried Michael, trying to make a high, windy voice like Miss Lark's.

"Andrew, you naughty little boy!" said Jane, and her voice, because she was a girl, was much more like Miss Lark's.

But Andrew just looked at them both very haughtily and barked sharply in the direction of Mary Poppins.

"Yap-yap!" said Andrew several times very quickly.

"Let me see. I think it's the first on your right and second house on the left-hand side," said Mary Poppins.

"Yap?" said Andrew.

"No—no garden. Only a backyard. Gate's usually open."

Andrew barked again.

"I'm not sure," said Mary Poppins. "But I should think so. Generally goes home at teatime."

Andrew flung back his head and set off again at a gallop.

Jane's eyes and Michael's were round as saucers with surprise.

"What was he saying?" they demanded breathlessly, both together.

"Just passing the time of day!" said Mary Poppins, and shut her mouth tightly as though she did not intend any more words to escape from it. John and Barbara gurgled from their perambulator.

"He wasn't!" said Michael.

"He *couldn't* have been!" said Jane.

"Well, you know best, of course. *As* usual," said Mary Poppins haughtily.

"He must have been asking you where somebody lived, I'm sure he must——" Michael began.

"Well, if you know, why bother to ask me?" said Mary Poppins sniffing. "*I'm* no dictionary."

"Oh, Michael," said Jane, "she'll never tell us if you talk like that. Mary Poppins, do say what Andrew was saying to you, *please*."

"Ask *him*. He knows—Mr. Know-All!" said Mary Poppins, nodding her head scornfully at Michael.

"Oh no, I don't. I promise I don't, Mary Poppins. Do tell."

"Half-past three. Teatime," said Mary Poppins, and she wheeled the perambulator around and shut her mouth tight again as though it were a trapdoor. She did not say another word all the way home.

Jane dropped behind with Michael.

"It's your fault!" she said. "Now we'll never know."

"I don't care!" said Michael, and he began to push his scooter very quickly. "I don't want to know."

But he did want to know very badly, indeed. And as it turned out, he and Jane and everybody else knew all about it before teatime.

Just as they were about to cross the road to their own house, they heard loud cries coming from Next Door, and there they saw a curious sight. Miss Lark's two maids were rushing wildly about the garden, looking under bushes and up into the trees as people do who have lost their most valuable possession. And there was Robertson Ay, from Number Seventeen, busily wasting his time by poking at the gravel on Miss Lark's path with a broom as though he expected to find the missing treasure under a pebble. Miss Lark herself was running about in her garden, waving her arms and calling: "Andrew, Andrew! Oh, he's lost. My darling boy is lost!

We must send for the Police. I must see the Prime Minister. Andrew is lost! Oh dear! Oh dear!"

"Oh, poor Miss Lark!" said Jane, hurrying across the road. She could not help feeling sorry because Miss Lark looked so upset.

But it was Michael who really comforted Miss Lark. Just as he was going in at the gate of Number Seventeen, he looked down the Lane and there he saw——

"Why, there's Andrew, Miss Lark. See, down there—just turning Admiral Boom's corner!"

"Where, where? Show me!" said Miss Lark breathlessly, and she peered in the direction in which Michael was pointing.

And there, sure enough, *was* Andrew, walking as slowly and as casually as though nothing in the world was the matter; and beside him waltzed a huge dog that seemed to be half an Airedale and half a Retriever, and the worst half of both.

"Oh, what a relief!" said Miss Lark, sighing loudly. "What a load off my mind!"

Mary Poppins and the children waited in the Lane outside Miss Lark's gate. Miss Lark herself and her two maids leaned over the fence, Robertson Ay, resting from his labors, propped himself up with his broom handle, and all of them watched in silence the return of Andrew.

He and his friend marched sedately up to the group, whisking their tails jauntily and keeping their ears well cocked, and you could tell by the look in Andrew's eye that, whatever he meant, he meant business.

"That dreadful dog!" said Miss Lark, looking at Andrew's companion.

"Shoo! Shoo! Go home!" she cried.

But the dog just sat down on the pavement and scratched his right ear with his left leg and yawned.

"Go away! Go home! Shoo, I say!" said Miss Lark, waving her arms angrily at the dog.

"And you, Andrew," she went on, "come indoors this minute! Going out like that—all alone and without your overcoat. I am very displeased with you!"

Andrew barked lazily, but did not move.

"What do you mean, Andrew? Come in at once!"

Andrew barked again.

"He says," put in Mary Poppins, "that he's not coming in."

Miss Lark turned and regarded her haughtily. "How do *you* know what my dog says, may I ask? Of course he will come in."

Andrew, however, merely shook his head and gave one or two low growls.

"He won't," said Mary Poppins. "Not unless his friend comes, too."

"Stuff and nonsense," said Miss Lark crossly. "That *can't* be what he says. As if I could have a great hulking mongrel like that inside my gate."

Andrew yapped three or four times.

"He says he means it," said Mary Poppins. "And what's more, he'll go and live with his friend unless his friend is allowed to come and live with him."

"Oh, Andrew, you can't—you can't, really—after all I've done for you and everything!" Miss Lark was nearly weeping.

Andrew barked and turned away. The other dog got up.

"Oh, he *does* mean it!" cried Miss Lark. "I see he does. He is going away." She sobbed a moment into her handkerchief, then she blew her nose and said:

"Very well, then, Andrew. I give in. This—this common dog can stay. On condition, of course, that he sleeps in the coal cellar."

"He insists, ma'am, that that won't do. His friend must have a silk cushion just like his and sleep in your room too. Otherwise he will go and sleep in the coal cellar with his friend," said Mary Poppins.

"Andrew, how could you?" moaned Miss Lark. "I shall never consent to such a thing."

Andrew looked as though he were preparing to depart. So did the other dog.

"Oh, he's leaving me!" shrieked Miss Lark. "Very well, then, Andrew. It will be as you wish. He *shall* sleep in my room. But I shall never be the same again, never, never. Such a common dog!"

She wiped her streaming eyes and went on:

"I should never have thought it of you, Andrew. But I'll say no more, no matter what I think. And this—er—creature —I shall have to call Waif or Stray or———"

At that the other dog looked at Miss Lark very indignantly, and Andrew barked loudly.

"They say you must call him Willoughby and nothing else," said Mary Poppins. "Willoughby being his name."

"Willoughby! What a name! Worse and worse!" said Miss Lark despairingly. "What is he saying now?" For Andrew was barking again.

"He says that if he comes back you are never to make him wear overcoats or go to the Hairdresser's again—that's his last word," said Mary Poppins.

There was a pause.

"Very well," said Miss Lark at last. "But I warn you, Andrew, if you catch your death of cold—don't blame me!"

And with that she turned and walked haughtily up the steps, sniffing away the last of her tears.

Andrew cocked his head towards Willoughby as if to say: "Come on!" and the other two of them waltzed side by side slowly up the garden path, waving their tails like banners, and followed Miss Lark into the house.

"He isn't a ninkypoop after all, you see," said Jane, as they went upstairs to the nursery and Tea.

"No," agreed Michael. "But how do you think Mary Poppins knew?"

"I don't know," said Jane. "And she'll never, never tell us. I am sure of that . . ."

From MARY POPPINS
Illustrated by Mary Shepard

The Door
of the Train

Helen Clare, who has made the five dolls in their dolls' house so real, is Pauline Clarke, whose story, "The Return of the Twelves," shows the same meticulous view of small things. When, in "The Return," Jane gets out the best dolls' house glasses for the banquet in honor of the wooden soldiers, they come from the same nursery as the toy train in which Vanessa and her family have the exciting ride described in this story. The Five Dolls stories started from the games played by Christina, adopted daughter of Cecil Leslie, who has illustrated the series, and as Christina made or was given new pieces of furniture, or invented new games, so new stories were suggested. The monkey, who provides "a breath of masculine air in a feminine household", is still extant, the author says, and "sits about with his paper hat on." Elizabeth Small, who owns the dolls' house in the stories, suddenly finds she is small enough to go in at the front door. But she goes as a visitor, and finds out that bossy Vanessa and the rest are fascinating people in their own right. Here is an author who understands children because she never forgets the wishes and delights of childhood.

A Trip by Train

ELIZABETH's old fur gloves, which had been patchy for a long time, were really no use any longer after playing in the snow. Her mother said that she could make anything she liked out of them for the dolls. They were a pretty pale gray color, and parts of them were still quite furry when she had brushed them out. First she cut the fingers and thumbs off. The furriest of the backs would make a lovely rug for the drawing room fireplace. Then she turned the two thumbs inside out, folded the tops over in a cuff, and there was a pair of fur boots for somebody. (She wondered who). She cut the best fur parts from five of the fingers, sewed them into muffs, and stitched a different colored silk on each, to hang 'round the dolls' necks. The three longest fingers could be made into scarves. There was one back left. This she shaped a little, like a cape, and sewed a hook and eye on at the top. Then she wrapped them all up in a piece of tissue paper and left the parcel outside the door, for it would be too big to carry when she was small.

As she went up the path, the monkey called out as usual from the roof.

"Parcel from London 'ere," he said.

149

"Yes, I know," said Elizabeth. "I had it sent."

"What is it?" he asked with interest.

"It's some fur clothes for the cold weather."

"I hopes there's one for me. Eskimoes always have fur clothes."

"But you've got fur clothes already."

The monkey looked gloomy.

"They gets everything," he said. "At least I ought to have a Davy Crockett cap."

Elizabeth had hardly tapped at the door before it was opened. All the dolls were waiting in the hall, as if they were just going out. Vanessa was wearing her bedspread and Jacqueline carrying her parasol.

"Oh, Mrs. Small," began Vanessa, "you've just caught us . . . Why, whatever is that large white parcel?" she said eagerly.

"Just you look what I've had made for you," said Elizabeth.

"What, what?" said Amanda.

"Bring it in," said Lupin.

"Is it presents?" asked Jane.

Jacqueline clasped her hands, "Ees eet to eat?" she said.

The dolls carried the large parcel into the diningroom and fell upon it to tear the paper off. The kitten helped.

"Bless my soul! Bless my soul!" said the parrot, walking along his perch.

"I'll open it, I'm the eldest," said Vanessa.

"I'm the quickest," said Amanda, who already had the paper off.

"Oh, Mrs. Small!"

"Bless my soul!" said Vanessa. "Fur things. Somebody, your brother, I suppose, has been big game hunting and shot a bear! How very generous and genteel of you to bring them."

"They're for the cold weather . . ." began Elizabeth.

"It went as quickly as it came, that snow," said Vanessa, in

150

a loud whisper. "Overnight. But these will be just as useful in the not-cold weather. Why, what a beautiful traveling rug!"

"Or a hearth rug."

"Mrs. Small! Muffs!"

"One each," said Elizabeth. "No, no, Lupin, you hang it round your neck to keep your hands in." For Lupin was pushing the muff onto her head.

"How very genteel!" said Vanessa with delight. "I always had a muff when I was a girl."

"Boots!" said Amanda. "I bags the boots!"

"No, I want them," Lupin said.

There was rather a quarrel as to who should have the boots, the scarves and the cape. In the end the three eldest dolls had the scarves, Amanda had the boots, and Lupin had the cape. ("To cover up her vest, you know," Vanessa said). The dolls put all the things on at once.

"You couldn't have brought them at a better time, Mrs. Small," said Vanessa, "as we were just planning an outing . . ."

"Yes, Mrs. Small," said Jane, "you'll never guess what's come past our door!"

"These fur things quite put it out of my head . . ." Vanessa said.

"What?" said Elizabeth.

"A railway! Jane saw it from the bedroom window. I'm not at all sure that I approve of it going past our door without permission . . ."

"A railway? Oh, I know what you mean." Elizabeth had suddenly remembered Edward's Hornby railway, which he had set up in the nursery.

"You knew about it, and you allowed them to build it?" Vanessa said, her feather beginning to bob. "Fancy letting them run it so close! We shall be deafened by the noise, and the smuts will get on the milk pudding."

"Serves the milk pudding right. I love the railway," said Amanda.

"Let's go," said Lupin. "We'll miss the train."

"And Mrs. Small," went on Jane, "how did they build it so quickly?"

"I think," Vanessa whispered, "they must have had slaves. But since it's there we may as well use it."

"What a good idea," Elizabeth said. "Come on then."

All the dolls, gathering their fur things around them (Vanessa had brought the traveling rug, "because trains are always cold, you know, so this is just the thing") tumbled out of the front door and made for the railway. Shuffle, shuffle, came Amanda, whose boots were too big.

"Going to the North Pole?" jeered the monkey.

"That vulgar animal! Take no notice," Vanessa said.

"I'm coming," he called, when he saw where they were going. "I'm the guard."

"I don't suppose the railway people will have you," Vanessa snapped.

But the railway seemed deserted. Edward had a circular track and several sets of points, a signal, two engines, a tender, three passenger cars and two freight cars. He had made a station out of a box lid. The dolls walked onto it, and the monkey went and stood by the signals.

"Nobody here," sniffed Vanessa. "Where do we get the tickets, pray?"

"We needn't bother about tickets," said Elizabeth, "as it's a private railway."

Amanda came hobbling back from the train.

"Vanessa!" she shrieked. "The car door won't open!"

"*Very* private," Vanessa sniffed. "Locked, I suppose. No doubt somebody with measles has been in that car and they've locked the door. Try another."

"Why do they lock it?" asked Lupin.

"To lock the germs in, of course,"

"Lots of people have had measles," called Amanda, tugging at the doors. "All the doors are locked."

"Then it's a most unhealthy train," Vanessa snorted, "and I doubt if we ought to go in it."

"Oh, it's all right," said Elizabeth, "but I'm afraid we'll have to travel in the freight cars, Vanessa, as the doors won't open. Climb in."

Lupin and Amanda thought that this was all the better. They climbed into a freight car, helped by Elizabeth. Lupin was swallowed up in her cape, and Amanda lost one of her boots.

"Bless my soul," said Vanessa, "it's not very genteel. Anyone would think we were cows. Or coal," she remarked.

"Yes, or sugar beets," said Elizabeth.

Vanessa stared. She was too old-fashioned to know about sugar beets.

"I suppose you mean sugar cane," she said. "Though I agree there's not much to choose between beating and caning. Come along, Jane, hold up your skirts." And she held out her hand to help Jane in. "My, that paying-guest will get her flounces dirty, and serve her right."

Poor Jacqueline smiled, not understanding, and clambered into the truck. The dolls all stood gazing over the edge.

"Now, when it starts, you must help pull me in," Elizabeth said. It was a good thing she remembered how to set the train going.

"But when does it start?" Jane said. "I haven't a watch."

"It goes when we like," Elizabeth explained.

Vanessa patted her scarf and smoothed her muff.

"How very genteel," she said, smiling. "Just like Royalty. I notice Her Majesty has her train run when she likes. And where she likes, too, for all I know. By the way, where are we going, Mrs. Small?"

"Dover!" said Jane.

"*La France*," screamed Jacqueline.

"The Isle of Wight," said Lupin.

"That's the only place she knows, she's very ignorant," whispered Vanessa.

"Oh, we just go around and around till it runs down," Elizabeth said.

"Runs down where?" Vanessa said. "Warn us, Mrs. Small, and we'll jump out."

"No, I mean you have to wind it up."

"Wind it up!" said Vanessa. "I never heard of a train before that you have to wind up. But I suppose it's some new-fangled notion," she sniffed.

"And we shall be going on a circular tour," Elizabeth said hastily. "Around and around."

"Ready?" called the monkey from the signals. And he put the signal up.

"Yes," shouted Elizabeth, and she let the catch go, and leaped at the freight cars as the little train began to move.

All the dolls seized Elizabeth and tugged her into the car.

"Good gracious me," Vanessa panted, "a most dangerous train, Mrs. Small, but you seem to be able to jump very well, I must say."

"Oh, isn't it lovely!" Amanda said, jigging up and down in the cattle truck. "Much better than the mouse-and-trap! Faster."

"It's very pleasant. Quite the thing," Vanessa said.

"There's a lovely view," said Jane. "We're going around the corner."

"There's the coal mine," Lupin said, as they passed the nursery coal box.

A Trip by Train

"What a charming house!" Vanessa said, smiling sweetly, as the Hornby train ran past the dolls' gate. "I wonder who lives there?"

"Vanessa," Amanda giggled, "you are silly. We live there."

"Well, there's no harm in wondering," Vanessa snapped, her cheeks going a shade redder.

"We've been past here before," Lupin said. "There's the monkey."

"Never mind. It never hurts to see things twice, especially for somebody as young and foolish as Lupin, you know," Vanessa said.

Elizabeth was wondering how many times the train would go around before it slowed down. She hoped very much that it would not topple off the rails as she had sometimes known it do. It was rocking slightly.

At this minute, Amanda, who was leaning out as far as she could lean and looking ahead, announced with interest:

"Mrs. Small, there's another train coming."

"Oh, how exciting," said Jane.

"It can't be," Elizabeth said. "There's no guard to set it going."

"Well, it is. Quite fast. I can see it."

"I can hear it!" Lupin yelled.

Elizabeth saw what had happened. The monkey had set the other engine going in the other direction. It had no cars on it, and was traveling fast.

"Hold tight, everybody!" she called. "There may be a smash!"

"Oh! Oh!" screamed all the dolls.

"Keep calm!" Vanessa ordered. "Be ready to jump! At least we are not penned in!"

But there was no need to jump. The other engine hummed along and bumped SMASH into their own! Their own toppled and wavered, and then, over it went, off the rails, bringing the three passenger cars and the two freight cars with it. All the dolls were tipped in a heap on the floor.

"Help!" screamed Lupin.

"*Au secours*," yelled Jacqueline.

"Don't make such a fuss," Vanessa said. "It was a very gentle spill indeed and nobody is hurt," she went on rather breathlessly, as she sorted out Lupin (who looked like a squirrel) and Amanda and Jane and Jacqueline and Elizabeth.

"That's wot comes of trains running when they like," jeered the monkey, walking along the line. The other engine had fallen too, and its works still whizzed.

"It's what comes of having a guard like you who knows nothing about it. Guard indeed!"

"Never mind, I loved it," Amanda said.

"So did I," said little Lupin. "I'm not a bit bruised because of my fur cape."

"Come along," said Vanessa. "Home again. Most convenient that the accident happened quite near our door, but I only hope the neighbors weren't looking. I don't know who will put the poor railway to rights. Perhaps they'll call in the slaves."

"Mrs. Small, I love my muff," said Jane, as she walked beside Elizabeth.

"So do I," chorused all the others.

"Most delightful," Vanessa said cheerfully. She did not seem at all put out by the accident.

"I'm glad you like them," Elizabeth said. "I must go now, Vanessa, but I shall come again soon."

"Do, do," said all the dolls at the gate.

When they were inside their house Elizabeth looked up at the monkey, who had climbed back on to the roof.

'What did you think of the railway strike?" he said, hugging himself.

"That's not a strike, that's a smash."

"One engine struck the other, what's that but a strike?" he said. And he waved his green cap, and blew through his teeth a long, wild whistle like a train.

From FIVE DOLLS IN THE SNOW
Illustrated by Cecil Leslie

When Laura Ingalls Wilder died in 1957, in her ninetieth year, she was perhaps the best-loved of all American authors, and for many years children have read and re-read her books. They are "her" stories. It is her own family that sets out from the forests of Wisconsin to travel by covered wagon through Kansas and Minnesota and settle finally in Dakota. It is her future husband, Almanzo Wilder, whose boyhood is described so vividly in "Farmer Boy". In middle age Mrs. Wilder recalled and set down the day to day happenings of that pioneer childhood, with a detail and a freshness that showed she was truly living the years over again.

LAURA INGALLS WILDER

Riding in the Cars

THEY could not talk very well, because all the time they were waiting, and listening for the train. At long, long last, Mary said she thought she heard it. Then Laura heard a faint, faraway hum. Her heart beat so fast that she could hardly listen to Ma.

Ma lifted Grace on her arm, and with her other hand she took hold of Carrie's. She said, "Laura, you come behind me with Mary. Be careful, now!"

The train was coming, louder. They stood by the satchels on the platform and saw it coming. Laura did not know how they could get the satchels on the train. Ma's hands were full, and Laura had to hold onto Mary. The engine's round front window glared in the sunshine like a huge eye. The smoke-stack flared upward to a wide top, and black smoke rolled up from it. A sudden streak of white shot up through the smoke, then the whistle screamed a long wild scream. The roaring thing came rushing straight at them all, swelling bigger and bigger, enormous, shaking everything with noise.

Then the worst was over. It had not hit them; it was roaring by them on thick big wheels. Bumps and crashes ran along the freight cars and flat cars and they stopped moving. The train was there, and they had to get into it.

"Laura!" Ma said sharply. "You and Mary be careful!"

"Yes, Ma, we are," said Laura. She guided Mary anxiously, one step at a time, across the boards of the platform, behind Ma's skirt. When the skirt stopped, Laura stopped Mary.

They had come to the last car at the end of the train. Steps went up into it, and a strange man in a dark suit and a cap helped Ma climb up them with Grace in her arms. "Oopsy-daisy!" he said, swinging Carrie up beside Ma. Then he said, "Them your satchels, ma'am?"

"Yes, please," Ma said, "Come, Laura and Mary."

"Who is he, Ma?" Carrie asked, while Laura helped Mary up the steps. They were crowded in a small place. The man came pushing cheerfully past them, with the satchels, and shouldered open the door of the car.

They followed him between two rows of red velvet seats full of people. The sides of the car were almost solidly made of windows; the car was almost as light as outdoors, and chunks of sunshine slanted across the people and the red velvet.

Ma sat down on one velvet seat and plumped Grace on her lap. She told Carrie to sit beside her. She said, "Laura, you and Mary sit in this seat ahead of me."

Laura guided Mary in, and they sat down. The velvet seat was springy. Laura wanted to bounce on it, but she must behave properly. She whispered, "Mary, the seats are red velvet."

"I see," Mary said, stroking the seat with her fingertips. "What's that in front of us?"

"It's the high back of the seat in front, and it's red velvet too," Laura told her.

The engine whistled, and they both jumped. The train was getting ready to go. Laura knelt up in the seat to see Ma. Ma looked calm and so pretty in her dark dress with its white lace collar and the sweet tiny white flowers on her hat.

"What is it, Laura?" Ma asked.

Laura asked, "Who was that man?"

"The brakeman," Ma said. "Now sit down and———"

The train jerked, jolting her backward. Laura's chin bumped hard on the seat back, and her hat slid on her head. Again the train jerked, not so badly this time, and then it began to shiver and the depot moved.

"It's going!" Carrie cried out.

The shivering grew faster and louder, the depot slid backward, and under the car the wheels began to beat time. A rub-a-dubdub, a rub-a-dubdub, the wheels went, faster and faster. The lumberyard and the back of the church and the front of the schoolhouse went by, and that was the last of that town.

The whole car swayed now, in time to the clackety-clacking underneath it, and the black smoke blew by in melting rolls. A telegraph wire swooped up and down beyond the window. It did not really swoop, but it seemed to swoop because it sagged between the poles. It was fastened to green glass knobs that glittered in the sunshine and went dark when the smoke rolled above them. Beyond the wire, grasslands and fields and scattered farmhouses and barns went by.

They went so fast that Laura could not really look at them before they were gone. In one hour that train would go twenty miles—as far as the horses traveled in a whole day.

The door opened, and a tall man came in. He wore a blue coat with brass buttons, and a cap, with

CONDUCTOR

in letters across its front. At every seat he stopped and took tickets. He punched round holes in the tickets with a small

161

machine in his hand. Ma gave him three tickets. Carrie and Grace were so little that they could ride on the train without paying.

The Conductor went on, and Laura said low, "Oh, Mary! so many shining brass buttons on his coat, and it says CON-DUCTOR right across the front of his cap!"

"And he is tall," Mary said. "His voice is high up."

Laura tried to tell her how fast the telegraph poles were going by. She said, "The wire sags down between them and swoops up again," and she counted them. "One—oop! Two —oop! Three! That's how fast they're going."

"I can tell it's fast, I can feel it," Mary said happily.

On that dreadful morning when Mary could not see even sunshine full in her eyes, Pa had said that Laura must see for her. He had said, "Your two eyes are quick enough, and your tongue, if you will use them for Mary." And Laura had promised. So she tried to be eyes for Mary, and it was seldom that Mary need ask her, "See out loud for me, Laura, please."

"Both sides of the car are windows, close together." Laura said now. "Every window is one big sheet of glass, and even the strips of wood between the windows shine like glass, they are so polished."

"Yes, I see," and Mary felt over the glass and touched the shining wood with her fingertips.

"The sunshine comes slanting in the south windows, in wide stripes over the red velvet seats and the people. Corners of sunshine fall on the floor, and keep reaching out and going back. Up above the windows the shiny wood curves in from the walls on both sides, and all along the middle of the ceiling there's a higher place. It has little walls of tiny, long, low windows, and you can see blue sky outside them. But outside the big windows, on both sides, the country is going by. The stubble fields are yellow, and haystacks are by the barns, and little trees are yellow and red in clumps around the houses.

"Now I will see the people," Laura went on murmuring. "In front of us is a head with a bald spot on top and side whiskers. He is reading a newspaper. He doesn't look out of the windows at all. Farther ahead are two young men with their hats on. They are holding a big white map and looking at it and talking about it. I guess they're going to look for a homestead too. Their hands are rough and calloused so they're good workers. And farther ahead there's a woman with bright yellow hair and, oh, Mary! the brightest red velvet hat with pink roses——"

Just then someone went by, and Laura looked up. She went on, "A thin man with bristly eyebrows and long moustaches and an Adam's apple just went by. He can't walk straight, the train's going so fast. I wonder what—Oh, Mary! He's turning a little handle on the wall at the end of the car, and water's coming out!

"The water's pouring right into a tin cup. Now he's drinking it. His Adam's apple bobs. He's filling the cup again. He just turns the handle, and the water comes right out. How do you suppose it—Mary! He's set that cup on a little shelf. Now he's coming back."

After the man had gone by, Laura made up her mind. She asked Ma if she could get a drink of water, and Ma said she might. So she started out.

She could not walk straight. The lurching car made her sway and grab at the seat backs all the way. But she got to the end of the car and looked at the shining handle and spout, and the little shelf under them that held the bright tin cup. She turned the handle just a little, and water came out of the spout. She turned the handle back, and the water stopped. Under the cup there was a little hole, put there to carry away any water that spilled. Laura had never seen anything so fascinating. It was all so neat, and so marvelous, that she wanted to fill the cup again and again. But that would waste the water. So after she drank, she only filled the cup part way, in order not to spill it, and she carried it very carefully to Ma.

Carrie drank, and Grace. They did not want any more, and Ma and Mary were not thirsty. So Laura carried the cup back to its place. All the time the train was rushing on and the country rushing back, and the car swaying, but this time Laura did not touch one seat that she passed. She could walk almost as well as the Conductor. Surely nobody suspected that she had never been on a train before.

Then a boy came walking along the aisle, with a basket on his arm. He stopped and showed it to everyone, and some people took things out of it and gave him money. When he reached Laura, she saw that the basket was full of boxes of candy and of long sticks of white chewing gum. The boy showed them to Ma and said, "Nice fresh candy, ma'am? Chewing gum?"

Ma shook her head, but the boy opened a box and showed the colored candy. Carrie's breath made an eager sound before she knew it.

The boy shook the box a little, not quite spilling the candy out. It was beautiful Christmas candy, red pieces and yellow pieces and some striped red-and-white. The boy said, "Only ten cents, ma'am, one dime."

Laura and Carrie, too, knew they could not have that candy. They were only looking at it. Suddenly Ma opened her purse and counted out a nickel and five pennies into the boy's hand. She took the box and gave it to Carrie.

When the boy had gone on, Ma said, excusing herself for spending so much, "After all, we must celebrate our first train ride."

Grace was asleep, and Ma said that babies should not eat candy. Ma took only a small piece. Then Carrie came into the seat with Laura and Mary and divided the rest. Each had two pieces. They meant to eat one and save the other for next day, but some time after the first pieces were gone, Laura decided to taste her second one. Then Carrie tasted hers, and finally Mary gave in. They licked those pieces all away, little by little.

They were still licking their fingers when the engine whistled long and loud. Then the car went more slowly, and slowly the backs of shanties went backward outside it. All the people began to gather their things together and put on their hats, and then there was an awful jolting crash, and the train stopped. It was noon, and they had reached Tracy.

"I hope you girls haven't spoiled your dinners with that candy," Ma said.

"We didn't bring any dinner, Ma," Carrie reminded her.

Absently Ma replied, "We're going to eat dinner in the hotel. Come, Laura. You and Mary be careful."

From BY THE SHORES OF SILVER LAKE
Illustrated by Garth Williams

The
Kitchen Door

Walter de la Mare always trusted children to accept terror and sadness, as well as joy and excitement, in the stories he wrote for them—stories creating a world of magic with an absolute reality of its own. There will never be another like it. In the story of "Dick and the Beanstalk" he lets fancy play around a familiar old nursery tale and adds his imaginings to it. A farmer's son, riding far from home on a frosty day, finds the dried remains of the beanstalk and climbs up to see what he can see. The giant Grackle, when he has recovered from his suspicions, persuades Dick to take him down to earth to see if he can discover the fate of his ancestor, and this makes difficulties for Dick's family. The extract given here comes from an earlier part of the story, where Dick is still in some danger.

WALTER DE LA MARE

Dick and the Beanstalk

BUT she led him in none the less through the great gates of the Castle and down into the kitchen, where a fire was burning on the hearth. This kitchen, Dick reckoned, was about the size of (but not much bigger than) a little church. It was warm and cozy after the dark and cold. A shaded lamp stood burning on the table, and there were pewter candlesticks three feet high for fat tallow candles on the dresser. Dick looked covertly about him, while he stood warming his hands a few paces from the huge open hearth. Here, beside him, was the very cupboard in which in terror Jack had hidden himself. The shut oven door was like the door of a dungeon. Through a stone archway to the right of him he could see a copper boiler. A chair stood beside the table. And on the table, as if waiting for somebody, was a tub-sized soup tureen. There was a bowl beside it, and a spoon to fit. And next to the spoon was a chunk of bread of about the size of a quartern loaf. Even though he stood at some distance, it was only by craning his neck that Dick could see what was on the table.

He looked at all this with astonished eyes. He had fancied Jack's giant's kitchen was a darker and gloomier place. But in Jack's day there was perhaps a fire less fierce burning in the hearth and no lamp alight; perhaps, too, in summer the shadows of the Castle walls hung coldly over its windows. Not that he felt very comfortable himself. Now that he had managed to get into the Castle, he began to be anxious as to what might happen to him before he could get out again. The ways and looks of this woman were not at all to his fancy and whoever was going to sup at that table might look even worse!

She had taken off her shawl now, and after rummaging in a high green cupboard had come back with a common-sized platter and an earthenware mug—mere dolls' china by comparison with the tureen on the table. She filled the mug with milk.

"Now get you up onto that stool," she said to Dick, bringing the mug and a platter of bread over to him. "Sit you up there and eat and drink and warm yourself while you can. My husband will be home at any moment. Then you can tell him who you are, what you want, why you have come, and where from."

Dick quaked in his shoes—not so much at the words, as at the woman's mouth when she said them. But he looked back at her as boldly as he dared, and climbed up onto the stool. There, clumsy mug in one hand and crust in the other, he set onto his bread and milk. It was pleasant enough, he thought to himself, to sit here in the warm eating his supper, though a scrape of butter would have helped. But what kind of dainty might not this woman's husband fancy for *his* when *he* came home!

So, as he sipped, he peeped about him for a way of escape. But except for the door that stood ajar, some great pots on the pot-board under the dresser, and a mouse's hole in the wainscot that was not much bigger than a fox's in a hedgerow, there was no crack or cranny to be seen. Besides, the woman was watching him as closely as a cat. And he decided that for the present it would be wiser to keep his eyes to himself, and to stay harmless where he was.

At last there came the sound of what Dick took for footsteps, from out of the back parts of the Castle. It was as if a man were pounding with a mallet on a tub. They came nearer. In a moment or two the kitchen door opened, and framed in the opening stood the woman's husband. Dick could not keep from squinting a little as he looked at him.

He guessed him to be about eighteen to twenty feet high—not more. Apart from this, he was not, thought Dick, what you could call a fine or large-sized giant. He was lean and bony; his loose unbuttoned leather jacket hung slack from his shoulders; and his legs in his stockings were no thicker than large scaffolding poles. There was a long nose in his long pale face, and on either side of his flat hat dangled dingy straw-colored hair, hanging down from the mop above it.

When his glance fell on Dick enjoying himself on his stool

by the kitchen fire, his watery green-gray eyes looked as if they might drop at any moment from out of his head.

"Head and choker! What have we here, wife?" he said at last to the leaden-faced woman. "What have we here! *Hm, hm.*"

Before she could answer, Dick spoke up as boldly as he knew how, and told the young giant (for though Dick could not be certain, he *looked* to be not above thirty)—he told the young giant how he had lost his way, and chancing on the withered Beanstalk, had climbed to the top of it to have a look around. He told him, too, how grieved he had been to hear that the woman's great-grandfather had never come back to the Castle after he had chased the boy called Jack away, and how much he wondered whether the Little Hen was buried, and what had become of the Harp. Dick went on talking because it was easier to do so than to keep silent, seeing that the two of them continued to stare at him, and in a far from friendly fashion.

"I expect it played its last tune," he ended up, "ages and ages before I was born."

"Aye," said the woman. "That's all pretty enough. But what *I* say is that unless the tale I have heard is all fable, this ugly imp here must be little short of the very spit of that wicked thief himself. Anywise, he looks to me as if he had come from the same place. What's more—" she turned on Dick, "if you can tell us where that is, you shall take my husband there and show it him. And he can look for the grave of my great-grandfather. And perhaps," and her thin dark lips went arch-shaped as she said it, "perhaps if you find it, you shall learn to play a tune on his Harp!"

Dick, as has been said, liked neither the looks nor the sound of this woman. She was, he decided, as sly and perhaps as treacherous as a fox. "I can show you where *I* came from easily enough," he answered. "But I know no more about Jack than I have—than I have heard."

"Nor don't we," said the woman. "Well, well, well! When he has supped you shall take my husband the way you came, and we shall see what we *shall* see."

Dick glanced at the giant, who all this while had been glinting at him out of his wide and almost colorless eyes. So, not knowing whether he followed his great-grandfather's habits, or how long his wife would remain with them, he thought it best to say no more. He smiled, first at one of them, and then at the other, took a sip of milk, and rank greasy goat's milk it was, and said, "When you are ready, I am ready too." The difficulty was to keep his tongue from showing how fast his heart was beating.

At this the giant sat down to the table and began the supper his wife had prepared for him. Spoon in hand he noisily supped up his huge basin of soup, picking out gingerly with his fingers, and as greedily as a starling, the hot steaming lumps of meat in it. He ate like a grampus. His soup finished, he fell to work on what looked like a shepherd's pie that had been sizzling in the oven. Then, having sliced off a great lump of greenish cheese, he washed it all down with what was in his mug. But whether wine, ale, cider, or water, Dick could not tell.

Having eaten his fill, the young giant sat back in his chair, as if to think his supper over. And soon he fell asleep. Not so did the woman. She had seated herself on the other side of the hearth in a great rocking chair, a good deal closer to him than Dick fancied, and she had begun to knit. Like the clanking of fire irons her needles sounded on and on in the kitchen, while the young giant, his mouth wide open, now and again shuddered in his slumbers or began or ceased to snore. Whereas if Dick even so much as opened his mouth

to yawn, or shifted his legs out of the blaze of the fire, the woman's slow heavy face turned round on him, and stared at him as if she had been made of stone.

At last, much to Dick's comfort, the young giant awoke and stretched himself. He seemed to be in a good humor after his nap, and not sulky or sharp as some people are. "What *I* say," he said with a laugh on seeing Dick again, "what *I* say is, there's more than one kind of supper!"

"Ha, ha, ha!" echoed Dick, but not very merrily. The giant then fumbled for a great club of blackthorn that stood behind the kitchen door. He put on his flat hat again, wound a scarf of sheep's wool around his neck, and said he was ready. Never had Dick, inside a book or out, heard before of a giant that wore a scarf. He clambered down from his stool and stood waiting. Her hand over her mouth, and her narrow sallow face showing less friendly than ever, the woman took another long look at him. Then she turned to her husband, and looked him over too.

"Well, it's a cold night," she said, "but you will soon get warm walking, and won't need your sheepskins." At mention of *cold* her husband stepped back and lifted the curtain that concealed the kitchen window. He screened his eyes with his hands and looked out.

"Cold!" he said. "It's perishing. There's a moon like a lump of silver, and a frost like iron. Besides," he grumbled, "a nap's no sleep, and I don't stir a step until the morning."

The two of them wrangled together for a while and Dick listened. But at last after drawing iron bars across the shutters and locking him in, leaving him nothing to make him comfortable, and only the flames of the fire for company, they left him—as Dick hoped, for good. But presently after, the woman came back again, dangling a chain in her hand.

"So and *so!*" she said, snapping together the ring at the end

175

of it on his ankle. "There! That kept safe my old Poll parrot for many a year, so it may keep even *you* safe until daybreak!"

She stooped to fix the other end of the chain round a leg of the great table. Then, "Take what sleep you can, young man," she said, "while you can, and as best you can. You'll need all your wits in the morning."

Her footsteps died away. But long afterwards Dick could hear the voices of the two of them, the giant and his wife, mumbling on out of the depths of the night overhead, though he himself had other things to think about. After striving in vain to free his leg from the ring of the chain, he examined as best he could with the help of his stool the locks and bolts of the shutters over the windows—stout oak or solid iron every one of them. He reckoned the walls of this kitchen must be twelve feet thick at least and the bolts were to match.

And while more and more anxiously he was still in search of a way out, he heard a sudden scuffling behind him, and a squeak as shrill as a bugle. He turned in a flash, and in the glow of the fire saw what he took to be a mouse that had come out of its hole, though it was an animal of queer shape, lean and dark, and half as large again as a full-sized English rat. Next moment, a score or more of these creatures had crept out of the wainscot. They gamboled about on the kitchen floor, disporting themselves and looking for supper.

By good fortune, when the squeak sounded, Dick had been standing on his stool by the window. He held his breath at sight of them, and perhaps had held it too long, or the giant's pepper had got into his nose, for he suddenly sneezed. At which a jubilee indeed went up in the kitchen. And if, in spite of his chain, by a prodigious leap from the stool to the table he had not managed to land on it safely, it might well have been the last of him. Luckily, too, the margins of the table jutted out far beyond its legs, so that though the sharp-nosed hungry animals scrabbled up the legs in hopes to get him, they could climb no further.

Now and again, squatting there, through the long hours that followed—half-hidden between the giant's tureen and mug—Dick drowsed off, in spite of these greedy noisy rodents, and in spite, too, of the crickets in the outer cracks of the oven, which kept up a continuous din like a covey of willow wrens. He was pestered also by the cunning and curiosity of a wakeful housefly, though others like it, straddling as big as cockroaches on the walls in the dusky light of the fire, remained asleep. It must be a fusty airless place, Dick thought, that had flies in winter. And so he passed a sorry night.

From PENNY A DAY
Illustrated here by Charles Keeping

JOYCE
LANKESTER BRISLEY

Bunchy and the Pastry Dough

ONCE upon a time there was a little girl called Bunchy, who lived with her grandmother in a cottage in the country.

It was a pretty little cottage, with roses climbing over it; and it had a pretty little garden with sweet peas and sunflowers growing in it; and there was beautiful country with woods and meadows lying around it.

So Bunchy was a happy little girl, living there with her kind old grandmother.

There was only one thing missing, which was that she had nobody to play with.

The cottage was a long way from the village, and hardly anyone came so far along the road except the miller with his sacks of flour, or the peddler with his tray of needles and buttons, or the grocer with his packets of tea and sugar.

But never anyone who could stop and play with a little girl like Bunchy.

One day Grandmother had to go to market, leaving Bunchy to keep house alone, for it was rather rainy for her to go along too.

Grandmother put on her cloak and her bonnet, her galoshes and her mittens, took her big basket and her big umbrella, and set forth. And Bunchy stood in the little rose-covered porch, waving good-by, feeling rather lonely, for she didn't know how she could manage to pass the hours by herself till Grandmother returned.

Grandmother got as far as the gate, and then she suddenly remembered something. And she stopped and called back to her granddaughter.

"There's a small lump of uncooked pastry dough on the larder shelf, which was left over when I made the pie this morning. If you would like to have it to play with while I am gone, you may, my dear." (For she knew how Bunchy always enjoyed standing by the kitchen table making things with little bits of dough while her grandmother was rolling the pastry.)

"Thank you, Granny," called Bunchy, still waving from the doorway; and Grandmother waved her umbrella for the last time before she went out of sight behind the hedge, on her way to market.

Then Bunchy turned back into the house.

She wandered upstairs, and she wandered downstairs, and she looked out of all the windows (not that there were many stairs or windows in the little cottage). And then, not finding anything interesting to do anywhere there, she thought that perhaps she would get out Grandmother's piece of dough and play with it.

So she went to the larder. And there on a plate on the shelf was a little round lump of pastry dough, soft and cold, waiting to be molded into anything a little girl could fancy.

Bunchy took it into the kitchen, rolling it between her hands, and she put it on the table, and pressed it out flat and rolled it up again several times.

"What fun it would be," said Bunchy to herself, "to make a little pastry girl to play with!"

So she got a knife from the basket and, standing on a stool, started cutting out a little girl from the flattened dough on the table, beginning at the top of the head, all down one side, arm, and leg; then up the other leg and the other arm, up till she reached the head again.

And when the knife reached the place where it had made the first cut, and the little pastry girl was quite complete—what *do* you think happened? Why, the little pastry girl lifted her head from the table and sat up; and while Bunchy, still standing on the stool, watched with her mouth wide open in surprise, the little pastry girl pulled her legs from off the table and jumped down with a soft thump onto the kitchen floor!

"Well!" said Bunchy to herself, staring with all her might. "Well, well, well!" (Which was what her grandmother always said when surprised, but there didn't seem to be anything else to say!)

The little pastry girl began stretching herself as if she were doing exercises, but Bunchy soon saw that she was trying to get her arms and legs more to the same length, for Bunchy had really made them rather odd. Then the pastry girl began feeling her pastry head with her pastry hands, and Bunchy suddenly thought:

"Why, I haven't given her any face!"

So she quickly got the currant box from the cupboard, took out two currants, and pressed them into the little pastry girl's head, for eyes. Then she took a tiny knob of dough from the table and pressed it into the center of the pastry girl's face for a nose. And then with a spoon she made a line below it for a mouth.

And in a trice the little pastry girl was smiling and twinkling at her in the friendliest way possible!

Here was a quaint playfellow!

181

Bunchy was delighted and amused herself for some time by making pastry buttons down the front of her dress, to finish her off; and as each one was set in place the little pastry girl looked so pleased.

Presently Bunchy gathered all the odd scraps of dough together in a ball. And, strangely enough, they made a lump which seemed as big as the first one. She rolled it out flat again.

This time she thought she would make a pussy cat; so she cut out a fine big one, head and ears and paws and tail all complete. And when it was done, up it got and down it jumped onto the floor, waving its white pastry tail from side to side.

This *was* fun!

Bunchy stood rolling together the leftover bits of dough while she watched her pastry girl and pastry cat making friends.

Strangely enough, the dough ball seemed still to be quite as big as before, so Bunchy rolled it out yet again on the table.

This time she thought she would make a house. So she cut out a house, with a roof and chimneys, and a door and windows, all complete, while the little pastry girl and the cat looked on, very interestedly. And when the last window was cut out and the house was finished it reared itself upright on the table and slipped down onto the floor; and it grew and grew, until at last it was quite of a size to admit people like Bunchy herself.

As she stood there staring up at it the little pastry girl slipped one chilly hand into hers and drew her towards the front door. The pastry cat ran in before them, leading the way into a little white kitchen, with a table and chairs and a dresser and crockery all made of pastry dough (which surprised Bunchy, for she had not made any "inside" to the house).

182

The pastry girl pulled out a chair for her, and Bunchy sat down carefully. She felt as if she were sitting on a piece of cold, soft rubber.

There was a shining black kitchen range at one end of the room, with a warm glow of fire in it, just like the one in Grandmother's kitchen; in fact, somehow Bunchy thought it *was* that same one, though how it got into the pastry house, or whether the kitchen itself had turned into pastry, or if the pastry house were still standing in the kitchen, she couldn't make out.

While she was puzzling over it the little pastry girl picked up the pastry cat and sat it on top of the stove. Bunchy was afraid it would be too hot there, but it settled down quite contentedly, while the little pastry girl fetched plates from the dresser and set them on the table.

Bunchy sat watching them both, and presently she noticed that the pastry cat was slowly turning to a golden-brown color. The next minute the pastry girl had taken it from the stove, broken it into crisp pieces, and piled them on the plates on the table.

Then she signed to Bunchy to draw up her chair and eat, and in some surprise Bunchy did so.

The pastry cat tasted very good, and Bunchy crunched away until she had eaten up all the pieces; for the pastry girl only pretended to eat (having, of course, no proper mouth), and when she had pretended enough over one piece would slip it onto Bunchy's plate and take another.

When the meal was finished the pastry girl led the way up some funny soft rubbery stairs to the little bedroom above.

Here was a white pastry bed, with a thick pastry coverlet; and the little pastry girl at once pulled her buttons off

(which were the only things she could remove) and got into bed, making room for Bunchy to get in beside her.

But Bunchy didn't want to get in—the bedclothes looked so cold and sticky. Still the little pastry girl kept beckoning and patting the lump of pastry which served for a pillow.

Just at that moment there was a distant bang of a door shutting. Was it Grandmother, come home from market?

Bunchy turned and ran from the room down the pastry stairs and out into the kitchen.

She had a sudden glimpse of the pastry house falling together and rolling up into a little ball as soon as she got outside it; and then the kitchen door opened and Grandmother came in, with her umbrella and her basket and a great number of parcels.

"Well, my dearie, have you managed to amuse yourself while I've been gone?" asked Grandmother, setting her things down on the kitchen table.

"Oh, yes, Granny!" said Bunchy. "I had such fun with the dough! I made a house, and a cat, and a little pastry girl."

"Ah!" said Grandmother knowingly, "I thought so, when I saw the dough ball!"

Now how *did* Grandmother know?

From BUNCHY
Illustrated by the author

"Understood Betsy," first published in the magazine "St. Nicholas" in 1916, is the only book written specifically for children by the novelist Dorothy Canfield, but it is in the same mood as her auto-biographical volumes in which she remembers with affection her Vermont childhood. Betsy, who is nine, has been sent from a shel-tered home in a town with elderly relatives (to whom she has always been Elizabeth Ann) to an aunt and uncle who have no time to spoil her in their busy life on a Vermont farm. At first, as this extract shows, Betsy is afraid of almost everything in her new surroundings. Gradually she learns to be a useful and happy member of the house-hold, and the author, describing the change, uses just those details and situations which would really be important to a child.

DOROTHY CANFIELD

Betsy Goes to School

ELIZABETH ANN was very much surprised to hear Cousin Ann's voice calling, "Dinner!" down the stairs. It did not seem possible that the whole morning had gone by. "Here," said Aunt Abigail, "just put that pat on a plate, will you, and take it upstairs as you go. I've got all I can do to haul my own two hundred pounds up, without any half-pound of butter into the bargain." The little girl smiled at this, though she did not exactly know why, and skipped up the stairs proudly with her butter.

Dinner was smoking on the table, which was set in the midst of the great pool of sunlight. A very large black-and-white dog, with a great bushy tail, was walking 'round and 'round the table, sniffing the air. He looked as big as a bear to Elizabeth Ann; and as he walked his great red tongue hung out of his mouth and his white teeth gleamed horribly. Elizabeth Ann shrank back in terror, clutching her plate of butter to her breast with tense fingers. Cousin Ann said, over her shoulder: "Oh, bother! There's old Shep, got up to pester us begging for scraps! Shep! You go and lie down this minute!"

To Elizabeth Ann's astonishment and immense relief, the great animal turned, drooping his head sadly, walked back

187

across the floor, got up on the couch again, and laid his head down on one paw very forlornly, turning up the whites of his eyes meekly at Cousin Ann.

Aunt Abigail, who had just pulled herself up the stairs, panting, said, between laughing and puffing: "I'm glad I'm not an animal on this farm. Ann does boss them around so." "Well, *some*body has to!" said Cousin Ann, advancing on the table with a platter. This proved to have chicken fricassee on it, and Elizabeth Ann's heart melted in her at the smell. She loved chicken gravy on hot biscuits beyond anything in the world, but chickens are so expensive when you buy them in the market that Aunt Harriet hadn't had them very often for dinner. And there was a plate of biscuits, golden brown, just coming out of the oven! She sat down very quickly, her mouth watering, and attacked the big plateful of food which Cousin Ann passed her.

At Aunt Harriet's she had always been aware that everybody watched her anxiously as she ate, and she had heard so much about her light appetite that she felt she must live up to her reputation, and had a natural and human hesitation about eating all she wanted when there happened to be something she liked very much. But nobody here knew that she "only ate enough to keep a bird alive," and that her "appetite was *so* capricious!" Nor did anybody notice her while she stowed away the chicken and gravy and hot biscuits and currant jelly and baked potatoes and apple pie—when did Elizabeth Ann ever eat such a meal before? She actually felt her belt grow tight.

In the middle of the meal Cousin Ann got up to answer the telephone, which was in the next room. The instant the door had closed behind her Uncle Henry leaned forward, tapped Elizabeth Ann on the shoulder, and nodded toward the sofa. His eyes were twinkling, and as for Aunt Abigail she began to laugh silently, shaking all over, her napkin at her mouth to stifle the sound. Elizabeth Ann turned wonderingly and saw the old dog cautiously and noiselessly letting himself down from the sofa, one ear cocked rigidly in the direction of Cousin Ann's voice in the next room. "The old tyke!" said Uncle Henry. "He always sneaks up to the table to be fed if Ann goes out for a minute. Here, Betsy, you're nearest, give him this piece of skin from the chicken neck." The big dog padded forward across the room, evidently in such a state of terror about Cousin Ann that Elizabeth Ann felt for him. She had a fellow feeling about that relative of hers. Also, it was impossible to be afraid of so meek and guilty an animal. As old Shep came up to her, poking his nose inquiringly on her lap, she shrinkingly held out the big piece of skin, and though she jumped back at the sudden snap and gobbling gulp with which the old dog greeted the tidbit, she could not but sympathize with his evident enjoyment of it. He waved his bushy tail gratefully, cocked his head on one side, and, his ears standing up at attention, his eyes glistening greedily, he gave a little, begging whine. "Oh, he's asking for more!" cried Elizabeth Ann, surprised to see how plainly she could understand dog talk. "Quick, Uncle Henry, give me another piece!"

Uncle Henry rapidly transferred to her plate a wing bone from his own, and Aunt Abigail, with one deft swoop, contributed the neck from the platter. As fast as she could, Elizabeth Ann fed these to Shep, who wolfed them down at top speed, the bones crunching loudly under his strong, white teeth. It did your heart good to see how he enjoyed it!

There was the sound of the telephone receiver being hung up in the next room—and everybody acted at once. Aunt Abigail began drinking innocently out of her coffee cup, only her laughing old eyes showing over the rim; Uncle Henry

189

buttered a slice of bread with a grave face, as though he were deep in conjectures about who would be the next President; and as for old Shep, he made one plunge across the room, his toenails clicking on the bare floor, sprang up on the couch, and when Cousin Ann opened the door and came in, he was lying in exactly the position in which she had left him, his paws stretched out, his head laid on them, his brown eyes turned up meekly so that the whites showed.

I've told you what these three did, but I haven't told you yet what Elizabeth Ann did. And it is worth telling. As Cousin Ann stepped in, glancing suspiciously from her sober-faced and abstracted parents to the lamb-like innocence of old Shep, little Elizabeth Ann burst into a shout of laughter. It's worth telling about, because, so far as I know, that was the first time she had ever laughed out heartily in all her life. For my part, I'm half surprised to know that she knew how.

Of course, when she laughed, Aunt Abigail had to laugh too, setting down her coffee cup and showing all the funny wrinkles in her face screwed up hard with fun; and that made Uncle Henry laugh, and then Cousin Ann laughed and said, as she sat down, "You are bad children, the whole four of you!" And old Shep, seeing the state of things, stopped pretending to be meek, jumped down, and came lumbering over to the table, wagging his tail and laughing too; you know that good, wide dog smile! He put his head on Elizabeth Ann's lap again and she patted it and lifted up one of his big black ears. She had forgotten that she was terribly afraid of big dogs.

From UNDERSTOOD BETSY
Illustrated here by Heather Copley

*On one occasion Barbara Euphan Todd dressed up as a scarecrow
for an impromptu fancy dress dance, so she can claim firsthand
knowledge of her best-known character. The first book about Worzel
Gummidge was written partly in a trailer in Cornwall, partly in
a garden hut, and was refused by more than one publisher; but, once
launched, the future popularity of the scarecrow was assured. At
home anywhere, Worzel Gummidge is the eternal clown, at war with
convention and orthodoxy. By his very nature he represents that
energetic earthy aspect of the country which appeals most to this
author. Her children are always doing things—camping, exploring,
acting, running. The books about Worzel Gummidge are as full of
incident as they are of humor.*

   *This extract comes from the beginning of his history. Susan and
her brother John have been sent to the Braithewaites' farm to con-
valesce after whooping cough. On their first day in the fields they are
caught in the rain and they borrow an umbrella they find leaning
against a scarecrow. Susan did think she heard this creature say
something, while they were arguing about whether they ought to
borrow the umbrella; now, as she sits by the fire alone in the evening,
she finds that she was right.*

BARBARA
EUPHAN TODD

The Scarecrow of Scatterbrook

WHEN the farmer and his wife had left the kitchen, the latch rattled again.

The tortoise-shell cat stopped washing her ears, and glanced over her shoulder. Then the door opened very slowly, and a strange-looking visitor shambled into the kitchen.

Susan recognised him almost at once.

"Evenin'!" said the scarecrow, and Susan wondered where she had heard his voice before. He stared round the room, then he coughed as sheep do on misty autumn nights. Presently he said, "Evenin'!" again.

"Good evening!" said Susan politely.

"You needn't be scared," he told her. "It's only me!"

"I'm not scared. Only just at first, before I remembered. I thought you might be a tramp."

"Not me!" he replied. "I'm a stand-still, that's what I am. I've been standing still, rain and fine, day in and day out, roots down and roots up."

He began to walk crabwise across the kitchen; one arm was stretched out sideways, and the other one was crooked at the elbow. As he walked, his bottle-straw boots made scratching noises on the stone floor.

"You'll wonder what I've come for!" he said.

But Susan didn't particularly wonder, for it seemed perfectly natural for him to be there. She stared at him, and decided that his straw boots could not be really comfortable for walking in.

"I've come to save you a journey," said the scarecrow. "At least, partly to save you a journey and partly to save myself from missing it."

"From missing what?" asked Susan.

"The umbrella. Where is it?"

Susan was so astonished that she could only point to the row of pegs on the door. The farmer's coat hung on one, and Mrs. Braithewaite's apron was on another. The third peg held a cap and the scarecrow's umbrella, or what was left of it.

"I'm so sorry," said Susan at last, "but you didn't seem to be using it, and so—"

"I know all about that," replied the scarecrow. "I heard you argufying."

"If we'd known you could talk, we'd have asked you to lend us the umbrella," explained Susan. "I did think though that I heard you speak, just as we were going away."

"That's right. But I'm not much of a talker except now and again."

The scarecrow took his umbrella down from the peg, and stroked it once or twice. Then he dropped it with a clatter.

"I might as well sit down," he said, and moved towards the fireplace. "How do you?"

"Very well, thank you," said Susan politely, though she couldn't think why he was asking the question *then*.

The scarecrow looked puzzled. "I mean," he explained. "I mean how do I sit? Is it difficult the first time you do it?"

But Susan couldn't remember, for she was so very used to sitting. She continued to look at the scarecrow. His face

certainly was remarkably like a turnip, and yet his widely-grinning mouth had a kindly expression. As he waited, the lump in the middle of his face began to look quite like a real nose. Just as Susan was wondering what to say next, he lifted the little hen robin from his pocket, and gently rubbed his cheek with her wing feathers. "It's still a bit damp outside," he explained, as he popped the bird back into its place. "I always use her as a hankychiff."

Then he suddenly moved backwards, lifted both feet together and sat down on the hearth rug with his legs sticking straight out in front of him.

"So that's how they sit," thought Susan.

The tortoise-shell cat looked very offended, and stalked out into the scullery.

The robin fluttered back into his pocket and began to make rustling noises inside it. Susan remembered then that the scarecrow in Ten-acre Field had had a robin's nest in its breast pocket. Just as she was wondering if there was a father robin, another little bird suddenly hopped out from his hiding place under the scarecrow's widely-brimmed hat, looked round importantly, straddled his legs, jerked his tail. Then, encouraged by the reflection of the fire gleaming on the sunny surface of a warming pan, he began a mad little song.

Susan leaned forward and touched the scarecrow on the knee. She longed to be friendly with anybody who kept robins in a coat pocket.

"What's your name?" she asked.

"Gummidge," he replied. "I'm Worzel Gummidge. I chose the name this morning. My granfer's name was Bogle."

"Gummidge isn't a very pretty name," objected Susan.

"No," he replied. "It's as ugly as I am."

Susan looked at him. His hat was awry over his turnipy face. A shabby black coat hung from his shoulders, and one arm was still akimbo. But she noticed that he had managed to bend his knees a little, and that his fingers, which two minutes before had looked like bits of stick, were more human now; they even showed lumps that might possibly be mistaken for knuckles. He was growing less like a scarecrow every minute. Soon, thought Susan, he might look more like a man than Farmer Braithewaite.

"Gummidge isn't pretty," she said, "but it's a very interesting name."

"Ooh aye!" he agreed. "But then, I've a power of things to interest me—roots tickling and shooting, rooks lifting in the wind, rabbits here, there, and scattered in a minute. Stop that now, do!" This last remark was made to the cock robin, who was pecking at his green-bearded chin.

"How old are you?" asked Susan.

"All manner of ages," replied the scarecrow. "My face is one age, and my feet are another, and my arms are the oldest of all."

"How very, very queer," said Susan.

"'Tis usual with scarecrows," replied Gummidge. "And it's a good way too. I get a lot of birthdays, one for my face and another for my middle and another for my hands, and so on."

"But do you get presents?"

"Well, I haven't had many so far," confessed Gummidge, "but then I've seldom thought about having birthdays. *Will* you stop that!" He raised a hand and pushed the little bird back again under the shadow of his hat.

"Do you often walk about?" asked Susan.

"Never done it before!" declared Gummidge. "But I says to myself last night, when I was standing in Ten-acre Field, I says to myself, 'You ought to go about the world and see things, same as the rabbits do. What's the use of having smart legs,' I said, 'if you don't use them!'" Gummidge stroked his shabby trousers proudly. "I says to myself, 'You might as well be rooted for all the traveling you do.' So this evening, after the rooks had stopped acting silly, I pulled up my feet and walked about a bit. Then I went up to the sheep pens and had a bit of a talk with one of the ewes."

"Which one?" asked Susan.

"Eliza, her that has the black face," replied Gummidge. "But she was a bit short with me; she was so taken up with her son and daughter."

"Has she got lambs?" asked Susan.

"Ooh aye! She's got a black son and a white daughter. She says they're the finest lambs in Scatterbrook and that they're wearing the best tails *she's* ever seen. I said to her, I said, ' You needn't talk; there's a hazel bush at the corner of Ten-acre which is fair covered with lambs' tails, and she doesn't make such a song about it.' After that the ewe turned her back on me."

"Why did you come here?" asked Susan.

"Well, I had thought about going to London instead," replied the scarecrow. "I thought I'd go to London, till I met a mouse in the lane and she changed my mind for me."

"Why did she?"

"She had been to London herself. She was a field mouse, and she'd heard tell of stowaways. So she stowed herself away in a market basket and she saw Piccadilly."

"Did she like it?" asked Susan.

"Well, I don't know about that," replied Gummidge. "But she saw a policeman, and he was dressed just the same as the one in Scatterbrook, and she said if they couldn't do better than that in Piccadilly, she'd come home again. And she said they told such lies. There's a place they call St. Martin-in-the-Fields, and it isn't in the fields at all. There's another place called Shepherd's Market, and she said there wasn't a shepherd there. So she said London was all a sham and that it was trying to copy Scatterbrook, so she came home again. And I've come here to fetch my umbrella."

"Are you going to stay in Scatterbrook?" asked Susan eagerly. She had taken a fancy to Worzel Gummidge and she hoped that he'd teach her how to talk to sheep and how to tame robins.

"I might," said Gummidge carelessly. He raised a hand and lifted a piece of mud from the place where his right ear should have been. Susan saw that his fingers moved stiffly as scissors and that his thumbs were like sticks. Then his head drooped forward and he fell asleep again.

The crackling of the fire, the singing of the kettle, and the soft powdery shuffle of falling ashes blended themselves into a jumble of sound, and Susan, too, fell asleep.

When she awoke, morning had slipped unnoticed into her bedroom, and she remembered having been tucked into bed very late indeed because Mrs. Braithewaite had forgotten all about her, and because Emily had not returned until eleven o'clock.

She was so sleepy that it was not until she was halfway through her breakfast, and John had finished eating the islands in his porridge that she remembered anything at all about Worzel Gummidge.

"Had the scarecrow gone away when you came home, Emily?"

"The what?" asked Emily.

"Eat up your bread and marmalade, for goodness' sake do," said Mrs. Braithewaite. "I must get cleared away if I'm to do anything this morning. We're late as it is."

Susan sighed, for she knew it would be no use to ask any more questions while Mrs. Braithewaite was in that sort of mood.

After breakfast she told John all about Worzel Gummidge, but he said she must have been dreaming, and that the scarecrow was still in the field.

"How do you know where he is?" asked Susan.

"I saw him before breakfast. I went out to look at that robin's nest, but I didn't get far enough. The scarecrow was there though."

"Oh look!" said Susan. "He's forgotten his umbrella." She pointed to the pegs on the kitchen door. The old umbrella was hanging from one of them.

"That proves he didn't come at all," said John in his most provoking voice.

If it hadn't been for the lambs, Susan herself might have thought that the scarecrow's visit was only a dream. But when Farmer Braithewaite came into the kitchen, and said,

"Hey! What do you think the ewe with the black face has got?"
Susan knew the answer.

"I know! I know!" she cried. "She's got a black son and a
white daughter, and they're wearing the best tails she's ever
seen!"

"Well, I never! Who's been telling you that?" asked the
farmer.

"Gummidge," said Susan.

"Gummidge?" the farmer looked puzzled. "There's nobody
of the name of Gummidge hereabouts."

Susan was saved from answering because Mrs. Braithewaite
called, "George, George! There's a strange cat slinking round
the chicken coops." So away went the farmer leaving Susan
to triumph over John.

"What did I say! What did I say!" she shouted, and as if

Barbara Euphan Todd

she hadn't said enough to prove that Worzel Gummidge really had paid a visit to the farm, a tiny brown feather fluttered down from the kitchen mantelpiece.

"That belongs to the robin!" said Susan.

From WORZEL GUMMIDGE
Illustrated here by George Adamson

Trapdoor
to
the Roof

Modwena Sedgwick helps her husband, a writer and broadcaster, to run their antique shop in Essex, England, and writes at the back of the shop. Her two sons went to boarding school when they were very young and she used to send them stories instead of letters. So began those tales of Pebblings Village and its animal inhabitants that soon afterwards found a place on the British radio. The stories of Galldora (the name is an anagram of "a rag doll") also started life as a radio series. They owe their beginnings perhaps to two wishes never granted to the author—for a rag doll (when she was a child) and for a daughter. Then, too, there is added her observation of the English countryside, and of a small niece who always imagined her doll as a naughty child who needed spanking. Modwena Sedgwick has written radio plays, poetry, articles and short stories for adults, but among her happiest creations will always be reckoned the brave little rag doll who believes experience is education, and who gets lost and trodden on and roughly treated, but always comes triumphantly out of her troubles.

Galldora and the Little Cat

ONE day Galldora found herself sitting on top of a house. It's a good thing I'm not afraid of heights, she thought, as she sat there propped up against the side of a chimney. The sun blazed, and the green trees stirred very gently, and the whole summery hot, hazy garden spread out below, like a dream. Galldora watched the swallows flying about, and heard them chattering away to themselves and, looking up, she could see the swifts. Miles and miles up they winged, racing each other and screaming with joy. Looking far down, she could see a family of long-tailed tits flying here and there like little wound-up toys.

I suppose, thought Galldora, it must be rather nice to be a bird and fly. If only I could fly all my troubles would be over. I could just fly down onto the lawn.

Just then two wood pigeons came and sat on the roof beside her. They looked at her with one eye and then with the other. Funny, thought Galldora, they can't look at me with both eyes at once.

A little later, when the sun was dipping and the shadows stretched out and out, Galldora saw the little boy who had thrown her up from the nursery window and onto the roof.

He was saying good-by to his cousin Marybell and to Marybell's mummy and daddy. His own mummy and daddy were with him. They were all laughing and talking and saying, "Good-by, and thank you for a lovely day," over and over again, or so it seemed to Galldora, who was watching. The little boy did cast a look up at Galldora, a hurried look. I hope, thought poor Galldora, he will say something about me before he goes. But he didn't.

All was peaceful in the garden once again. All the birds, and the sleepy, hot flowers, and the full-leaved trees were happy and all in their right places—all except Galldora.

For sitting on a roof is no place at all for a rag doll, thought Galldora. It's all right for birds, but not for rag dolls. Still, perhaps that little boy didn't mean me to get stuck.

A blackbird came and sat on an old apple tree in the garden and started up a clear, tuneful evening song. Marybell's mother and Marybell came and tidied up deck chairs and cushions that were lying on the lawn.

"Listen, Marybell, that blackbird is singing beautifully," and both Marybell and her mother stood for a moment and looked up at the bird and listened.

"If I had a worm I would give it to that blackbird for singing so beautifully," said Marybell. Then, having tidied up the lawn, both Marybell and her mother went back into the house.

The long shadows mingled one with another, and soon the night wind blew a star into the sky. The moon came out to ride her long lone ride in the heavens and see that all was in order, and all the little stars hurried to their places.

This is terribly sad, thought Galldora, and the saddest thing of all is that there is nobody here to know how sad I am.

Just then Galldora's attention was caught by a strange noise—a scratching noise and a faint purr. Then more

scratching noises came, then a soft meow. Galldora saw a
small furry face coming around the chimney, whiskers first.

"It is a dear little white-and-black cat," said Galldora to
herself. "I'm so glad. Now I will have somebody to know
how sad I am.'

One white paw, then a black paw, came round the stack,
and the little cat's shoulders came too. It was creeping

silently and cautiously, gazing about with great wide eyes. At first, because Galldora didn't move, it didn't see the rag doll, but as soon as it saw Galldora, the little cat was so startled it nearly fell off the roof.

"It's all right, really, it's all right, it's only me," called Galldora.

"Oh! it's you, is it?" answered the cat. It came and sniffed Galldora, then it looked about, and it whispered: "Where are THEY?"

"Who?" asked Galldora.

"The gang," whispered the little cat. Galldora was just going to say, "What gang?" when she noticed the little cat had gone. Suddenly the little cat appeared around the other side of the brick chimney, and it whispered: "They are not here yet——"

"Must you be so mysterious?" asked Galldora. "Who is the gang?"

"The gang are the big cats," answered the little cat, speaking very softly, "and I do hope, now that I've managed to climb the roof, they'll let me in on all their secrets. They discuss very important things, you know, but they never let on—well, anyway, not when they're down there. Even if I say "hello" they look straight through me, really they do—straight through me, as if I was a baby still—and it's most upsetting. But I have climbed the roof now, so—oh! what was that?" suddenly exclaimed the little cat.

An appalling caterwauling had started. The little cat smiled. "That's them," he whispered. "Oh, dear, I do feel all of a quiver."

"If I were you," Galldora started, "I should ask them politely——" but she got no further, for the noise the cats were making was deafening. It grew louder and louder, and then a low whinny started up. The little cat was grinning.

'They're gathering—they're gathering!" he purred, excitedly."Don't they sing beautifully? Excuse me, I'll go and join them now." Galldora hoped all would be well with the little cat, but there was such a hissing and screaming and snarling and grumbling and fur flying, that Galldora was afraid the big cats had all set on the little cat as soon as they saw him.

Oh, I do hope they don't hurt him, thought Galldora, getting very motherly.

Suddenly the little cat came around the chimney again. "Well?" asked Galldora curiously.

"Oh, dear!"gasped the little cat,"it's worse and worse."

"How?" asked Galldora.

"Because," said the little cat,"I've got to answer questions before I can join the gang. The first one is ever so difficult. I simply don't know what the answer is."

"Well, what's the question?"asked Galldora, and added proudly,"I may be able to help you."

"I hope you can," whispered the cat."It is: 'What looks with one eye but has two?' "

"Oh, but I know," cried Galldora excitedly.

"Oh, please don't talk so loudly," begged the little cat; "they'll hear you."

"I do know,"Galldora whispered."It's birds."

"Are you sure?"asked the little cat.

"Why, yes," said Galldora,"for two pigeons came and sat on the roof here beside me, this very afternoon. And they could only look at me with one eye at a time, I noticed specially." The little cat said nothing. He licked his paw and then licked around his face. "I know that's right, really I do," said Galldora."Go on, go and tell them" The little cat still took no notice, then he got up, stretched, and went around the chimney without a word.

A low chanting started from the big cats. This went on for

a terribly long time. Then the screeching and hissing started up again. The little cat came back to Galldora. He was looking scared again, but this time there was a little glint of cockiness in his wide, gold eyes.

"Well?" asked Galldora.

"I gave the right answer," was all the little cat said. He might thank me, thought Galldora, but the little cat didn't thank her, he only said: "They asked me another question."

Well, he can jolly well think of the answer for himself, thought Galldora.

"The question was: 'How can you get milk and food from humans?' I said 'I just cry,' but they said that wasn't the right answer."

"Of course it wasn't right," said Galldora, and though she didn't have any intention of helping the little cat, she couldn't help saying: "If I could sing I'd sing, and then my dear Marybell—the girl who owns me, you know—she'd say, 'Why, Galldora, how beautifully you sing,' and she'd give me anything I wanted."

"How do you know?" asked the little cat, sitting very straight and squinting at the moon.

"When the blackbird sang in the garden," went on Galldora, "Marybell looked up at him and said: 'If I had a worm I would give it to that blackbird for singing so beautifully.'"

"Ah!" smiled the little cat.

"But, of course, you can't sing," said Galldora.

"I can purr," answered the little cat, and he padded away over the roof. Galldora listened, but this time no whining or caterwauling happened. The little cat appeared again, very quickly. It sat down and started to try and lick behind its ears.

"I'm not going to talk to that little cat," Galldora told herself, "he's getting more conceited every moment. He can talk to me first if he wants to."

He did—and the little cat said, "I'm getting very clever at this guessing game." Then he had another lick, and he said, as if it wasn't anything very important, "I've got to answer a third and last question," and the little cat went on licking himself, and Galldora went on being silent. The little cat couldn't get its paws behind its ears, try as it might.

"Ah, so it's not going to rain," said Galldora. She never could keep quiet for long.

"And why do you think that?" asked the little cat, turning his head slightly away.

"Because you haven't licked behind your ears. Cats only lick behind their ears when it's going to rain. That's what Marybell told me, anyway."

"Now I know," said the little cat, and it put its little pink tongue out and licked its black nose. Then it got up, and walked away, with its tail held high in a question mark.

"Oh, bother!" said Galldora to herself. "I believe that was the answer to the third question. He wanted to know what cats do when it's going to rain." It must have been the right answer to the third question, for all the rest of the night, the little cat sat with the big cats on the far side of the roof, and listened to them discussing high secrets. To Galldora it sounded a terrible noise, and she was quite pleased when a window below her was opened, and Marybell's daddy looked out and shouted: "Shoo! Shoo!" and then clapped his hands. The cats, in a great flurry, hissed and screamed as they leaped and scrambled and jumped off the roof. They made such a din that they set Sparks, the cocker spaniel, barking in the kitchen, and they set another dog barking, too. It was a long way off, but it barked dolefully, on and on. The long barking of the distant dog upset the owls. A little owl started his stark cry that wasn't unlike a bark. *Ah-uk, Ah-uk, Ah-uk*, went the little owl. *Whooo!* called a great tawny owl, as it scooped low over the roof and, seeing Galldora's eyes glint in the moon-light, dived and then flew away.

My eyes must be shining, thought Galldora. The owl turned, coming back for another look.

"Help! Hide me—I'm frightened of that owl," came a little voice, and Galldora saw the little cat, cringing against the chimney. Galldora's motherly instincts were roused. She forgot how rude and conceited the little cat had been.

"Quick!" she called." Come and hide with me—snuggle up, as close as you can, under my arm."

"Thank you," whimpered the little cat.

"Now, keep your head down," ordered Galldora, "and don't cry or make a move," The great owl came a third time over the chimney, and it alighted on the chimney and stared down at Galldora.

"What in the world are you?" it asked.

"I'm a rag doll," answered Galldora, bravely.

"Fur," said the owl." Fur—what's that fur?"

"Oh, that!" and Galldora laughed, gaily, "that's my fur coat, and I find it comfortable to lean against, you know."

"Really?" said the owl." Really? And why are you on the roof, sitting up here so boldly? Don't you hide when you see me—or try to? I'm a great hunter, much feared."

"But why should I hide? I'm very unpleasant to eat," said Galldora, smiling brightly." I'm so unpleasant to eat that even one bite at me would make you feel sick."

"Really?" said the owl, and blinked." The things one learns," he said, and he flew off. As soon as the owl had gone, the little cat licked Galldora's face all over.

"Oh, thank you, thank you," he cried." You're a real lady."

That's better, thought Galldora. "And are you one of the gang now?" she asked. The little cat hung his head.

"Yes," he said, in a very low voice, "yes."

"Well, cheer up, then," said Galldora. "What are you so miserable about? You're a big cat now, and isn't that grand?"

"I suppose so," murmured the little cat, "only—only——"

"Only what?" asked Galldora.

"Only"—and the little cat looked at the rag doll with its wide eyes—"only, I can't get down. I did try, honestly I did. And when the big cats called out and told me to follow them, I pretended I was going the other way. But I hid, 'cause I didn't want to shame myself, and let them know that I couldn't get down, not after answering all those difficult questions—the ones you answered for me, I mean."

"That's a very sad story," said Galldora. "Well, I suppose you'll just have to stay up here."

"Yes," answered the little cat, "I'll have to stay until I grow big enough to climb down."

But the little cat wasn't very patient. As soon as a cock crowed the little cat said, "Oh, dear, I am thirsty." And when the robin woke, and sang loudly in the apple tree below, the little cat said, "Oh, I would love some milk." And when the blackbird started up and woke the chaffinch, and he woke the wood-pigeons, and they woke a great many other birds, the little cat said, "I don't think I can wait until I grow up." And when Sparks, the spaniel, came rushing out of the back door and barked at the milkman in a friendly, tail-wagging way the little cat said, "I know I can't wait till I grow up," and he started to meow.

Once he had started to meow, the little cat went on meowing and meowing. Soon Sparks pricked up his ears and he sat on the lawn and looked up at the roof, then he barked. He could see the little cat walking around and around the chimney, and in between his barks he could hear the little cat meowing. The barking brought out Marybell and Marybell's daddy. "What is it, old man?" asked Marybell's daddy.

"Look," Sparks barked, "look up there."

"Look, Daddy—look!" cried Marybell, who understood Sparks, "on the roof—it's a poor little pussy." Marybell's mummy joined them, then, and she looked up too. There they all stood and wondered what to do. But none of them saw Galldora. Galldora was very afraid nobody would notice her, so she said to the cat, "I've done you two good turns, haven't I?"

"Yes," said the little cat, "but I wish you could do me another and get me off this roof. I know I can't wait till I'm grown up."

"Oh, they'll get you down all right," said Galldora, "now that they've seen you, but do me a good turn, will you, and stand by me; then, when they come and get you, they'll notice me, too."

"All right," said the little cat, "you have been very kind to me, but oh! I must get down. I hate it here, I hate it here; I want some milk," and on and on cried the little cat, louder and louder.

Marybell's daddy fetched a ladder and, with the help of two neighbors and the owner of the little cat, he climbed up to the roof and, just as he lifted the little cat, he saw the rag doll.

"Good gracious—Galldora—fancy finding you here." He picked Galldora up and brought her down, too.

He handed the little cat to the little cat's owner, who was delighted to have him back, and hurried him away to a big saucer of milk. Then he handed Galldora to Marybell, saying: "Of all your dolls, Marybell, Galldora is the strangest. Fancy getting on top of the roof!"

"I know," answered Marybell calmly. "Galldora is very strange, but she can't help it. I think it's because she's a rag doll."

From ADVENTURES OF GALLDORA
Illustrated by **Diana John**

Meindert DeJong was given the Newbery Award in 1955 for "The Wheel on the School." In his acceptance speech he spoke of his childhood in Wierus, the Frisian fishing village on the North Sea which lies behind the book. In the village (which he calls Shora here) the school has only six pupils—Jella, Eelka, Auka, Pier, Dirk, and Lina, the only girl. One day they ask the schoolmaster why no storks nest in Shora as they do in other Dutch villages. The roofs are too steep, they decide, and they must find a wheel for a base before they can hope to attract storks to the village. The story tells how they all hunt for a wheel and how, after a storm, two drowned storks are washed up and two others, still alive, are sighted standing on a sandbank not far away. These birds are brought back safely in a rowboat with the help of crippled Janus; and while the extract I have chosen ends the story, it promises a new beginning for Shora with its pair of storks. DeJong's story was written not just from memory, but from that reliving of childhood in imagination which is his special achievement. He is not talking at children "over a nine-foot fence," as he puts it, but saying to them, "Come gather around me and listen . . . There was this village of Shora, and in it were five houses, and in the five houses were six children. Oh, there were other houses and other littler children, and older people, but that's not important, and all that matters is that in these six children of Shora are you and all the children of the world. I know, for I have been back, and I have been a child again."

MEINDERT DEJONG

The Wheel on the School

IN THE group that set off for the school, no one had a thought for anything but the storks. Eelka, Dirk, and Auka were trying to tell Pier and Lina what they had done to get ready for the storks but kept interrupting themselves with eager questions about the storks. The five boys and Lina raced on. They left the women far behind. Still farther behind, the teacher and Douwa were inching the wheel chair down the dike. Janus sat fuming and raging, as eager and impatient as any of the children. "I could have drowned or starved there in that boat, so long as those storks were all right," he said.

"Calm yourself, Janus. You did your part," Grandmother Sibble III told him. But she was doing her own level best, with the aid of Douwa's stick, to hurry before the wheel chair.

At the school Janus came into his own again. The whole group was waiting for him, uncertain whether or not to put the half-drowned, bone-cold storks up on the wheel or to warm them first in the schoolroom by Eelka's fire. They shouted the perplexing question at Janus.

Janus made them wait until his wheel chair had been pushed right among them. Then he had to consider for a maddeningly long time. "Well, if I was a stork, and had just come out of

217

Africa, and had a storm knock the stuffing out of me for five days and nights, and on top of that had sat on a cold sand bar with the water spitting me in the eye . . . If I was a stork, I'd want to sit *on* that stove."

Lina and Pier immediately carried the storks inside. Janus was the authority. Chairs were hastily shoved near the stove for Pier and Lina. They seated themselves and held the storks carefully in their laps.

"What did I tell you? Get one hand around those necks!" Janus suddenly bellowed from the doorway. "When those fellows come alive, they could peck your eyes out."

"You carried them all the way," Auka and Eelka were begging Pier and Lina, "now let us hold them awhile." Lina looked so tight-lipped and stubborn, they centered their attention on Pier. "Come on, Pier!" Dirk said. "If you can't even let your own brother—"

"Let him alone, all of you," Janus told them fiercely. "He risked his neck to get them off that sand bar."

Lina sat quietly, looking down at her stork. She had to hold herself very quiet, absolutely still, or she'd burst out and scream and laugh and cry. It was so unbelievable, so wonderful, sitting in school with a stork in her lap. Storks in school, storks in Shora! She bent deep over her stork and cried a little and stroked its long, white neck.

Behind Lina, old Douwa was explaining to Janus what they had done to get ready for the storks—how they'd broken into Janus' shed and used his ladders, rope, and shovels. Janus did not seem to be too attentive. When the teacher, standing beside him, heard about the burial of the storks in the churchyard, he was shocked. "But, Douwa, it's Government land! That's against the law. That's punishable. It belongs to the State and the Queen." He was scandalized. "They'll have to come out of there."

Janus twisted his wheel chair to face him. "So it's Government property, so they dug a little hole, so the Queen won't like it! Well, let the Queen come and dig them up and drag them off to Amsterdam and bury them behind the palace!"

Janus suddenly realized what he was saying. He guffawed. The picture of the Queen dragging the storks down all the roads to Amsterdam and digging a little hole behind the palace filled him with delight. He roared with laughter.

Everybody tried to quiet him. "Janus, the storks! You'll scare the storks!"

"Huh," Janus said. "If they're used to lions roaring all around them, they won't mind Janus." He threw his head back again to laugh.

At the stove Lina's stork struggled in her arms, struggled wildly. Its long neck and wild eyes rose high above her. Janus' laugh stopped in his mouth. "Grab him, Jella! Grab that neck," he cried. "And up with them on the wheel. Quick! Now that the blood's running in their veins again. Come on, Pier!"

Pier and Jella jumped to his orders. They remembered Janus' cautioning and kept a hand around the long necks. The stork under Jella's arm struggled wildly, trying to twist free from his grasp.

"Don't choke him, you young idiot," Janus said sternly.

Up on the ladder Jella had to let go his hold on the stork's neck; he needed both hands to climb the ladder. With the big stork tucked under one arm, he climbed up. Pier followed right behind him. On the roof they had to crawl slowly along the ladder. Suddenly Jella's stork began fiercely pecking at his head. Jella closed his eyes and let him peck. The sharp jabs knocked off Jella's cap. The stork's hard bill hammered down on his bare head. A tuft of hair came away in his bill. Jella squealed. He could take no more. He braced himself against the ladder, grabbed the stork with both hands and tossed him up towards the wheel.

Big white wings opened. Jella's stork landed on the rim of the wheel. Pier handed his stork to Jella who reached high to place the stork on the wheel. Stretching his long neck down, the big male stork angrily pecked at Jella. Jella hastily released his mate. The male stepped over and stood above her defensively. Slowly her head lifted, her long neck came up, she looked at her lord and master.

"Loosen that rope and down with the ladders," Janus called from below. "While they're still all in. Later it might scare them away."

Jella lay flat on the ladder as he untied the knot in the rope underneath the wheel. Everybody helped to pull the ladders down. They laid them along the school wall. Then all retreated to the road and stood, without speaking or moving, staring up at the two storks on the wheel. The male stork stood tall and white, looking down at them. His mate had gathered her legs under her and sat squat against the hub of the wheel.

The male stork circled the wheel with slow, stately steps, studying it and now and then tapping the rim with his bill. When he had completed his inspection of the wheel, he stood tall and dignified again, looking up at the sky. His long bill opened and he began making hard clapping sounds up into the sky. The female tilted her head and listened; she struggled to get to her feet.

The male gently ran his bill along her white neck. Suddenly he spread his wings and flew down from the roof. He landed in the playground, right before the hushed crowd gathered in the road. His sharp eyes had seen a long twig. He seized it in his bill. Flapping his wings heavily in his weariness, he rose to the roof and dropped the twig on the wheel before his mate. Gravely he bowed before her and pushed the twig closer to her.

Still sitting in her exhausted huddle, she touched the twig with her bill and drew it towards her. She seemed to accept the twig as a promise of the nest they were going to build there. The male stork settled down on the wheel close beside her and closed his eyes.

Down in the road nobody said a word. The little group stood silent, staring up at the roof of the school. Then Janus whispered, "They've shown us they're grateful. They've shown they're going to stay and build their nest. Now let's all quietly get away from here and leave them alone."

They tiptoed away, solemnly turning to look back at the storks, and Janus rode in their midst.

"You can't believe it," Janus kept whispering. "You can't believe it—storks in Shora."

"Not since I was a little child," Grandmother Sibble III said softly to herself.

"Storks in Shora," Lina repeated. "But I can believe it, Janus! It's so impossibly impossible, I can believe it now."

"Ah, yes, little Lina," the teacher said. "So impossibly impossible that it just had to be. And the long dream—storks on every roof in Shora—is beginning to come true."

From THE WHEEL ON THE SCHOOL
Illustrated by Maurice Sendak

Claude Aveline was born Eugène Avtsine, in Paris in 1901, and legalized a name which he first used as a pseudonym. The story I have included here comes from "De quoi encore?," which was published in 1946: the translation, by Margaret Ledésert, "The Bird that Flew into the Sea, and Other Stories," came out in England in 1961. These delicately nonsensical fantasies play around the idea of changing. A white kitten in a litter of black ones—how can it become like the others? A toy lion on a visit to Africa wishes he were a real live lion; a bird really thinks he can live under water like a fish; and in the story I have included here, an elephant believes he can be taken for a mosquito. Aveline's two other books for children, "Baba Diène et Morceau-de-Sucre" (1936) and "L'Arbre Tic-Tac" (1950) have not yet been translated into English. These are fantasies too, and perhaps he escaped in them, as he did in detective stories, from the world which he tackled seriously in so many novels, articles, essays, and lectures. His nonsense tales have a sparkle and elegance all their own.

CLAUDE AVELINE

The Story of the Elephant Who Pretended to be a Mosquito

ONCE upon a time there was an elephant who wanted to go on a journey. He had wanted for a long time to go and stay with his cousins, the hippos, who lived on the far side of the jungle, on the banks of the Great River. But it would take days and days to get there by walking, and Topoho, our elephant, was rather lazy. He could take the train, of course; but, unfortunately for him, on the Jungle Train the bigger you are the more you pay for your seat. A journey that costs a penny for a flea costs fifteen dollars for a lion, and even more if he has any fleas to pay for. So you can guess what it would cost an elephant! And Topoho was as stingy as he was lazy.

One day he had a bright idea.

What if I pretend to be a mosquito? he thought.

He knew that on the Jungle Train mosquitoes travel at an especially cheap rate, not only because they are small, but because they are needed in the jungle to bite the men who come to kill or capture the animals who live there. Often a whole regiment of mosquitoes are given special orders to travel on the train, and then they don't pay anything for their seats.

Topoho went trotting gaily down to the station, trying on the way to make a noise like the buzzing of a mosquito. Of course, he made a *terrible* din! All the animals of the village whom he passed shouted to him:

"Oh, Topoho! Whatever *is* the matter?"

But Topoho was making so much noise that he didn't even hear them.

The ticket agent at the station, an old monkey, was *very* short-sighted and *very* deaf. But all the same he heard the noise that Topoho was making.

"Who are you?" he asked.

Topoho answered: "A mosquito."

"Impossible!" exclaimed the old monkey. "Can I really hear a mosquito buzzing? Well! I can't be deaf any more!"

He lifted up the shutter of his little window and peered out, but, being so shortsighted, he couldn't see anything.

"Where do you want to go to, Little One?" he asked.

Topoho replied: "To the banks of the Great River." And, without thinking, he added: "I'm going to stay with my cousins the hippos."

The old monkey burst out laughing. "That's a good joke, that is! A mosquito, cousin to the hippos!"

And he handed Topoho a green ticket. On the Jungle Train mosquitos always have *green* tickets.

To get onto the platform travelers had to show their tickets to a ticket collector, who was also a monkey. But he was a *young* monkey, with excellent eyesight and *very* good hearing.

"Your ticket, Fatty!" he said to Topoho.

Topoho replied indignantly: "Who are you calling 'Fatty'? Is that the way to address a mosquito?"

And he showed the ticket collector his *green* ticket, which he was holding in his trunk. The young monkey looked at it in amazement. Then he said: "I beg your pardon!"

The Elephant Who Pretended to be a Mosquito

There were lots of travelers on the platform. When the train came in Topoho looked for the Mosquito Car. But the car was divided into the *tiniest* of compartments, each big enough for five hundred mosquitoes. Topoho, of course, couldn't even put one foot inside. So he climbed up on the roof, and the train started off.

At each station a monkey ticket collector would run to the Mosquito Car and shout at Topoho: "Get down from there! That's no place for an elephant!"

Topoho would just show his green mosquito ticket, and the ticket inspector would say right away: "I beg your pardon!"

But the mosquitoes, who got out of the train at each station to stretch their wings, saw what was going on. So they held a council in their compartments, and decided to teach Topoho a lesson—all the more so because the roof of the Mosquito Car was beginning to crack under his weight. Topoho's trunk was hanging down in front of the windows, so they flew onto the end of it and began to crawl right inside.

First a hundred, then a thousand, then ten thousand mosquitoes climbed into Topoho's trunk and began to walk about inside, just as you or I do in the subway. It was very dark in there, but right at the end they could see a tiny bit of daylight, such as you see when you are in a tunnel. Topoho could feel something tickling, and he began to wave his trunk about. That was just what the mosquitoes were waiting for. Their chief gave a signal, and they *all* bit him at the same time. And an elephant's skin, inside his trunk, is as soft and tender as our skin. The ten thousand bites made poor Topoho sneeze so violently that he lost his balance. He fell right off the roof of the Mosquito Car and landed on the ground. Meanwhile, the train continued on its way.

Inside Topoho's trunk the mosquito chief gave the order: "About turn! Fly!"

All the mosquitoes flew straight out of Topoho's **trunk** and hurried towards the train to find their seats **again.** Topoho was left all alone in the jungle, stunned by his **fall,** and feeling a terrible pain in his trunk. When he began **to** feel a bit better he got up, and slowly made his way on **foot** back to the village.

The next day our Topoho turned up again at the station, with his trunk all bandaged in a great red scarf. Everybody had heard of his adventures.

The young monkey ticket collector said to him: "Good morning, Mr. Mosquito! Have you hurt yourself?"

Topoho replied very humbly, speaking very oddly **through** his nose because of the mosquito bites.

"Please don't make fun of me! If only you knew how **my** trunk hurts!"

Then he went up to the ticket office and said to the **old** monkey: "Please give me an elephant ticket for the banks of the Great River—a ticket for a

VERY LARGE ELEPHANT!

From THE BIRD THAT FLEW INTO THE SEA
AND OTHER STORIES
Translated from the French by Margaret Ledésert

The
Door of the School

"The China Spaniel" is one of many stories which were first told impromptu to children, and afterwards written down. They come from a writer who was brought up on Edward Lear and believes nonsense to be an important ingredient in poetry. Certainly they appeal to something secret and instinctive in all of us, besides being so entertaining to read. As certainly, they belong to a writer who, in a lifetime's work in prose and verse, has never produced anything that was not unique, unexpected and haunting.

RICHARD HUGHES

The China Spaniel

THERE was once a school that was rather cross and dull, and it was run by one old woman.

Now it so happened that one of the children at this school was a china spaniel, the kind that has a gold chain 'round its neck, and doesn't look as if it had much sense. As a matter of fact, this one had practically no sense at all, he was easily the stupidest pupil in the whole school, and could never learn his lessons properly.

One day they were all given some poetry to learn for home-work, and the china spaniel really did try his hardest: but when he came into school the next day he couldn't remember a single line of it.

In fact, the only thing that came into his head to say was:

> *Pink and green silver-paper toffee-paper!*
> *Pink and green silver-paper toffee-paper!*
> *Pink and green . . .*

"What!" screamed the old woman: "*That* isn't what I gave you to learn!"

But there must have been some sort of magic in the words, for immediately all the other children in the school, the good ones and the clever ones and everybody, rose up from the desks, and all began chanting together at the tops of their voices:

Pink and green silver-paper toffee-paper!
Pink and green silver-paper toffee-paper!

—and out into the street they all rushed, dancing and singing at the tops of their voices.

"What's this? What's this?" said a policeman. "What's all the row about?"

"Pink and green silver-paper toffee-paper!" shouted the children.

And thereupon the policeman began to dance too, and chanted it with the children.

"What's this? What's this?" cried the Chief of Police, who happened to be passing: "One of my policemen dancing? What does this mean, sir!"

"Pink and green silver-paper toffee-paper!" replied the policeman: and no sooner did he hear it than the Chief of Police started chanting it too, with all the rest, for by now there were quite a lot of other people of the town who had joined the procession and went along chanting:

Pink and green silver-paper toffee-paper!

with the china spaniel, who had started it all, marching proudly at their head.

At last they came to the royal palace, whereupon the King came out on his balcony ready to make a speech.

"My loyal subjects, I see you gathered together before my palace in great numbers. Well, as you know, I am a kind king and always anxious to give you what you want, so what is it?"

"Pink and green silver-paper toffee-paper!" cried the people; "pink and green silver-paper toffee-paper!"

"*What* did they say they wanted?" whispered the Prime Minister, who was a little deaf, at the King's elbow.

"Pink and green silver-paper toffee-paper?" asked the Prime Minister's secretary in polite surprise.

And then, in a twinkling, they were all dancing and chanting and shouting in the palace as well as outside it:

> *Pink and green silver-paper toffee-paper,*
> *Pink and green silver-paper toffee-paper,*
> *Pink and green silver-paper toffee-paper,*
> *Pink and green silver-paper toffee-paper,*
> *Pink and green silver-paper toffee-paper,*
> *Pink and green silver-paper toffee-paper!*

Nor was it long before the whole nation was singing it: and some enemies who were besieging the town at the time, hearing it, thought it must be some sort of national anthem, till they found themselves starting to sing it too; and, in short, it wasn't long before the whole world was singing it—the whole world, that is to say, except the old woman who kept the school.

"It would take more than the whole world going mad," she said very firmly, "to make *me* start dancing and playing the goat!"

And she went on trying to run her school just as before it happened, the silly old thing.

From THE SPIDER'S PALACE

William Mayne lives in the North Riding district of England, and many of his stories reflect the Yorkshire scene, moors and hill roads and valleys, in snow and in sunshine. They owe much also to his experience as a teacher and his active interest in children. This is the opening of a short vivid book that describes an afternoon in a primary school—or out of it, for Miss McGregor is taking her pupils to catch crayfish in a stream and cook them on an open fire. Mayne writes with immediacy and he writes most of all to please himself; in doing so he pleases many readers.

WILLIAM MAYNE

Counting the Class

Miss McGregor rang the bell. Everybody stopped running about and shouting. Tommy Routh was climbing down the gate in and out of the bars. Mary thought he was like a length of wool being woven. He was last in the line, pulling himself together at the waist and dusting his back where it had been on the dusty playground.

The bottom class went into school and the door closed behind them. The voice of Mrs. Meadows came out through the open window. The door opened again and Miss McGregor came out with a ball of string. She had put the bell away. Mary could see it inside the window next to a big jar holding the stems of meadowsweet. The meadowsweet looked like heaps of snow. A fly flew through the window to look at it.

Miss McGregor blinked her eyes to get them used to the brightness of the sunshine in the yard.

"It's one o'clock," she said. "Is everybody here?"

Carolyn was the eldest, and she had to count them up. Mary counted as well. Carolyn said they were all there, twenty-one. Mary could only count twenty, and she did it again, but it was still twenty.

"Come on, then," said Miss McGregor. "Let's start off."

"Miss McGregor, you'll need your cushion," said Carolyn.

233

"No, she won't," said somebody else, "she can sit on the grass, we've got to go."

"I think I would like my cushion," said Miss McGregor. "Thank you, Carolyn."

Carolyn ran in for the cushion, into the empty classroom. She caught up with the others at the gate. Then they were out in the empty road between the houses of the village. Nobody was about in the sunshine, because they were all having their dinners. Carolyn carried the cushion. Mary took the ball of string, and they walked together beside Miss McGregor, down the lane and into the market place, and then down the road towards the river.

"Caro," said Mary. "I could only count twenty people. Why did you count twenty-one?"

"That's what there are," said Carolyn. "Perhaps you forgot Tommy Routh."

"Me?" said Tommy Routh. "What did you forget about me?"

"I didn't forget him," said Mary. "You needn't fuss, Tommy."

"Count them again," said Carolyn. "And I will, too, and we'll see what it is."

"They're all here," said Tommy. "The lot of them."

234

"Twenty," said Mary, pointing at Carolyn, because she was the last to be counted. Carolyn said twenty-one, and she was pointing at herself, too, with her finger on her chest.

"You've done something daft, then," said Carolyn. "Do it all again. You say them, and I'll count them."

They were at the front of everybody, so Mary had to walk backwards to see them all. She said each name, and Carolyn counted them on her fingers, putting the cushion well under her arm to leave her hands empty for the job.

"Tommy Routh, that's nineteen, and you, Caro, twenty," said Mary. "I can't make it more."

"You can," said Carolyn, "because I know what you did. You forgot somebody."

"Kate," said Mary. "No, I got her, because I keep counting her and then uncounting her. Tommy Routh, have you got out again?"

"I'm nineteen," said Tommy Routh. "What are you?"

"Me?" said Mary. "I wasn't in. I'm twenty-one. I forgot to count myself."

"I always count myself, even if I'm alone," said Carolyn.

From THE FISHING PARTY
Illustrated by Christopher Brooker

In this extract Jerry Pye's dog, Ginger, puzzled about the way his master vanishes five days a week, sets out to discover where he goes. This and much else in "Ginger Pye" is partly true. Eleanor Estes bases her stories on a sure knowledge of children, earned during her career as a librarian and also from her own daughter; but when she began to write she went back also to that essential source, memories of childhood. A few years ago she wrote in "The Horn Book": "The search for Ginger is the theme of 'Ginger Pye.' Our dog, Ginger, really was stolen on Thanksgiving Day when he was a few months old . . . and he did return, full-grown, dragging a ragged long rope behind him, and with terrible scars on his face, in the month of May. This book, being a search, permitted me to include in it many impressions that I had not yet been able to get into any other book, such as those of tramps and sunny fields, and walking along behind a cow switching its tail to get rid of flies, and the eerie sound of a certain whistle, a sort of wailing siren, that blew each evening at five o'clock, usually, it seemed to me, when I was in the sunny field. It always frightened me unbearably, and my sister told me it was the gipsies' whistle, summoning them home, at five o'clock."

ELEANOR ESTES

Ginger on the Fire Escape

THIS time, as Ginger steered his nose past the Carruthers' and the Gaines' tempting houses, all he permitted himself was a slight reminiscent wag of the tail. That was all. Not even a peep from the corners of his eyes. And from his mind he banished thoughts of all the eyes of all the hidden cats that probably were on him. Scrunching up his nose, pushing it on up the street, he lost himself completely in following the trail of Jerry Pye.

At a certain point, going through a small field, the scent led Ginger to a little crab apple tree. He stood on his hind legs and inhaled the scent as far up the tree as he could thrust his nose. Jerry had been up this tree but he certainly was no longer there for, of course, there would be a much keener scent if he were. The quest was by no means over.

Ginger remained poised there against the tree in contemplation. Jerry's going up the tree might be what was known as a decoy. Decoys were difficult, though not impossible, to outwit. For instance, the person a dog was trailing might leap from treetop to treetop. A dog had to work double hard and might have to explore in every direction before finding the trail again. But then, that is all part of tracking.

Ginger wagged his tail in appreciation of his master's cleverness and he keenly anticipated matching his wits against his. No doubt, Jerry had suspected that Ginger would try to trail him. So, up the tree he had gone to throw Ginger off his tracks.

Thus Ginger analyzed the difficult situation before leaping down. He then began spiritedly to go around and around the tree in ever-widening circles. By the time he was ten dog-lengths away from the tree his nose picked up the scent again. And the decoy was over.

Apparently Jerry had swung out of the tree on a branch and had landed way over here on all fours. Here, also, was one of Jerry's pencils with Ginger's tooth marks on it as well as Jerry's own. Jerry had then proceeded in the same direction as before the tree decoy, and this Ginger did likewise, with the pencil in his mouth.

The pencil made trailing considerably more difficult than hitherto, if not well-nigh impossible. In the end, Ginger had to drop the pencil, find the trail, go back for the pencil, and bring it to the farthest point of trailing. Of course he could not abandon the pencil. The going, therefore, was slower now, not only because of the complication of the pencil, but also because suddenly there seemed to be a very great many more smells to weed out before locating Jerry's.

Ginger snorted and blew and carefully cherished the faint but certain scent that was Jerry's. So close to the ground did he keep his nose, he bumped right into the cement step of a sweet shop. He raised his head, sniffing expertly and gently. He allowed the enticing chocolate and peanut smells to mingle with Jerry's.

Was it possible that here was the end of the trail, the end of the long quest? Did Jerry spend all those hours away from him in a sweet shop? How marvelous, if true. He wagged his tail expectantly. His mouth drooled, for he loved sweets and he trotted into the shop.

Jerry was not there, Ginger soon found out as he sniffed busily around the floor, eating bits of sweet that had been dropped and giving an excited bark when he found a piece of sticky paper Jerry had thrown down. It had had licorice in it—not one of Ginger's favorites; one of Jerry's though.

Ginger chewed all the sweetness out of the paper and reluctantly let that go. After all, he had still to push his nose and Jerry's pencil up the street and that was just about all he could manage. The trail was certainly hot now, what with having found Jerry's pencil and then this piece of sticky paper. Yes, this was what was known as being "hot on the trail".

Sniff, sniff, here. Snort and blow there. A great, great many feet had passed this way and Ginger lost the trail. He just followed the lead of all those feet and at last he paused to take his bearings. He looked about him. He had come through the wide open gate of a tall brown wooden fence and here he was, in an enormous yard, half pavement and half worn-down grass. He lay down on a little patch of this grass close to a big brick building. His nose stung and his neck ached from the long push and hard concentration. The pencil lay safely between his paws. He licked his tongue over his dry nose until it became moist and cool again, and he studied the building before him.

The building was big, hard, and brick. If this was where Jerry came every day and spent his time, Ginger was no longer envious. Why come here, though? Why come here when he and Jerry could tramp up Shingle Hill or tear through the woods around the reservoir picking up acorns and finding frogs? Still, inside might be pleasanter than outside, and Ginger toured the building to find a way in.

All doors were closed. All Ginger could do now was to sit and wait for Jerry to come out. Imagine Jerry's pleasure when he saw his faithful dog waiting here for him, choosing to wait here for him instead of chasing cats, moreover.

Ginger lazily crossed his front paws the way he always did while resting. He felt drowsy. Now and then he twitched his back to get rid of a fly circling around in the warm October sunshine. He listened to the sounds coming from the big building. There was a sound as of many bees droning. A sharp voice gave a command and this droning stopped. The sharp voice gave another command and there was a burst of singing. "Hats off, hats off, the flag is passing by." This was pleasant and Ginger was sorry when it stopped. After the singing there was quiet for a time, with only an occasional sharp command from the one in charge of all these goings on.

The long quest, the warm sunshine, the quiet, all contributed to Ginger's sleepiness. With one vigilant eye half open, he began to nod.

Then—was he dreaming? He heard Jerry's voice. Jerry's voice loud and clear and all by itself. Ginger sat up. His tail began uncertainly to wag. Then it wagged uncontrollably, for he was not dreaming. Jerry's voice was coming loud and clear from one of the high windows. Jerry was not using his regular voice that he used with Ginger or with any of the Pyes. He was using a high and loud and clear voice. But it was Jerry's voice, even so.

Ginger listened, in a transport of delight. Then he gave a short bark announcing, if Jerry cared to know, that he, Ginger, was right out here. Not only was he out here, he would manage to get to Jerry somehow, so there would be no more separation.

Ginger no longer felt tired. He tore around the building,

barking and wagging not only his tail, wagging his whole body. He was looking again for a way in. All entrances were closed. He came back and longingly stared up at the window from which he judged Jerry's voice was coming. Jerry was still talking, though the one in command kept butting in.

There was a perilous-looking iron stairway leading up to the open window through which Jerry's voice was floating. Standing beneath this curious stairway Ginger could see sky through the open work of the steps. Cautiously Ginger put one paw on the bottom step. It was hard to get a grip on but at least it did not wobble. He put his other front paw on the bottom step and carefully pulled his body up onto it.

The main difficulty was that his paws kept sliding through the iron bars. What peculiar stairs. No carpets at all, as at home. Even so, by being extremely cautious, he might be able to drag himself to the next story, pencil and all.

Carefully, step by step, Ginger crawled up the extraordinary stairs. This was not a decoy. This was a dangerous undertaking. He did not dare look down between those iron bars. He had looked down once and nearly dropped Jerry's pencil out of terror. Up, up, he crept until there at last he was—at the open window. Gasping in relief, Ginger climbed onto the window sill and stood there, drooling, pencil in mouth, tail wagging in delighted expectation.

This room happened to be filled with boys and girls all seated at little desks. They looked sleepy and the place did not seem anywhere nearly as enticing as up at the reservoir. But anyway, there was Jerry, standing by his seat, his voice coming out clear and high and loud again.

The teacher issued a command. "Read it again, Jerry, more distinctly, and pay more attention to your final g's."

"My dog, Ginger," read Jerry Pye and he cleared his throat.

Well. When Ginger heard Jerry say his name he let out one short yelp of greeting. Ginger! "Yes, here I am, right here, Jerry," was what his bark meant. Of course he dropped Jerry's pencil, but fortunately it dropped on the window sill and not down below. Ginger quickly picked it up again and held it triumphantly in his mouth.

The minute Ginger let out that little yelp of greeting, what a hullabaloo came over the place. Some little girls screamed and some laughed. All the boys cheered. The person in command clapped her hands but no one paid any attention to her. Jerry dropped the paper he was holding and for a moment he stared at Ginger, too stunned for words or action. Then he rushed to the window and patted his dog to make him feel at home.

Ginger jumped into the room, dropped Jerry's pencil at his feet and looked up at Jerry. He was inviting him to throw it so he could run after it and bring it back, the way they played the rock game at home, or ball, or stick.

Jerry picked up his pencil. "He even found my pencil I lost on my way to school this morning," he said in greater astonishment than ever. "What a clever dog!"

"Your dog?" asked Oliver Peacock, a boy with glasses, in admiration.

"Yes," said Jerry proudly. "My dog. Trailed me here."

"The dog brought a pencil with him because it's school," shrilled one little girl.

"Whew!" whistled Oliver Peacock.

Ginger wagged his tail and looked as though he were laughing, the way he always did when he understood that pleasant things were being spoken of him. He licked Jerry's hand. So. Here he was! It was not much of a place but if Jerry could put up with it, so could he. He trotted around the room, his paws making a pitter-patter. He smelled here and sniffed

there. In one corner by a cupboard he kept his nose glued for some time. There was the possibility of mice there.

He detoured around the tall person who was still clapping and giving orders that no one was obeying any more than he obeyed anyone when he was off after a cat.

Suddenly the tall one took a long stick and she brought this down on her desk with such a bang it broke in two and went sailing through the air.

"Quiet!" she bellowed.

The hullabaloo stopped short then. This was a welcome relief to Ginger who did not see how Jerry stood this sort of a noisy life. His ears hurt him.

"Jared Pye!" the tall one said. "Either take your dog home or make him lie down under your desk until dismissal time which is, thank merciful heavens, only a few minutes away. And, Jared," she added, "see that this disgraceful performance is not repeated or I shall have to report you to Mr Pennypepper. Even so, you shall stand in the corner all this afternoon," she promised.

"Always the same old punishments," groaned Dick Badger wearily to Jerry.

"Come here, Ginger," said Jerry. As though he could help it, he thought, if the dog he owned happened to be so clever he could trail him all the way to school. You would think the teacher could see that, wouldn't you? he asked himself. "Come here, pup," he urged.

Ginger recognized the pleading note in Jerry's voice and he pattered over to him, for he wanted nothing to do with the tall one and her sticks and shrill voice.

"Lie down, Ginger," said Jerry. "Dead dog," he begged.

Being awfully tired, Ginger was happy to lie down. He licked his nose with loud smacking noises and he washed his torn and bleeding ear, and he washed himself all over.

He was right under Jerry's desk and every now and then Jerry gave him a nice pat with his foot.

There was complete silence now except for Ginger's loud paw-licking and the occasional loud nose-blowing of the tall one. In this quiet Ginger stopped licking himself. With a contented sigh he slipped into a thoughtful doze. He scarcely did more than twitch his ears when, from another room, he heard some more of the droning, as of bees, that he had heard outside. Now he could hear what the droning was saying, though.

R-A-T rat, C-A-T cat. Apparently the boys and girls were being instructed in the best way to manage these creatures. As for Ginger, he was too tired to listen and, besides, he knew the best way to handle them. As though one had to come to a place like this to learn such things.

From GINGER PYE
Illustrated by Margery Gill

The
Bedroom Door

The two pieces which follow reflect the concern for the well-being of working class children which was so strong in mid-Victorian England. Richard Hengist Horne, who wrote "Memoirs of a London Doll" under the pseudonym "Mrs.Fairstar", was a versatile and original man whose work ranged from innumerable articles and reviews to "Orion", an epic in three books, and "The Death of Marlowe", a play in a Jacobean style. Horne spent most of the year 1841 investigating conditions of child labor in the northwest of England, for a large-scale government commission—it was after she had read his report that Elizabeth Barrett wrote her poem "The Cry of the Children". Horne's four stories for children are obviously written by a man who enjoyed their company but, like his friends William and Mary Howitt, he let his sympathy for them come through as well, and the tenderness for them which made him condemn the horrific in children's books. The narrator of "Memoirs of a London Doll" is Maria Poppet herself, made in Holborn by old Sprat the toymaker, and the property, at one time or another, of a Jewish rag merchant, of the Countess of Flowerdale's little daughter in Hanover Square, of an Italian brother and sister who push a barrel organ through the streets, and, last of all, of little Lucy of Ashbourn Hall. Her first owner, Ellen Plummy, the heroine of this extract, is only seven when she is sent to live with her Aunt Sharpshins, and Nanny Bell is ten years old.

RICHARD HENGIST HORNE
("MRS. FAIRSTAR")

My First Frock and Trousers

THERE were plenty of little odds and ends of silks, and stuffs, and velvets, and muslins, which Ellen had already collected, and which her aunt had told her she might have, and with these they knew they could make me a beautiful dress. They finished their dinner as fast as possible, and ran upstairs again, in order to be alone for this pleasant work.

They accordingly began by carefully measuring me around the waist and around the shoulders; and then across the back down to the waist, measuring from the right shoulder crossing down to the middle of the left side. Their little fingers were busy about me in all directions, they did so tickle me. Then they measured my arms, first from the top of the shoulder to the elbow when bent, and next from the tip of the elbow to the wrist. Lastly, they measured me from the back of my neck down to the middle of the waist, just where there is, or ought to be, the most bend in a doll's back; and from this they measured for the skirt right down below my knees, and for the trousers they measured down as low as my ankles.

But how were these two little girls to find time to do all this work for me? The whole day they were engaged, from six o'clock in the morning till bedtime. So as it was now summer, and quite light at five o'clock, Ellen and Nanny both determined to get up at that time, and thus have an hour every morning to themselves, in order to make me a frock and trousers. And they calculated that by doing this for a week, they could easily finish the task they had set themselves. But the poor little girls had to work so hard for more than thirteen hours every day, that neither of them could awake in time. After several mornings, however, Ellen did manage to wake up enough just to speak, and call Nanny; and Nanny woke up enough just to answer. After which down sunk their cheeks upon the pillow, and they were fast asleep in a moment.

The next morning Nanny Bell called Ellen at half past five o'clock, and Ellen made a great effort, and sat up in bed with her eyes shut. At last she half opened one eye, and then she saw poor Nanny as fast asleep again as if she had never called her. So back fell Ellen upon her pillow.

Now, for several nights, they both made great resolutions before they went to sleep; but when the morning came they could not keep them, though they tried very much to do so; and one morning Ellen, as soon as Nanny called her, rolled herself out of bed upon the floor. But there she lay, and when the other girls were going past the door to their work at six o'clock, and came in to see if Ellen and Nanny were dressed, there they found Ellen fast asleep upon the floor in her nightgown.

Something, however, happened in consequence of this. Ellen had caught a bad cold and sore throat with sleeping upon the floor, and the doctor said she must remain in bed for two days to get rid of it. Ellen was, therefore, sent to bed again soon after dinner, and as it was necessary that somebody should be with her to give her medicine, or barley water to drink, Nanny Bell was chosen by her own request.

Here was a chance! Now was the time to work at my frock and trousers.

But there was something to be done first. There was medicine to be taken. It was brought by Aunt Sharpshins in a teacup, and it had a dark red and yellow color, and oh, such a strong smell! Poor Ellen looked at her aunt so pitifully, as much as to say, "Must I really take this nasty medicine?"—then she looked into the teacup, and made a face—then she looked around the room making the same face, only sadder—then she gave a little frown as much as to say, "Why should I be afraid? I know it is good for me—I am determined to take it!" then she shut her eyes—put the teacup to her lips—and down went the medicine!

As soon as Mrs. Sharpshins left them, Nanny produced some sugarplums out of a little paper for Ellen to take after her medicine; and as they ate the sugarplums, Nanny laughed at the horrid faces my mamma had made before she took her medicine and just after it was down, and then they both laughed very much.

Ellen now sat up in bed, and Nanny helped her to prop herself up with pillows at her back, and covered her shoulders with a large shawl. Nanny then brought all the bits of muslin, and silk, and stuffs, and velvet, together with a pair of scissors, and needles and thread, and spread them out upon the quilt before Ellen. I was placed on the bed beside her with my head raised high, so that I might see them working. When all was ready, Nanny got upon the bed and sat down opposite Ellen, and to work they both went.

The measurements had already been made, and the slips of paper with the marks were laid upon the quilt. Then they began cutting out.

First they cut out my underclothes, and these were all of cambric muslin, which they said was necessary in order to be soft to the skin of such a little creature as I was. I could not help laughing to myself when I heard them say this, because I was made all of wood, and my skin was only the fine hard-polished varnish of the celebrated Mr. Sprat. I was not quite so tender as they fancied. They next cut me out a small under-bodice of white jean instead of stays. Then came the trousers, which were cut long and full, and were of soft white muslin trimmed with openwork. Then they cut out a petticoat of fine cambric muslin, the body quite tight and the skirt very full all around. My frock was made to fit nicely to the shape, but not too tight. It was of fine lemon-colored merino, with a sash of violet-colored velvet, and very full in the skirt, and they said it must have some stiff muslin inside the hem to make it set off, and not hang too loosely in the folds.

When all was cut out and arranged, my mamma and Nanny both went to work with their needles, and they worked all the day, as long as they could see. The underclothes and the trousers were all quite finished, and the body and one sleeve of the frock were begun.

The next morning, after my mamma had taken her medicine and made the same horrid face as before, only not quite so bad this time, they went to work again. But this second morning the weather was not so warm as the day before; so Nanny went to the bed of one of the other girls and took off the top sheet, and tied up a bit of it in the middle with a long and strong tape in a strong knot, and then with a chair upon the bed she managed to tie the other end to a nail in the wall just over the head of the bed; she then spread out all the sheet that hung down so as to cover them both in, like a little tent. And in this pleasant manner they worked all the second day, by which time my frock was quite finished.

Besides this they had made me a pair of silk stockings, which were sewed upon my legs to make them fit better; and

as I was naturally from my birth rather stiff in the ankles and instep, they made the stockings without feet, but sewed black satin over both my feet in the shape of the prettiest boots possible, with stitches of cross work in front. When all was done, and everything put upon me, nothing would do but they must take me out for a walk around the room.

Out we all got from the tent; my mamma in her nightgown and shawl, with a bit of flannel around her throat, and slippers, and I walking between the two little girls, each holding me by the hand.

But we had hardly walked twice round the room, talking like ladies who are out in the park, when suddenly we heard Aunt Sharpshins coming upstairs! In a moment we were all upon the bed—down came the tent—underneath the bed it was thrown—into the bed we all three got as quick as possible—and when Mrs. Sharpshins came into the room we all seemed fast asleep.

She stood at the foot of the bed, looking at us. After a minute or two she went down again.

"How you laughed and shook the bed," said my mamma to Nanny. "I thought she would have found us out, and somehow I wished she had. I don't like to have pretended to be asleep."

"But," answered Nanny, "she would have been so unkind if she had seen us walking in the park."

"I wish people would not be unkind," sighed my mamma; and then she added, "How dear and kind *you* are, Nanny; and how you have worked for me, and nursed me all these two days."

At this they threw their arms 'round each other's necks, and so we all three went to sleep in reality, quite forgetting the tent which had been thrown under the bed. But it was a good-natured, merry girl that it belonged to, and she only gave my mamma and Nanny a good tickling when she found it, after a long search, at bedtime.

> *From* MEMOIRS OF A LONDON DOLL
> *Illustrated here by Leslie Marshall*

Charles Kingsley, born and bred in Devonshire, England, son of a clergyman and in orders himself, scholar, theologian and reformer, was deeply in sympathy with the hardships of the poor in his own time but he also respected the best elements of the squirearchy. So, in this extract from "The Water Babies", he obviously takes the part of little Tom the chimney sweep's boy, who is bullied and overworked by his cruel master Grimes; but his picture of the family at Hall Place is an affectionate one. Into this book Kingsley put arguments about evolution, education, politics and other controversial issues, but children would hardly go on reading it if the story had not such a sure understanding of a little boy, his troubles and joys and excitements. Then, too, I have chosen this as a superb piece of writing, with a peaceful opening skillfully changed to the rhythms of speed and chase.

CHARLES KINGSLEY

The Little Sweep

BUT Tom and his master did not go in through the great iron gates, as if they had been dukes or bishops, but around the back way, and a very long way around it was; and into a little back door, where the ash boy let them in, yawning horribly; and then in a passage the housekeeper met them, in such a flowered chintz dressing gown, that Tom mistook her for My Lady herself, and she gave Grimes solemn orders about "You will take care of this, and take care of that," as if he was going up the chimneys, and not Tom. And Grimes listened, and said every now and then, under his voice, "You'll mind that, you little beggar?" and Tom did mind, all at least that he could. And then the housekeeper turned them into a grand room, all covered up in sheets of brown paper, and bade them begin, in a lofty and tremendous voice; and so after a whimper or two, and a kick from his master, into the grate Tom went, and up the chimney, while a housemaid stayed in the room to watch the furniture; to whom Mr. Grimes paid many playful and chivalrous compliments, but met with very slight encouragement in return.

How many chimneys Tom swept I cannot say; but he swept so many that he got quite tired, and puzzled too, for they were not like the town flues to which he was accustomed, but such as you would find—if you would only get up them and look, which perhaps you would not like to do—in old country houses, large and crooked chimneys, which had been altered again and again, till they ran one into another, anastomosing (as Professor Owen would say) considerably. So Tom fairly lost his way in them; not that he cared much for that, though he was in pitchy darkness, for he was as much at home in a chimney as a mole is underground; but at last, coming down as he thought the right chimney, he came down the wrong one, and found himself standing on the hearth rug in a room the like of which he had never seen before.

Tom had never seen the like. He had never been in gentle-folks' rooms but when the carpets were all up, and the curtains down, and the furniture huddled together under a cloth, and the pictures covered with aprons and dusters; and he had often enough wondered what the rooms were like when they were all ready for the quality to sit in. And now he saw, and he thought the sight very pretty.

The room was all dressed in white —white window-curtains, white bed curtains, white furniture, and white walls— with just a few lines of pink here and there. The carpet was all over gay little flowers; and the walls were hung with pictures in gilt frames, which amused Tom very much. There were pictures of ladies and gentlemen, and pictures of horses and dogs. The horses he liked; but the dogs he did not care for much, for there were no bull dogs among them, not even a terrier. But the two pictures which took his fancy most were, one a man in long garments, with little children and their mothers around him, who was laying his hand upon the children's heads. That was a very pretty picture, Tom thought, to hang in a lady's room. For he could see that it was a lady's room by the dresses which lay about.

The other picture was that of a man nailed to a cross, which surprised Tom much. He fancied that he had seen something like it in a shop window. But why was it there? "Poor man," thought Tom, 'and he looks so kind and quiet. But why should the lady have such a sad picture as that in her room? Perhaps it was some kinsman of hers, who had been murdered by the savages in foreign parts, and she kept it there for a remembrance." And Tom felt sad, and awed, and turned to look at something else.

The next thing he saw, and that, too, puzzled him, was a washing stand, with ewers and basins, and soap and brushes, and towels, and a large bath full of clean water—what a heap of things all for washing! "She must be a very dirty lady," thought Tom, "by my master's rule, to want as much scrubbing as all that. But she must be very cunning to put the dirt out of the way so well afterwards, for I don't see a speck about the room, not even on the very towels."

And then, looking toward the bed, he saw that dirty lady, and held his breath with astonishment.

Under the snow-white coverlet, upon the snow-white pillow, lay the most beautiful little girl that Tom had ever seen. Her cheeks were almost as white as the pillow, and her hair was like threads of gold spread all about over the bed. She might have been as old as Tom, or maybe a year or two older; but Tom did not think of that. He thought only of her delicate skin and golden hair, and wondered whether she was a real live person, or one of the wax dolls he had seen in the shops. But when he saw her breathe, he made up his mind that she was alive, and stood staring at her, as if she had been an angel out of heaven.

No. She cannot be dirty. She never could have been dirty, thought Tom to himself. And then he thought, "And are all people like that when they are washed?" And he looked at his own wrist, and tried to rub the soot off, and wondered whether it ever would come off. "Certainly I should look much prettier then, if I grew at all like her."

And looking round, he suddenly saw, standing close to him, a little ugly, black, ragged figure, with bleared eyes and grinning white teeth. He turned on it angrily. What did such a little black ape want in that sweet young lady's room? And behold, it was himself, reflected in a great mirror, the like of which Tom had never seen before.

And Tom, for the first time in his life, found out that he was dirty; and burst into tears with shame and anger; and turned to sneak up the chimney again and hide; and upset the fender and threw the fire irons down, with a noise as of ten thousand tin kettles tied to ten thousand mad dogs' tails.

Up jumped the little white lady in her bed, and, seeing Tom, screamed as shrill as any peacock. In rushed a stout old nurse from the next room, and seeing Tom likewise, made up her mind that he had come to rob, plunder, destroy, and burn; and dashed at him, as he lay over the fender, so fast that she caught him by the jacket.

But she did not hold him. Tom had been in a policeman's hands many a time, and out of them too, what is more; and he would have been ashamed to face his friends forever if he had been stupid enough to be caught by an old woman; so he doubled under the good lady's arm, across the room, and out of the window in a moment.

He did not need to drop out, though he would have done so bravely enough. Nor even to let himself down a spout, which would have been an old game to him, for once he got up by a spout to the church roof—he said to take jackdaws' eggs, but the policeman said to steal lead—and, when he was seen on high, sat there till the sun got too hot, and came down

by another spout, leaving the policemen to go back to the stationhouse and eat their dinners.

But all under the window spread a tree, with great leaves and sweet white flowers, almost as big as his head. It was magnolia, I suppose; but Tom knew nothing about that, and cared less; for down the tree he went, like a cat, and across the garden lawn, and over the iron railings, and up the park towards the wood, leaving the old nurse to scream murder and fire at the window.

The under gardener, mowing, saw Tom, and threw down his scythe; caught his leg in it, and cut his shin open, whereby he kept his bed for a week; but in his hurry he never knew it, and gave chase to poor Tom. The dairymaid heard the noise, got the churn between her knees, and tumbled over it, spilling all the cream; and yet she jumped up, and gave chase to Tom. A groom cleaning Sir John's hack at the stables let him go loose, whereby he kicked himself lame in five minutes; but he ran out and gave chase to Tom. Grimes upset the soot sack in the new-graveled yard, and spoiled it all utterly; but he ran out and gave chase to Tom. The old steward opened the park gate in such a hurry, that he hung up his pony's chin upon the spikes, and, for aught I know, it hangs there still; but he jumped off, and gave chase to Tom. The ploughman left his horses at the headland, and one jumped over the fence, and pulled the other into the ditch, plough and all; but he ran on, and gave chase to Tom. The keeper, who was taking a stoat out of a trap, let the stoat go, and caught his own finger; but he jumped up, and ran after Tom; and considering what he said, and how he looked, I should have been sorry for Tom if he had caught him. Sir John looked out of his study window (for he was an early old gentleman) and up at the nurse, and a marten dropped mud in his eye, so that he had at last to send for the doctor; and yet he ran out, and gave chase to Tom. The Irishwoman, too, was walking up to the house to beg—she must have got around by some byway—but she threw away her bundle, and gave chase to Tom likewise. Only my Lady did not give chase; for when she had put her head out of the window, her night wig fell into the garden, and she had to ring up her lady's-maid, and send her down for it privately, which quite put her out of the running, so that she came in nowhere, and is consequently not placed.

In a word, never was there heard at Hall Place—not even when the fox was killed in the conservatory, among acres of broken glass, and tons of smashed flowerpots—such a noise, row, hubbub, babel, shindy, hullabaloo, stramash, charivari, and total contempt of dignity, repose, and order, as that day, when Grimes, gardener, the groom, the dairymaid, Sir John, the steward, the ploughman, the keeper, and the Irishwoman, all ran up the park, shouting "Stop thief", in the belief that Tom had at least a thousand pounds' worth of jewels in his empty pockets; and the very magpies and jays followed Tom up, screaking and screaming, as if he were a hunted fox, beginning to droop his brush.

And all the while poor Tom paddled up the park with his little bare feet, like a small black gorilla fleeing to the forest. Alas for him! there was no big father gorilla therein to take his part—to scratch out the gardener's inside with one paw, toss the dairymaid into a tree with another, and wrench off Sir John's head with a third, while he cracked the keeper's skull with his teeth as easily as if it had been a coconut or a paving stone.

However, Tom did not remember ever having had a father; so he did not look for one, and expected to have to take care of himself; while as for running, he could keep up for a couple of miles with any stagecoach, if there was a chance of a copper or a cigar end, and turn cartwheels on his hands and feet ten times following, which is more than you can do. Wherefore his pursuers found it very difficult to catch him; and we will hope that they did not catch him at all.

From THE WATER BABIES
Illustrated here by Harold Jones

The Gate
of
the Sports' Field

The stories in this section were all written to be told to children, and a polished conversational style makes them easy, as well as pleasant, to read. H. E. Todd began the stories about Bobby Brewster for his eldest son. Their first audience of more than one was a group of children on a beach in England, and it was one of the parents listening who insisted they ought to be written down. Two more sons, as Mr. Todd says, "came along to keep the inspiration fresh," and for many years he has been telling his tales at schools and Book Weeks, as well as on the radio and television. "Bobby Brewster himself is a mixture of all the small boys I have ever known, including my sons and myself. His appreciation of sardines dates from my early youth." The author can take something very ordinary and suddenly, and quite matter-of-factly, change it to something odd. You believe what happens because the author says so—and this is the art of the storyteller.

H. E. TODD

Football Boots

WHEN he was young the only football Bobby Brewster played was kicking about on the lawn with Mr. Henry Brewster—that's his father. They used a tennis ball, with two coats on the ground for goal posts, so Bobby wore his ordinary shoes for that.

Of course, before he went to Miss Trenham's school, Bobby Brewster had to buy some football boots. He was quite excited when he went to the shop with his mother, and they chose a very smart, brown pair with white laces and studs underneath. As a matter of fact, Bobby was so excited that he insisted on walking home in them, but the studs felt so funny on the hard pavement that he never tried that again.

At Miss Trenham's school, the boys play football every Monday and Thursday mornings. On Bobby Brewster's first Monday morning they stopped lessons at 11 o'clock, and all the boys took their white jerseys and their football boots off their pegs. Miss Trenham is most particular about their appearance and behavior outside, and she made them all tie their jerseys neatly around their necks by the sleeves and hang their football boots over their right shoulders by the laces. Then off they marched in twos down to the town ground. Miss

Trenham stopped the traffic in the High Street, and they really looked a most impressive sight marching over the crossing. They put on their jerseys and football boots in the pavilion, Miss Trenham led them onto the football field, and the game started.

As a matter of fact, Bobby Brewster was very disappointed with his first game of football. He was one of the smallest boys there, and he found it very difficult to run fast in his new football boots. Once, he even took a huge kick at the ball, missed it and fell down backwards, which made the other boys laugh and Bobby Brewster feel rather silly.

When his mother came to fetch him from the ground she asked him how he had enjoyed the game.

"Not much," he said.

"Why not?" asked Mrs. Brewster.

"Well," said Bobby, "for one thing these football boots are silly. They're much too stiff; I can't run properly in them and, what's worse, when I try to kick the ball they make me miss it."

Mrs. Brewster didn't say anything more. She thought to herself that, after all, Bobby Brewster was about the smallest boy in the game, so he couldn't expect to do very well at first. It would have been tactless to say so, though, particularly when he was so disappointed.

When they got home there were a few minutes before dinner time, so Mrs. Brewster said she would clean Bobby's football boots before putting them away.

"I shouldn't bother," said Bobby Brewster. "They're silly."

"Never mind. You'll soon get used to them if you look after them properly," said Mrs. Brewster. So she cleaned all the mud off and put them into the cupboard under the stairs.

The next Thursday morning before school a funny thing happened. When Mrs. Brewster gave Bobby his football boots, they were quite muddy. She was rather surprised, but it was time to get off to school, so she didn't say anything. Bobby enjoyed his football better that day. He still wasn't a very good player, but at least he didn't fall down instead of kicking the ball, and once he even managed to kick it twice before any of the other boys could touch it. When he got home after football, he thought he would clean his own boots, and his mother showed him how to do it.

Well, believe it or not, the following Monday morning when Bobby fetched his football boots to take to school, they were muddy again. He knew he had cleaned them after the last game, and he couldn't understand what had happened, but there was no time to ask his mother, so he went off to school and forgot all about it. Football that day was really quite exciting, and Miss Trenham even said "Well played, Brewster!" twice. When Bobby put the boots away that morning, he cleaned them carefully and gave them an extra polish.

Now comes the really funny part of the story. That night when Bobby was asleep, he was wakened up by a voice shouting "Goal!" He thought he was dreaming at first, but then the voice shouted "Goal!" again, and it sounded as if it came from the garden. Bobby jumped out of bed, went to the window and looked out. It was a bright, moonlit night, and he could see quite clearly. But you'll never guess what he did see. You won't, really.

Bobby Brewster's football boots were playing football with a tennis ball on the lawn. All by themselves. One was kicking one way and one the other, and they were running all over the place. They were doing the most tricky footwork, too—at least, it wasn't exactly footwork, because they hadn't got any feet in them, but it was ever so tricky! Bobby watched for a short time, and then felt cold, so he went back to bed and fell asleep.

When he woke the next morning, he thought again he may have been dreaming, but he dressed quickly and went downstairs. He looked in the cupboard, and can you guess what he saw? Two muddy football boots. He did, really.

"Well," said Bobby Brewster to himself, "there's only one explanation. They must be magic football boots."

At least he thought he said it to himself, but he can't have done, because a voice said, "We are."

"I beg your pardon?" asked Bobby Brewster.

"I said we are magic football boots," said the voice.

"You're even more magic than I thought, then," said Bobby Brewster. "You can talk as well as run."

"There's nothing magic about football

boots running," said the voice. "They wouldn't be much good if they couldn't."

"Perhaps not," answered Bobby Brewster, "but they usually have feet in them."

"That's true," said the voice. "Maybe I'd better explain. First of all, though, we must introduce ourselves. I'm the left boot and my name's Biff. My brother on the right is called Boff, but he can't talk."

"What a pity," said Bobby Brewster.

"Yes, it is rather," said Biff. "He's jolly good at football, though. Last night he beat me 3—2, and the game before that he won 4—0."

"It's a bit of a nuisance that you play football at night, you know," said Bobby Brewster. "I always have to go to school with muddy boots."

"That's what I was going to explain," said Biff. "We're only playing to help you."

"How do you make that out?" asked Bobby Brewster curiously.

"After your first game at Miss Trenham's," said Biff, "you told your mother we were silly boots and that we couldn't run or kick."

"I'm very sorry," said Bobby Brewster. "I'd never have mentioned it if I'd thought you were listening."

"Boff and I were very disappointed to hear it," said Biff, "because we'd taken a liking to you. So we decided to practice at nights until we got really good at football. Then you could play better in us, and you wouldn't need to complain any more."

"That was most thoughtful of you," said Bobby Brewster. "And, you know, I'm much better at football already."

"Just you wait till we've had more practice," said Biff. "You'll be the best player in the school. We're going to play every

Tuesday and Friday night so that we get better and better. I'm afraid, though," he added, rather sadly,"I shall never beat Boff. He's much better than I am."

"Never mind," said Bobby Brewster."I'll try to remember to use my right foot for kicking goals."

And that's exactly what Bobby Brewster has done ever since then. It's the end of the term now, and he's the best player in the school, even better than the bigger boys. He runs up the field kicking the ball first with Boff and then with Biff. When he gets near the goal, Boff! in it goes, and Miss Trenham cries,"Oh, well played, Brewster!"

There's just one other thing. Instead of cleaning his boots on Mondays and Thursdays, Bobby Brewster gets up early every Wednesday and Saturday morning after Biff and Boff have been practicing, and cleans them so that they're ready for his next game. He polishes them especially well, and while he's doing it he makes plans with Biff for playing their next game together. Even though he can't talk, Boff must be listening, too, because the plans always seem to work.

Football Boots

I know what you're thinking. What will Bobby Brewster do when he grows out of his football boots and has to buy a bigger pair? I'm afraid I can't answer that question. He'll have to go into the shop and ask the manager for a pair of magic football boots. I hope they have them in stock, don't you?

From BOBBY BREWSTER'S SHADOW
Illustrated by Lilian Buchanan

Elizabeth Chapman says Marmaduke the truck came into being because of illness. With two young sons going through measles and chicken-pox, one after the other, there came "the awful day of complete boredom, when every book in the nursery was known almost off by heart, and there was no one to go to the library. So I sat by their sides and made up a story about an old red lorry, or truck, who lived in a small town in England and traveled across the moors to Manchester. I had spent my childhood in a similar town in that county and had known and loved the desolate moors, which were practically on my doorstep, in all weathers. This had been my world, when I was young, and so this was where the old red lorry went on his first journey." In the stories of Marmaduke, everything that happens could happen to any lorry. It is Marmaduke himself, with his fits of ill-humor and his kind heart, who makes everyday things seem fresh and new.

ELIZABETH CHAPMAN

Marmaduke at the Races

"I THINK it's time we had a day's holiday," said Joe to Marmaduke one fine, sunny, summer's day. "We haven't any work which needs doing today. Would you like to go to the motor races?"

"What, and see the racing cars?" exclaimed Marmaduke. "Oh, I should like that. Is it far from here?"

"No, just a few miles. If we set off now, we shall be there for the start."

So Joe gave Marmaduke a quick polish so that he would look smart, and then off they went.

> "Merrily we go,
> Marmaduke and Joe,
> Singing high and low,
> Merrily we go –"

they sang as they rode along. It was so nice to have a day with no work to do.

"I wish I were a racing car," sighed Marmaduke. "I do like going fast, but I know it's not safe on the ordinary roads. It must be nice to be on a proper track and go as quickly as you like."

"Well, you're not really built for speed," laughed Joe. "But still, it would be nice to do it just once. However, there's no hope of that happening, so we may as well forget it."

On they went, singing their song, and looking at all the interesting things in the fields and the villages as they passed.

Then *Zoooooom* – Marmaduke nearly jumped off his wheels. A bright yellow racing car sped past them and was away up the road ahead.

"Oh, that must be one of them," said Marmaduke excitedly. "Oh, hurry up, Joe, I can't wait to get there."

"There's plenty of time," replied Joe. "We shan't be late, never fear."

So Marmaduke had to be content to travel steadily along. Then, as they were rounding a corner, there in front was the yellow racing car, drawn up to the side of the road, with the driver standing by the car, looking very dismal indeed.

"Hello, there! Is anything wrong?" asked Joe.

" 'Fraid so," sighed the driver. "It's such a little thing, really. She was all right when we left home this morning. I went over the engine myself. Now she won't go, and all because a screw's fallen out of one of the parts of the engine. What a silly thing to happen." He did look miserable. "Could you give me a lift to the next garage?" he went on. "I'll be able to get a screw there, and then I can probably get a lift back and put her right again. Still, by that time the race will be over."

"Why, of course we'll give you a lift," said Joe. "I'm sorry about the race, though. We are on our way there. We should have liked to have seen you take part."

Then Marmaduke had an idea.

"Couldn't we tow the car?" he asked. "We always keep a towing rope in the back, and we should save such a lot of time, then."

"Well, that *is* kind of you," said the racing man. "Do you know, if you'd be good enough to tow me to the race track, I think we could get there in time after all. There's sure to be a screw to fit this engine in the repair pits."

So Joe tied one end of the rope onto the back of the lorry, and the other end to the front of the yellow racing car, and off they went, slowly along the road.

"Oh dear! I do hope we get there in time," said Marmaduke. "This towing is a slow business, but it's the most we can do."

At last they were at the race track. Everyone stared at the sight of the old red lorry towing the gleaming yellow racing car, and then they began to cheer and make a way through the crowd for the little procession. Marmaduke felt very important, and more important than ever when the racing driver, after he had fixed a new screw in his engine, arranged for Marmaduke and Joe to watch the race from a specially good place.

In a little while, the cars lined up for the start, and then they were off.

How Marmaduke and Joe cheered as the little yellow car shot around the track at top speed.

"Hurrah! Hurrah! Toot-toot!" called Marmaduke. "He's going to win. Our driver's going to win. Oh, go on, yellow car, you *must* win."

Around and around they went. A red car was leading, then came a blue, and then the yellow one. Gradually the yellow one crept up till he was second, and on and on they raced. It was such a long race. Marmaduke was quite worn out with being excited for such a long time.

Then, the next time they came around, the yellow and red cars were side by side.

"Oh, do hurry, yellow car," cried Marmaduke.

And then, with a great burst of speed, the yellow car flashed past the winning post.

"Hurrah!" cried the crowd.

"Hurrah!" cried Marmaduke and Joe. "Three cheers for the yellow car."

They listened happily as a very important-looking man announced into a microphone that the yellow car was the winner, and they clapped furiously when he presented the driver with a grand silver cup.

The driver thanked the important-looking man and then went on talking to him for quite a long time.

The important-looking man listened, looked thoughtful, and then smiled, and stepped over to the microphone again.

"Ladies and gentlemen," he said. "I've just learned that our winner here would never have reached the course in time today if it hadn't been for a certain lorry by the name of Marmaduke. Now I understand that Marmaduke likes going fast very much, but his driver, Joe, quite rightly won't allow him to go too fast on the roads. So I think it would be a good idea if we gave Marmaduke a little reward for helping our gallant driver, and allowed him to drive around this track as fast as he likes."

How the crowd cheered as Marmaduke was driven onto the track. Then he felt a little nervous when he saw all the people looking at him. However, he felt very much better when he saw the yellow racing car come onto the track behind him.

"I'll follow you, Marmaduke," called the driver. "I'm to

have a victory run, so go on, as fast as you like, and I'll try to catch you."

Then Marmaduke forgot all about the crowd and saw only the broad empty track in front of him, and off he went. He had to slow down to go around the bends, of course, but when he was on the straight part he went very fast indeed.

How glorious it was. The sun shone, the fresh wind tore past his body, and Marmaduke felt wonderful.

At last, he had to come to a stop. The yellow racing car drew up beside him, and everyone clapped and cheered for fully two minutes, while Joe and the racing driver waved their hands and smiled. Marmaduke knew very well that the yellow car hadn't tried to catch him, as, of course, he could go much, much faster than the old lorry, but Marmaduke felt very happy indeed.

"Oh, what a wonderful holiday!" he said to Joe when they were on their way home. "Fancy, I never thought when we set out this morning that I'd be going as fast as I liked before the day was out."

"Well, it's the sort of thing that happens only once," said Joe. "Now you'll have to be content with going a bit slower, my lad."

And, of course, Marmaduke *was* quite, quite content.

From MARMADUKE AND HIS FRIENDS
Illustrated by Eccles Williams

Jennings is ten, and a new boy at Linbury Court Preparatory School, when this episode of the football field occurs. Since this story was written there have been many more books about Linbury Court. The characters in them are all composites drawn from boys the author has taught, or known, at various schools. It was for boys, in fact, in the dormitory or at the lunch table, that the stories started, developing afterwards into radio plays and later put into book form. We have all had some such cumulations of misfortune in our school days, but it takes an Anthony Buckeridge to put them in such a neat, vivid, comical form.

Jennings Arrives Late

THE crowd around the notice board parted to allow Mr. Carter to pass through and pin the football teams on the board. The first practice of the term was due to start when afternoon classes were over, and most of the new boys had been picked to play in"B"game; how they shaped in this would determine their football status for the next few weeks; the promising players would be promoted to"A"game, while the rabbits would find themselves relegated to the kick-and-rush contingent.

"Have you played much football, Jennings?"inquired Mr. Carter.

"Yes, quite a lot, sir,"Jennings replied."I'm not at all bad, really."

"That's for us to decide,"said Mr. Carter, silencing the cry of "Show-off" that went up on all sides. "And what about you, Darbishire?"

Darbishire had a profound distrust of ball games. His experience was somewhat limited as he had played football only once in his life, and what he chiefly remembered was that the ball traveled very fast and hurt when it hit you in the face and knocked your glasses off. This had happened early in the

281

game, and he had removed his glasses for safety, with the result that his only other recollection was of being continually knocked off his feet by a seething mob who rushed around in pursuit of some apparently invisible object.

"I'm trying Jennings at center-half," Mr. Carter was saying. "Where would you like to play, Darbishire?"

Positions on the field meant nothing in Darbishire's life and this seemed a silly question. Surely there was only one place?

"I'd like to play on that field behind the chapel, please, sir," he replied, " 'cause it's next to the road and I might be able to get some car numbers if they come close enough."

"What I mean is," explained Mr. Carter, "which position do you want to play in? Forward? Half-back? Or where?"

Darbishire understood at last. "I think I'd like to be wicket-keeper, sir," he said, surprising himself by his ready command of sporting terms. There was a howl of laughter from the rest of the group who echoed the remark at the tops of their voices for the benefit of those out of earshot on the fringe of the circle. But Mr. Carter kept a straight face.

"You'd better try outside-left, Darbishire," he said.

(*Afternoon classes follow, and Jennings is kept in after a crisis with an ink pot. We take up the story when Mr. Wilkins has let him go to change for games, for which he is already late.*)

He shot out of the classroom and, unmindful of school rules, scampered along the corridors to the changing room. As he ran, he practised imaginary shots at goal. Wham! A beautiful corner kick, he decided, as the imaginary ball swerved in mid-air and, eluding the imaginary goalkeeper's frenzied fingers, crashed with a resounding thud into the net. How the imaginary crowd cheered! "Good old Jennings!"

they yelled, clapping him on the back. "One-nothing." He smiled with becoming modesty at a fire extinguisher on the wall and prepared for the next phase. He decided on a penalty kick and, increasing his speed to the maximum as he rounded the corner to the changing room, he let fly with his foot, making perfect contact with the ball. The imaginary aspect of the kick ended with sudden abruptness as his foot made perfect contact with an object that was certainly not a football. It was the headmaster, and he received the full force of the penalty kick just below the kneecap.

"Ough!" said the headmaster in unacademic tones.

Martin Winthrop Barlow Pemberton-Oakes, Esq., M.A. (Oxon), Headmaster, was not normally a devotee of the ballet but, on this occasion, he executed a number of *pas de chats* and *grands jetés* that would have done credit to a prima ballerina. When the pain had abated somewhat, he placed his injured leg gently back on the ground and looked down to ascertain the cause of the trouble.

"I'm terribly sorry, sir," said Jennings. "I didn't know you were coming around the corner."

"This is a school," began the headmaster, "and not a bear garden. It has rules for the benefit of people who wish to turn corners without being kicked on the kneecap. If, therefore, I make a rule that no boy shall run in the corridors, I am at a loss to understand why my instructions are disregarded."

"No, sir," said Jennings.

The headmaster was not used to having odd remarks interpolated into his speeches.

"No, sir? What do you mean, ' No, sir? ' Are you disagreeing with what I said?" he demanded in the iciest of head-magisterial tones.

"No, sir. I mean, no, I didn't suppose you could understand –er– what you said, sir. I was agreeing with you, really, sir."

"Kindly note, Jennings, that when I make a remark that is not a question, neither comment nor answer is required."

"Yes, sir–er–I mean—no comment," said Jennings hastily.

"You will return to your classroom, Jennings, and meditate upon the fate that awaits small boys who run in corridors. Why on earth you can't behave like a civilized human being is beyond me!"

Jennings was not sure whether this one required an answer, or was another of those "no comments." The headmaster had certainly asked why, but Jennings decided that it might be rash to embark upon a lengthy explanation.

The teams had finished changing for games and were streaming out onto the field as Jennings returned to his classroom. He watched them gloomily from the window. This was the end; no football today and, if he went on like this, there probably wouldn't be any ever.

He was still thinking bitter thoughts three minutes later when he saw the headmaster standing in the doorway.

"Well, Jennings, have you meditated upon your misdeeds?" His kneecap was hurting less now and he felt more inclined to be lenient to a new boy, who perhaps had not had enough time to become used to school life.

"Yes, sir," replied Jennings.

"In that case you may once more proceed to the changing room, this time at a walking pace."

Jennings' first impulse was to say, "Gee, thanks, sir," but decided that it might be interpreted as a comment upon the headmaster's judgment, so he said nothing.

"Well," said the headmaster, "haven't you anything to say?"

"Yes, sir. Thanks very much, sir."

Masters were funny, Jennings thought, as he walked sedately to the changing room. One minute they ticked you off for answering and the next they ticked you off because you didn't. Golly, but he would have to hurry if he wanted to play football; the game had started hours ago, and, if he wasn't there soon, he wouldn't be allowed to play.

There wasn't time to change properly and take everything off, so he removed his jacket and put his white sweater on instead. He wasted precious seconds trying to pull his football shorts over the trousers he was already wearing, but they were too tight, so he rolled up his trouser legs a couple of inches and pulled his voluminous white sweater down till it reached nearly to his knees and gave no sign of what he was wearing underneath. Socks were easier; the second pair went over the top of the first without much difficulty and he had only to put his football boots on and he would be ready. Gosh, it must be nearly half time; everyone else had gone out ages ago!

Not quite everyone, though, for as he made a dive for his football boots, he saw Darbishire sitting on the floor in front of the boot lockers.

"What on earth are you doing here, Darbi?" he demanded.

"It's these stupid boots," replied Darbishire. "My mother tied them together by the laces when she packed them, so's I wouldn't lose one without the other—not that I wanted to lose both"—he went on in case his meaning should not be quite clear—"but she thought there'd be more chance of neither getting lost if—"

Jennings cut short the explanation.

"Well, you haven't lost them, so why don't you put them on?"

"I can't undo the knot," said Darbishire sadly. "I've been tugging at it for about twenty minutes, and the harder I tug, the tighter the knot gets."

"Gosh! Yes, you have got it into a mess," agreed Jennings, inspecting the four lace ends tied inextricably together. "I shouldn't think anyone could undo that, now, but you'll just have to put them on and put up with it. There'll be an awful how-d'you-do if you don't turn up, and you don't want that, do you?"

"No, I don't want a 'how-d'you-do'," said Darbishire, solemnly eying the laces."What I really want is a 'how-d'you-undo'."

Darbishire thought that his prowess as a footballer would be severely handicapped if he had to play with both feet tied together, but as this seemed preferable to the official wrath that his absenteeism would incur, he put on his boots and shuffled to the door. The tied laces permitted him to take a step of about ten inches and, assisted by Jennings, he proceeded in an ungainly shamble to the football field. They looked a queer pair, as Jennings' bulk was increased by his day clothes beneath his sweater, and as this capacious garment was pulled down almost to his knees, it appeared as though he had absent-mindedly forgotten to wear any trousers.

Mr. Carter was taking the game and decided not to waste any more time in demanding explanations of their late arrival.

"I've put Brown at center-half as you weren't here, Jennings," he said."You'd better play—let me see—what are we short of?"

They were standing near the goal and the goalkeeper, one Paterson, immediately chipped in.

"Can I come out of goal, sir? I'm getting super cold standing about and Jennings has got a sweater and goalkeepers always wear sweaters, sir, it says so in the laws of the game, honestly, sir, and as I haven't got a sweater, sir," he went on without pausing for breath,"I'm really breaking the rules, and Jennings ought to be jolly good in goal with a super sweater like that, oughtn't he, sir?"

As Paterson looked chilly, Mr. Carter despatched him to the forward line and sent Jennings to keep goal.

"And where did I say you were to play, Darbishire?" he asked.

"You said I was to be left out, sir," replied Darbishire.

"Left out of what?"

"I don't know out of what, sir; just left outside somewhere."

"Yes, I remember," said Mr. Carter, as light dawned. "Outside-left, not left outside."

The game was fast and furious and Mr. Carter was too busy to notice Darbishire's crippling progress to the left wing. It took him some time and much inquiry to get there, but finally he reached a spot near the touch-line where he was out of the hurly-burly and there he stood, somewhat awkwardly, at ease.

Jennings' goal was hard pressed by the opposing forwards and after saving eight shots in four minutes—three good saves and five lucky ones—he began to feel uncomfortably warm, but to remedy his overdressed condition would have been asking for trouble. He mopped his brow and saw that the opposing forwards were launching yet another attack. The ball came lolloping towards him—an easy shot to save—and he gathered it into his hands without difficulty, but before he could clear it to his forwards he was hemmed in on three sides by his determined opponents. What could he do?

Washbrooke major was winding up the whole of his ninety-one pounds for a tremendous barge which would have knocked Jennings and the ball far over the goal line. The goal posts were not fitted with nets, so Jennings decided to retreat and, still clasping the ball, he stepped back over his own goal line, skipped nimbly around the post and punted the ball up the field. The whistle blew.

"Goal," said Mr. Carter.

"But, sir, it can't be," argued Jennings, " 'cause I saved it; I caught it before it crossed the line."

"But you took it over the line when you dodged around the post," Mr. Carter explained.

"Oh, but that was just to get away from Washbrooke; I'd saved it hours before that."

Mr. Carter looked more closely at the perspiring goalkeeper.

"What are you wearing?" he demanded, and proceeded to investigate. "Vest, shirt, pullover, tie, underpants, suspenders, trousers—with bulging pockets—boots, two pairs of socks and an outsize sweater," he reeled off. "Are you sure you wouldn't like your overcoat as well?"

Jennings' explanation was unavailing, and for the third time that afternoon he headed towards the changing room as Mr. Carter restarted the game.

Darbishire rather liked playing outside-left. It was peaceful, he decided; the frantic battles of the mid-field seemed remote, and it was unlikely that anyone would disturb the serene stillness by kicking the ball to this quiet backwater near the touch-line.

There were some wild flowers growing on the bank a few yards away and he would have liked to wander off and pick them, but for the distressing handicap around his ankles. Never mind, he would pretend that he was a prisoner in a chain gang and was condemned to spend ten years with his feet securely . . . The train of thought jolted to a sudden halt. The worst was about to happen; some ill-advised athlete had sent a pass out to the left wing and the ball was coming straight at Darbishire. Now what was it that one was supposed to do? Oh, yes, kick the ball; the direction didn't matter, the main thing being to boot the beastly thing as far away as possible and hope that it didn't come back.

"Go on, Darbishire," called his captain. "Kick!"

It would be stretching the facts to say that Darbishire kicked the ball, but the spirit was willing even though the flesh was weak and held together at the ankles by boot laces. He drew his right foot back the full ten inches that the latitude of his laces allowed and swung his boot forward as hard as he could. The impetus of the forward swing dragged the other foot with it; up into the air went both feet, and Darbishire fell flat on his back while the ball rolled harmlessly over the touch-line.

The boys who assisted Darbishire to his feet were almost helpless with laughter.

"What happened, Darbishire?" they asked. "Did you have a stroke?"

"Oh, no, nothing so serious," Darbishire assured them. "It's merely a sort of temporary disability that I'm suffering from."

Mr. Carter took one look at the inextricable knots, and cut the temporary disability with his penknife. Two minutes later, as he blew his whistle to end the game, Jennings arrived, correctly changed and anxious for the fray.

From JÉNNINGS GOES TO SCHOOL
Illustrated here by Mary Dinsdale

Miniature
Doors

The Irish writer, T. H. White, died in 1964, leaving a handful of novels which no one else could have written—witty, fantastic, bursting with life. For a time he was a master at Stowe School, in Buckinghamshire, England, and the Vanbrugh mansion and its grounds, full of lakes and follies and Chinese Gothic summer houses, inspired "Mistress Masham's Repose," from which novel this extract is taken. To imagine oneself small is a dream (or a nightmare) which comes to everyone, adult and child alike; it is one of the classic themes of fantasy, like flying or being invisible. Sometimes such a fantasy suggests how vulnerable the small characters are, and how dangerous their lives. We can read "Alice in Wonderland", for instance, or the stories of the Borrowers, as almost a warning against the tyranny of force. T. H. White's book has a moral too. His young heroine Maria is oppressed by hardhearted guardians, Miss Brown the governess and the local vicar, and when she escapes and finds, on an island in the grounds, a colony of Lilliputians established there two hundred years before, she is tempted to exercise on them the power that her superior size gives her. But her friend the Professor, who alone knows her secret, gives her good advice, and here we see her putting it into practice. When Swift described the Lilliputians, in "Gulliver's Travels", he worked out all the details to scale, and T. H. White did the same.

T. H. WHITE

Maria Makes Friends

MARIA went around the green, with her eyes skinned, but without making any discoveries. She did find that there were four stone walls, about three inches high, which divided it into fields for the cattle. On her other visit she had taken them for drains. They looked as if they had been made of rubble from the inside of the temple, which, as she was beginning to suspect, was probably hollow. Ants, she knew, would sometimes eat away the furniture from inside, in tropical countries—or perhaps it was termites—and it looked as if the People had been doing the same thing. At any rate, there were no houses or other buildings of any sort, which might have given them away.

When she had finished with the green, she went and sat on the steps for nearly half an hour, but there was no sign of the conference in the cupola having come to an end. So she went around the green for the second time, visited the camouflaged dock for canoes, and took a look at the shrubbery. There was little to discover. It did seem that the lowest parts of the tangle, what we might call the undergrowth of the forest, had paths in it, leading in various directions toward the shore, but only a rabbit would have noticed these. One thing she found, and that was a robin caught by a noose of horsehair, on one of the higher branches. It was dead. Maria did not mind this, as she had no illusions about the habits of robins, and she saw that it had evidently been caught for somebody's dinner.

After these trips she sat on the steps again, for still another half hour, and wished very much that the Parliament would rise.

When it did rise at last, the original messenger came out alone, looking pleased, important, and slightly out of breath. He bowed politely, mopped his brow with a small handkerchief, and announced that the Professor's case was won! If she would kindly sit here, at a safe distance from the cowsheds, the People were prepared to show themselves.

She sat where she was told, holding her breath with excitement, and the messenger stood beside her, as if she were his private discovery. Wonderful things began to happen.

First the gate in the lowest step was opened, and out of this the cattle came, each one led by a cowman holding a rope, for fear that they should bolt on seeing Maria. They were black cattle, like Frisians, and, curiously enough, they showed no sign of being afraid. Probably she was too big for them to notice. They took her for a tree, and left it at that. The sheep came next, all baaing, with their lambs bleating and frisking. When the lambs had a drink, their tails went around like propellers, and this could be distinctly seen. The cattle were about four inches high, the sheep about an inch and a half. There were some small sheep dogs, like something out of a Noah's Ark, which ran around the sheep and yapped in squeaky voices, evidently enjoying the performance very much.

When the farm animals had been promenaded round the green and driven back for safety in the step, there came a procession of fishermen from the same entrance. These marched round, peeping sideways at the Giantess, carrying paddles for the canoes, harpoons like the one with which she had been attacked, small gaffs, and minnow rods with horse-hair lines complete. They had leather thigh boots, tanned from the skins of mice.

While the fishermen had been making their parade, the population of the island had been coming from the doors in the five pillars, without being noticed. She turned around when the last fisherman had disappeared, and there they were on the top step of the temple, in hundreds. (She found out later that there were more than five hundred. This was a greater number than could be supported by the green, but they lived by fishing and hunting and also by using secret pastures on the mainland at night, as we shall see.) When she turned around, all the People said with one voice: "Ooo!"

They were in rags.

It was not exactly rags, when she looked closer, but poor working clothes made of knitted wool from the sheep, and from mole skins or mouse skins. Some of the women had sewn themselves capes, from the breast feathers of small birds.

They all stood gazing at her with their mouths open, and the mothers held their children tightly by the hand, and the men stood rather in front, in case of emergency.

Nobody knew what to do.

Finally she remembered her instructions. She called out that she was going to stand up, so they must not be afraid. When she did stand, there was another "Ooo!" She told them to stay where they were, as she would be back in a minute, and then she rushed to the punt to fetch her package. When she got back, she warned the crowd to stand away from the middle of the pavement—some of the babies began to howl—and laid the package in the center, only staying to undo the string.

She stood off gently, being careful to look behind her for

fear of treading on somebody, and said: "See what it is."

The lawyer, or whatever he was, was the coolest person, for he had already passed his own fears, so he called up a team of fishermen, who pulled back the brown paper under his directions. Maria was interested to see that they did not tear the paper off, but treated it with care and admiration. Indeed, a piece of thick cardboard covering about half an acre seemed to them a useful article. When it was off, the People began to come forward slowly, hesitating between curiosity and suspicion, and the lawyer—he was the schoolmaster really—looked at her, to find out what was going to happen next. She pointed to him, to spread the presents out.

It was the silk handkerchiefs which did the trick. When the women saw these, they came quickly to finger them, and to love the bright, smooth colors. There were six three-penny ones, from Woolworth's, of artificial silk, the thinnest kind, for ladies, very gay.

They did not pull them about. They spread them reverently on the step. They were the loveliest things they had ever seen, since their forebears had been carried off from mighty Lilliput, two hundred years before.

Then there was the packet of needles. The men fingered these weapons, trying their temper and their points, with wagging heads and learned comment.

Two pennies' worth of nails were dragged aside by one party, evidently smiths, and these rang every bar of metal with a hammer, lifting separate nails and dropping them with the smallest clangs, pointing out their beauty in thoughtful tones.

A packet of razor blades, the useful kind with only one edge, so that one does not cut one's fingers when sharpening pencils, proved a puzzle to undo. But, when they had been undone, and their greasy paper stripped, there was a universal cry of admiration. For those two hundred years and more, there had been no metal for the People, except the rusty nails holding the laths inside the plaster dome: only these, and six cutlasses which had come with them from Lilliput, but which were now harpoons.

The final glory was in a paper bag. Maria opened it herself, the People standing back in wonder, and laid the contents out in rows. It was a shilling's worth of chocolate creams.

She had gone through a tussle with the Professor about these. He, with his giant's obsession about choosing small things for small people, had wanted to buy an old-fashioned sweet which was sometimes used on cakes, called Hundreds and Thousands. They were tiny pellets of hard sugar, colored pink or white or blue. Maria had insisted on full-sized chocolates. Which would you have preferred, then: a hard piece of sugar about the size of a toffee apple, or a chocolate cream the size of a pram?

There was no doubt about the kind which the people of Lilliput admired. Half the chocolates were quickly cut into slices with one of the razor blades, and in a minute everybody was nodding his head, smiling at his neighbor, rubbing his waistcoat, and taking another bite.

It was a pushover.

But suddenly there was a movement of dismay. All the eaters stopped eating the slice in their hands, all the ladies dropped tears on the silk handkerchiefs, everybody went off into a corner of the pavement and began to argue with the Schoolmaster. Maria watched them with a worried eye.

Presently the Schoolmaster came back.

"The People, Ma'am," he said awkwardly, "have call'd to Mind, that Transactions of this Complexion were carry'd out for Currency among the Nations of the civilized Globe. Four hundred Sprugs, Ma'am, Y'r Honor, Miss, were all the Treasure ever brought away from our unhappy Country, and these we have retain'd as old Mementoes of our former Greatness . . .''

Maria knew about sprugs. She had been reading the famous *Travels* madly, ever since she had found the People, and she knew that these were the golden coins of ancient Lilliput—each about the size of a seqⁱn or spangle.

"Goodness me," she said."But this is a present. Nobody has to pay. I robbed my money box, and the Professor bought them, and when Miss Brown finds me out she will take my life. We bought them for you freely, with our love."

"A Present, Ma'am," said the Schoolmaster with unexpected pathos, shedding a tear like the smallest dewdrop on a spider's web into his right sleeve, "a Gift of such Magnificence, Ma'am," he shed three more, "is, after all these Moons, is, Ma'am, Y'r Honor, Madam, Miss, is . . ."

And the poor fellow dissolved completely. It was from having too many shocks in one day.

Maria, very sensibly, turned 'round and left them to recover.

From MISTRESS MASHAM'S REPOSE
Illustrated here by Robin Jacques

The magic in "Doctor Boomer" is, in effect, the magic and magnificence of the Scottish Highlands. "Doctor Boomer" is set in Sutherland, Scotland, and the passages given here, though its details were noted on many occasions, depends most of all on a day when the author watched salmon leaping up the falls of the river Shin near Lairg. The three books reflect, as she says, "the other side of reality," the beneficent magic of music and the darker enchantments stirred in all of us by extremes of wind and weather. All kinds of associations and objects are woven into the stories—a house in the west of England which has a room full of wheels and clocks, a medieval leech book, a cousin knowledgeable in the occult, a ruined castle in Skye; and, in each book, imagination creates an unusual fairy land. The passage given here describes part of a journey undertaken by Lukey, the small ally of two human children, to seek help for the champions of the good against an evil horde of invaders from over the sea.

MARGARET J. MILLER

Conversation with a Salmon

LUKEY was running through wet grass, under the birch trees, in the direction of the river. As he ran, he hoped that Alal was as busy in the kitchen as the clatter of dishes had suggested. The Storyteller was likely to sleep for some time.

The rain had stopped now, and when Lukey looked up between the lacework of little birch leaves he saw white clouds spreading across a blue sky, free and untrammeled. As for him, he was a prisoner, for as the Storyteller had said, the birch wood was well fenced in. Through the trees he could see a high fence which seemed to be made of criss crossed strands of some gleaming metal. And now he remembered that when they had entered the wood Alal had closed a gate after them. There was only one unfenced side—the side by the river. He was imprisoned without hope of escape. Unless, that is, he could make use of his Great Idea.

The sound of the stream was growing louder in his ears every moment as he tripped over the moss and grass under the birch trees. Presently he came out from the trees and found himself on stony ground above the river, close to a splendid waterfall.

The water sped over the falls like smooth brown glass

broken and whirled in its lower reaches into a froth of tempestuous foam. Lukey smiled as he thought how Boomer would probably have described it. "Aspic jelly like wot we used to have in the Queen's day, with hard-boiled eggs and shrimps in it and such."

Yes, the upper part of the waterfall was like brown jelly, like liquid glass, like transparent brown taffeta with white lights in it. Lukey was fascinated by it. And when he turned his eyes away from the falls and looked at the flat stones beside the stream, they seemed to be fluid like the water—circling, shivering, and dissolving in a never-ending motion.

Lukey shook his head violently. This wouldn't do at all. While the Storyteller was still soundly asleep he must carry out his plan.

Just as he remembered this a wonderful thing happened. A magnificent salmon, gleaming in the sunlight, leapt out of the water at the foot of the falls, hung quivering in the air a moment, and then slipped into the glassy top of the falls and on to the smooth pools beyond.

This was exactly what Lukey wanted. Hurriedly and excitedly, he scrambled down the bank which rose above the stream. Even as he did so, another salmon shot out of the water and tried to leap the falls. But this one was beaten back by the force of the rapids. Lukey had no doubts, however, that it would try again.

By now Lukey was standing on a small flat stone close to the loud-voiced water which boiled and seethed with foam. Three times he watched as three huge salmon leapt the falls successfully. Then he made his way downstream a little to a comparatively peaceful pool away from the main force of the rushing stream.

He stood very still now and watched. For some time nothing happened, and he was just about to move to another place when a silvery salmon came gliding into the pool.

Lukey bent down and put his mouth as close to the water as he could.

"It's a friend what's speaking," he said rapidly. "A friend what's in need of help wot you can provide."

The salmon remained poised in the shallow brown water. Lukey spoke again.

"What sort of help? Why, just this. I'm a prisoner here with a sort of—a sort of magician. He'd do you harm as well as me if he had a chance, I've no manner of doubt. But I can escape from him if you'll just be so kind as to carry me up the waterfall on your back."

The water trembled into agitated ripples and bubbles.

"Couldn't do it? A course you could. I don't weigh more than—more than a new-born fly or such. Less, I shouldn't wonder."

Once more the smooth brown water was broken up by ripples.

"It's as much as you can do to get up that there pestiferous waterfall by yourself, let alone taking a passenger? Now I'm ashamed to hear you talking like that, a great handsome big fish like you.'

The water remained still now. The salmon was clearly thinking over the idea. Lukey was preparing to wait patiently, when all at once, above the din of the waterfall, he heard other sounds.

A voice calling, loud and insistent. And a crashing of feet through the broken branches which lay here and there under the birch trees.

Lukey became panic-stricken. Alal must have gone into the room where the Storyteller was, discovered Lukey's absence, and roused his master. If the Storyteller found him down by the river he would guess that he was trying to escape that

303

way. And never again would he be allowed freedom to wander in the birch wood.

"It's life and death," he whispered to the salmon lying still in the water. "Life and death, I tell you. Look, if you'll come to the edge of the river I'll get on your back. And you'll soon see that I don't weigh no more than a feather."

The shouts were getting nearer now. There was not time to be lost. No time at all.

But the salmon had made up his mind. For with one swift dart it came close to the border of the stream, and waited to allow Lukey to mount upon its back.

As Lukey stepped into the icy water and put a leg on each side of the cold, slippery body, he suddenly thought of the danger of what he proposed to do. Could he really cling on and keep his balance while the salmon did that tremendous leap? There was in fact nothing to hold onto—nothing on which he could get a good grip in order to stand the powerful onrush of the waterfall.

Leaning over, he clasped his arms as well as he could around the salmon.

"No, I'll do my best not to choke you," he replied in answer to the salmon's complaint. He relaxed his grip a little. It would never do to throttle his rescuer just when all its strength was needed for the leap.

"Alal! Alal!" came the shouting voice which was now immediately overhead on the bank. "Bring the net. Quick! Quick!"

The salmon had started to swim into midstream. The cold of the water was terrible, and Lukey felt that if he was not drowned he would certainly be frozen to death.

Water splashed into his face and eyes. But at one moment, as the salmon rose nearer to the surface, he saw that Alal was coming running along the shore very close to the stream.

And in his hand he carried a fish net with a remarkably long handle.

"You say you're just a-going to jump?" whispered Lukey to the salmon. "Very well, then. I'm ready."

The salmon sought deeper water now and curled its tail ready to leap. Lukey's head was submerged. He was holding his breath.

But the next second he was hanging dizzily in the air, with the terrible white foam in front of his eyes, and the thundering sound of it in his ears. With a smack he was plunged in the seething mass, and after that he forgot everything except that he must cling on, cling on, whatever happened.

Somehow he succeeded in doing this. It was fortunate that he did, for instead of finding himself at the top of the falls as he had hoped, when he regained consciousness it was only to find that the salmon had been flung back by the force of the water. Like many another before him, he had not made the leap at the first attempt.

The Storyteller was close to the river now, and Alal had joined him, stretching out his long net towards where Lukey sat with his head bobbing above the stream.

Breathless and exhausted, the salmon was telling him something.

"You say you can't do it?" Lukey had to shout to make himself heard above the din of the water. "A course you can. Just one more try. You'll do it like a bird a-soaring through the air, I shouldn't be surprised."

But the salmon had been tired out by its effort. And while it rested, trying to recover strength for the second leap, a dreadful thing happened. Suddenly Lukey found himself and his friend the salmon tumbling together in the great net which Alal had been stretching out from the bank. And now they were soaring into the air like birds—with this difference, that a bird in the air is free, while they were captives.

"Splendid, Alal! Magnificent work!" called the Storyteller from the upper bank as Alal stood on the flat stones near the river, triumphantly holding up his catch.

While Lukey trembled to think what would happen next, there was another sudden change in his situation. With a crack like the branch of a tree breaking off, the long handle of the net snapped in two, and Lukey, the salmon and the net were plunged together into the river again.

With a twist of its strong back the salmon was at once clear of the net. But for Lukey it was more difficult, since one of his legs had got caught in the wide mesh, and try as he would he couldn't free it. Meanwhile the Storyteller was stamping and gnashing his teeth on the bank, and Alal, with arms outstretched, was wading towards Lukey.

The salmon had been so angry at being netted that Lukey was sure it would swim away at the first opportunity. But again it showed itself to be kindly, for as Alal waded ever nearer and nearer, it waited for Lukey. As he lashed out wildly to free his leg, swallowing a great deal of water in the process, Lukey cast one terrified glance towards the shore. Those dark clutching hands were almost upon him.

I must kick again, thought Lukey. I mustn't give up! Just one more kick and—that's it! That's done it! Now I'm free! Free to go up them there falls once more.

Alal had been stumbling forward with hands stretched wide. But as Lukey hurled himself on to the salmon's back, a stone gave way beneath his pursuer's feet, and Alal was plunged, startled and angry, into the cold, rushing stream.

A leap into the air, with the salmon's body all a-quiver. A flash of golden sunlight and then the chaos of foam and brown, tumbled water. A fight against foam until it became

shallower and less powerful. And soon the foam disappeared altogether and the salmon was swimming upstream as though in clear brown molten glass, boring through the water powerfully and gladly, with sideways movements of its body.

"I'll finish you for this, Alal, you careless scoundrel!" shouted the Storyteller, stamping and shaking his fist upon the bank. And to Lukey he yelled: "I'll get you yet! See if I don't!" He trembled and shook with rage as Lukey's little head was borne away from him into the distance.

"As to that, we'll know later," muttered Lukey. "But anyhows I'm going to get to Garadon first, as quick as I can."

Half an hour later, he was deposited on the bank of the stream by the salmon. Having thanked his rescuer with deep gratitude, he walked on down a wide glen. Here he was lucky enough to come upon a stray pony. And he succeeded in persuading it to carry him on its back for the rest of the way in return for a reward of apples. The trotting of its hoofs was music in his ears as every mile drew him nearer to Bergar and the work he had to do.

From DOCTOR BOOMER
Illustrated by Robin Jacques

The
Stable Door

Dinah Maria Mulock (Dinah Craik) was born in 1826 into a parson's family. She was determined to succeed as a writer and went to London in the 1840s, where she soon became a well-known literary figure. Some of her stories for children described traditional fairy scenes, but "The Adventures of a Brownie," from which this extract comes, really belongs with Juliana Ewing's stories or the pictures of Randolph Caldecott, for the book reflects the English rural scene now almost vanished. This is first and foremost a realistic story, about cheerful children and busy grown-ups, and the Brownie plays his part in a pleasant domestic setting.

DINAH CRAIK

Brownie's Ride

FOR the little Brownie, though not given to horsemanship, did once take a ride, and a very remarkable one it was. Shall I tell you all about it?

The six little children got a present of something they had longed for all their lives—a pony. Not a rocking horse, but a real live pony—a Shetland pony, too, which had traveled all the way from the Shetland Isles to Devonshire—where everybody wondered at it, for such a creature had not been seen in the neighborhood for years and years. She was no bigger than a donkey, and her coat, instead of being smooth like a horse's, was shaggy like a young bear's. She had a long tail, which had never been cut, and such a deal of hair in her mane and over her eyes that it gave her quite a fierce countenance. In fact, among the mild and tame Devonshire beasts, the little Shetland pony looked almost like a wild animal.

But in reality she was the gentlest creature in the world. Before she had been many days with them, she began to know the children quite well; followed them about, ate corn out of the bowl they held out to her; nay, one day when the eldest little girl offered her bread and butter, she stooped her head and took it from the child's hand, just like a young lady.

Indeed, Jess—that was her name—was altogether so lady-like in her behavior that, more than once, cook allowed her to walk in at the back door, when she stood politely warming her nose at the kitchen fire, for a minute or two, then turned around and as politely walked out again. But she never did any mischief; and was so quiet and gentle a creature that she bade fair soon to become as great a pet in the household as the dog, the cat, the kittens, the puppies, the fowls, the ducks, the cow, the pig, and all the other members of the family.

The only one who disliked her, and grumbled at her, was the gardener. This was odd because, though cross to children, the old man was kind to dumb beasts. Even his pig knew his voice and grunted, and held out his nose to be scratched, and he always gave each successive pig a name, Jack or Dick, and called them by it, and was quite affectionate to them, one after the other, until the very day that they were killed. But they were English pigs—and the pony was Scotch—and the Devonshire gardener hated everything Scotch, he said; besides, he was not used to groom's work, and the pony required such a deal of grooming on account of her long hair. More than once, Gardener threatened to clip it short, and turn her into a regular English pony, but the children were in such distress at this that the mistress and mother forbade any such spoiling of Jess's personal appearance.

At length, to keep things smooth, and to avoid the rough words and even blows which poor Jess sometimes got, they sought in the village for a boy to look after her, and found a great rough shock-headed lad named Bill, who, for a few shillings a week, consented to come up every morning and learn the beginning of a groom's business; hoping to end, as his mother said he should, in sitting, like the squire's fat coachman, as broad as he was long, on the top of the hammercloth of a grand carriage, and do nothing all day but drive a pair of horses as stout as himself a few miles along the road and back again.

Bill would have liked this very much, he thought, if he could have been a coachman all at once, for if there was one thing he disliked, it was work. He much preferred to lie in the sun all day and do nothing; and he only agreed to come and take care of Jess because she was such a very little pony that looking after her seemed next door to doing nothing. But when he tried it he found his mistake. True, Jess was a very gentle beast; so quiet that the old mother hen with fourteen chicks used, instead of roosting with the rest of the fowls, to come regularly into the portion of the cow shed which was partitioned off for a stable, and settle under a corner of Jess's manger for the night; and in the morning the chicks would be seen running about fearlessly among her feet and under her very nose.

But for all that she required a little management, for she did not like her long hair to be roughly handled; it took a long time to clean her, and though she did not scream out like some little children when her hair was combed, I am afraid she sometimes kicked and bounced about, giving Bill a deal of trouble—all the more trouble, the more impatient Bill was.

And then he had to keep within calling distance, for the children wanted their pony at all hours. She was their own special property, and they insisted upon learning to ride— even before they got a saddle. Hard work it was to stick on Jess's bare back, but by degrees the boys did it, turn and turn about, and even gave their sisters a turn too—a very little one —just once around the field and back again, which was quite enough, they considered, for girls. But they were very kind to their little sisters, held them on so that they could not fall, and led Jess carefully and quietly, and altogether behaved as elder brothers should. Nor did they squabble very much,

though sometimes it was rather difficult to keep their turns all fair, and remember accurately which was which. But they did their best, being on the whole extremely good children. And they were so happy to have their pony that they would have been ashamed to quarrel over her.

Also, one very curious thing kept them on their good behavior. Whenever they did begin to misconduct themselves, to want to ride out of their turns, or to domineer over one another, or the boys, joining together, tried to domineer over the girls, as I grieve to say boys not seldom do, they used to hear in the air, right over their heads, the crack of an unseen whip. It was none of theirs, for they had not got a whip; that was a felicity which their father had promised when they could all ride like young gentlemen and ladies; but there was no mistaking the sound—indeed, it always startled Jess so that she set off galloping, and could not be caught again for many minutes.

This happened several times, until one of them said, "Perhaps it's the Brownie." Whether it was or not, it made them behave better for a good while: till one unfortunate day the two eldest began contending which should ride foremost and which hindmost on Jess's back, when *Crick—crack!* went the whip in the air, frightening the pony so much that she kicked up her heels, tossed both the boys over her head, and scampered off, followed by a loud "Ha, ha, ha!"

It certainly did not come from the two boys, who had fallen—quite safely, but rather unpleasantly—into a large nettle bed; whence they crawled out, rubbing their arms and legs, and looking too much ashamed to complain. But they were rather frightened and a little cross, for Jess took a skittish fit, and refused to be caught and mounted again, till the bell rang for school—when she grew as meek as possible. Too late—for the children were obliged to run indoors, and got no more rides for the whole day.

Jess was from this incident supposed to be on the same friendly terms with Brownie as were the rest of the household. Indeed, when she came, the children had taken care to lead her up to the coal cellar door and introduce her properly—for they knew Brownie was very jealous of strangers and often played them tricks. But after that piece of civility he would be sure, they thought, to take her under his protection. And sometimes, when the little Shetlander was restless and pricked up her ears, looking preternaturally wise under those shaggy brows of hers, the children used to say to one another, "Perhaps she sees the Brownie."

Whether she did or not, Jess sometimes seemed to see a good deal that others did not see, and was apparently a favorite with the Brownie, for she grew and thrived so much that she soon became the pride and delight of the children and of the whole family. You would hardly have known her for the rough, shaggy, half-starved little beast that had arrived a few weeks before. Her coat was so silky, her limbs so graceful, and her head so full of intelligence, that everybody admired her. Then, even Gardener began to admire her too.

"I think I'll get upon her back, it will save me walking down to the village," said he, one day. And she actually carried him—though, as his feet nearly touched the ground, it looked as if the man were carrying the pony and not the pony the man. And the children laughed so immoderately that he never tried it afterwards.

Nor Bill neither, though he had once thought he should like a ride, and got astride on Jess—but she quickly ducked her head down, and he tumbled over it. Evidently she had her own tastes as to her riders, and much preferred little people to big ones.

Pretty Jess! When cantering around the paddock with the young folk, she really was quite a picture. And when at last she got a saddle—a new, beautiful saddle, with a pommel to take off and on, so as to suit both boys and girls—how proud they all were, Jess included! That day they were allowed to take her into the market—Gardener leading her, as Bill could not be trusted—and everybody, even the blacksmith, who hoped by-and-by to have the pleasure of shoeing her, said what a beautiful pony she was!

After this, Gardener treated Jess a great deal better, and showed Bill how to groom her, and kept him close at it too, which Bill did not like at all. He was a very lazy lad, and whenever he could shirk work he did it; and many a time when the children wanted Jess, either there was nobody to saddle her, or she had not been properly groomed, or Bill was away at his dinner, and they had to wait till he came back and could put her in order to be taken out for a ride like a genteel animal—which I am afraid neither pony nor children enjoyed half so much as the old ways before Bill came.

Still, they were gradually becoming excellent little horsemen and horsewomen, even the youngest, only four years old, whom all the rest were very tender over, and who was often held on Jess's back and given a ride out of her turn because she was a good little girl and never cried for it. And seldomer and seldomer was heard the mysterious sound of the whip in the air, which warned them of quarreling—Brownie hated quarreling.

In fact, their only trouble was Bill, who never came to his work in time, and never did things when wanted, and was ill-natured, lazy, and cross to the children, so that they disliked him very much.

"I wish the Brownie would punish you," said one of the boys, "you'd behave better then."

"The Brownie!" cried Bill contemptuously, "if I caught him I'd kick him up in the air, like this! "

And he kicked up his cap—his only cap, it was—which, strange to relate, flew right up, ever so high, and lodged at the top of a tree which overhung the stable, where it dangled for weeks and weeks, during which time poor Bill had to go bareheaded.

He was very much vexed, and revenged himself by vexing the children in all sorts of ways. They would have told their mother, and asked her to send Bill away, only she had a great many anxieties just then, for their dear old grandmother was very ill, and they did not like to make a fuss about anything that would trouble her.

So Bill stayed on, and nobody found out what a bad, ill-natured, lazy boy he was.

But one day the mother was sent for suddenly, not knowing when she should be able to come home again. She was very sad, and so were the children, for they loved their grand-mother—and as the carriage drove off they all stood crying round the front door for ever so long.

The servants even cried too—all but Bill.

"It's an ill-wind that blows nobody good," said he. "What a jolly time I shall have! I'll do nothing all day long. Those troublesome children sha'n't have Jess to ride; I'll keep her in the stable and then she won't get dirty, and I shall have no trouble in cleaning her. Hurrah! what fun!'

He put his hands in his pockets, and sat whistling the best part of the afternoon.

The children had been so unhappy, that for that day they quite forgot Jess; but next morning after lessons were over, they came, begging for a ride.

'You can't get one. The stable door's locked, and I've lost the key." (He had it in his pocket all the time.)

"How is poor Jess to get her dinner?" cried a thoughtful little girl. "Oh, how hungry she will be!"

And the child was quite in distress, as were the two other girls. But the boys were more angry than sorry.

"It was very stupid of you, Bill, to lose the key. Look about and find it, or else break open the door."

"I won't," said Bill, "I daresay the key will turn up before night, and if it doesn't—who cares? You get riding enough and too much. I'll not bother myself about it, or Jess either."

And Bill sauntered away. He was a big fellow and the little lads were rather afraid of him. But as he walked, he could not keep his hand out of his trousers pocket, where the key felt growing heavier and heavier, till he expected it every minute to tumble through, and come out at his boots—convicting him before all the children of having told a lie.

Nobody was in the habit of telling lies to them, so they never suspected him, but went innocently searching about for the key—Bill all the while clutching it fast. But every time he touched it, he felt his fingers pinched, as if there was a cockroach in his pocket—or a little lobster—or something anyhow that had claws. At last, fairly frightened, he made an excuse to go into the cowshed, took the key out of his pocket and looked at it, and finally hid it in a corner of the manger, among the hay.

As he did so, he heard a most extraordinary laugh, which was certainly not from Dolly the cow, and, as he went out of the shed, he felt the same sort of pinch at his ankles, which made him so angry that he kept striking with his whip in all directions, but hit nobody, for nobody was there.

But Jess—who, as soon as she heard the children's voices, had set up a most melancholy whinnying behind the locked stable door—began to neigh energetically. And Boxer barked, and the hens cackled, and the guinea fowls cried "Come back, come back!" in their usual insane fashion—indeed the whole farmyard seemed in such an excited state, that the children got frightened lest Gardener should scold them, and ran away, leaving Bill master of the field.

319

What an idle day he had! How he sat on the wall with his hands in his pockets, and lounged upon the fence, and sauntered around the garden! At length, absolutely tired of doing nothing, he went and talked with Gardener's wife, while she was hanging out her clothes. Gardener had gone down to the lower field, with all the little folks after him, so that he knew nothing of Bill's idling, or it might have come to an end.

By-and-by Bill thought it was time to go home to his supper. "But first I'll give Jess her corn," said he, "double quantity, and then I need not come back to give her breakfast so early in the morning. Soh! you greedy beast. I'll be at you presently if you don't stop that noise."

For Jess, at sound of his footsteps, was heard to whinny in the most imploring manner, enough to have melted a heart of stone.

"The key—where on earth did I put the key?" cried Bill, whose constant habit it was to lay things out of his hand, and then forget where he had put them, causing himself endless loss of time in searching for them—as now. At last he suddenly remembered the corner of the cow's manger, where he felt sure he had left it. But the key was not there.

"You can't have eaten it, you silly old cow," said he, striking Dolly on the nose as she rubbed herself against him— she was an affectionate beast. "Nor you, you stupid old hen!" kicking the mother of the brood, who, with her fourteen chicks, being shut out of their usual roosting place, Jess's stable—kept pecking about under Dolly's legs. "It can't have gone without hands—of course it can't." But most certainly the key was gone.

What in the world should Bill do? Jess kept on making a pitiful complaining. No wonder, as she had not tasted food since morning. It would have made any kind-hearted person quite sad to hear her, thinking how exceedingly hungry the poor pony must be.

Little did Bill care for that, or for anything, except that he should be sure to get into trouble as soon as he was found out. When he heard Gardener coming into the farmyard, with the children after him, Bill bolted over the wall like a flash of lightning, and ran away home, leaving poor Jess to her fate.

All the way he seemed to hear at his heels a little dog yelping, and then a swarm of gnats buzzing round his head, and altogether was so perplexed and bewildered, that when he got into his mother's cottage he escaped into bed, and pulled the blanket over his ears to shut out the noise of the dog and the gnats, which at last turned into a sound like somebody laughing. It was not his mother, she didn't often laugh, poor soul!—Bill bothered her quite too much for that, and he knew it. Dreadfully frightened, he hid his head under the bed clothes, determined to go to sleep and think about nothing till next day.

Meantime, Gardener returned with all the little people trooping after him. He had been rather kinder to them than usual this day, because he knew their mother had gone away in trouble, and now he let them help him to roll the gravel, and fetch up Dolly to be milked, and watch him milk her in the cow shed—where, it being nearly winter, she always spent the night now. They were so well amused that they forgot all about their disappointment as to the ride, and Jess did not remind them of it by her whinnying. For as soon as Bill was gone, she grew quite silent.

At last one little girl, the one who had cried over Jess's being left hungry, remembered the poor pony, and peeping through a crevice in the cow shed, saw her stand contentedly munching at a large bowl full of corn.

"So Bill did find the key. I'm very glad," thought the kind

little maiden, and to make sure looked again, when—what do you think she beheld squatting on the manger? Something brown, either a large brown rat, or a small brown man. But she held her tongue, since being a very little girl, people sometimes laughed at her for the strange things she saw. She was quite certain she did see them for all that.

So she and the rest of the children went indoors and to bed. When they were fast asleep, something happened. Something so curious, that the youngest boy, who thinking he heard Jess neighing, got up to look out, was afraid to tell, lest he too should be laughed at, and went back to bed immediately.

In the middle of the night, a little old brown man, carrying a lantern, or at least having a light in his hand that looked like a lantern—went and unlocked Jess's stable, and patted her pretty head. At first she started, but soon she grew quiet and pleased, and let him do what he chose with her. He began rubbing her down, making the same funny hissing with his mouth that Bill did, and all grooms do—I never could find out why. But Jess evidently liked it, and stood as good as possible.

"Isn't it nice to be clean?" said the wee man, talking to her as if she were a human being, or a Brownie. "And I dare say your poor little legs ache with standing still so long. Shall we have a run together? The moon shines bright in the clear, cold night. Dear me! I'm talking poetry."

But Brownies are not poetical fairies, quite commonplace, and up to all sorts of work. So, while he talked, he was saddling and bridling Jess, she not objecting in the least. Finally, he jumped on her back.

"Off, said the stranger; off, off, and away!" sang Brownie, mimicking a song of the cook's. People in that house often heard their songs repeated in the oddest way, from room to room, everybody fancying it was somebody else that did it. But it was only the Brownie. "Now, ' A southerly wind and a cloudy sky proclaim it a hunting morning!' "

Or night—for it was the middle of the night, though bright as day—and Jess galloped and the Brownie sat on her back as merrily as if they had gone hunting together all their days.

Such a steeplechase it was! They cleared the farmyard at a single bound, and went flying down the road, and across the ploughed field, and into the wood. Then out into the open country, and by-and-by into a dark, muddy lane—and oh! how muddy Devonshire lanes can be sometimes!

"Let's go into the water to wash ourselves," said Brownie, and coaxed Jess into a deep stream, which she swam as bravely as possible—she had not had such a frolic since she left her native Shetland Isles. Up the bank she scrambled, her long hair dripping as if she had been a water dog instead of a pony. Brownie, too, shook himself like a rat or a beaver, throwing a shower round him in all directions.

"Never mind, at it again, my lass!" and he urged Jess into the water once more. Out she came, wetter and brisker than ever, and went back home through the lane, and the wood, and the ploughed field, galloping like the wind, and tossing back her ears and mane and tail, perfectly frantic with enjoyment.

But when she reached her stable, the plight she was in would have driven any respectable groom frantic too. Her sides were white with foam, and the mud was sticking all over her like plaster. As for her beautiful long hair, it was all caked together in a tangle, as if all the combs in the world would never make it smooth again. Her mane especially was braided into knots, which people in Devonshire call elf locks, and say, when they find them on their horses, that it is because the fairies have been riding them.

Certainly, poor Jess had been pretty well ridden that night! When, just as the dawn began to break, Gardener got up and looked into the farmyard, his sharp eye caught sight of the stable door, wide open.

"Well done, Bill," shouted he, "up early at last. One hour before breakfast is worth three after."

But no Bill was there; only Jess, trembling and shaking, all in a foam, and muddy from head to foot, but looking perfectly cheerful in her mind. And out from under her fore legs ran a small creature, which Gardener mistook for Tiny, only Tiny was gray, and this dog was brown, of course!

I should not like to tell you all that was said to Bill, when, an hour after breakfast time, he came skulking up to the farm. In fact, words failing, Gardener took a good stick and laid it about Bill's shoulders, saying he would either do this, or tell the mistress of him, and how he had left the stable door open all night, and some bad fellow had stolen Jess, and galloped her all across the country, till, if she hadn't been the cleverest pony in the world, she never could have got back again.

Bill dared not contradict this explanation of the story. Especially as the key was found hanging up in its proper place by the kitchen door. And when he went to fetch it, he heard the most extraordinary sound in the coal cellar close by— like somebody snoring or laughing. Bill took to his heels, and did not come back for a whole hour.

But when he did come back, he made himself as busy as possible. He cleaned Jess, which was half a day's work at least. Then he took the little people for a ride, and afterwards put his stable in the most beautiful order, and altogether was such a changed Bill, that Gardener told him he must have left himself at home and brought back somebody else.

Whether or not, the boy certainly improved, so that there was less occasion to find fault with him afterwards.

Jess lived to be quite an old pony, and carried a great many people—little people always, for she herself never grew any bigger. But I don't think she ever carried a Brownie again.

From THE ADVENTURES OF A BROWNIE
Illustrated by H. Paterson

*Kate Seredy was born in Budapest. She came to the United States
with her family in 1922. As illustrator and author, she uses the
country of her adoption very often, but her best stories are built around
memories of her childhood in Hungary. The heroine of "The Good
Master" is an excitable girl sent from the city to stay with her uncle
on a great farmstead where horses are supreme. Although she has only
just learned to ride, she takes an active part in the roundup which
is so brilliantly recorded here.*

KATE SEREDY

The Roundup

THEY rode out of the yard while the morning dew was still sparkling on the grass. The north road they took today wasn't at all like the one leading to the sheep herds. There were large wheat and rye fields on both sides. Narrow paths forked out of the main road, leading to white cottages nestling under shade trees. From the distance they looked like small white mushrooms under their heavy thatched roofs. The scenery was changing gradually. There were more and more trees. They crossed many small wooden bridges, spanning brooks. Soon they could see the river Tisza, like a wide blue ribbon on the green velvet of the fields. Jancsi rode ahead. Suddenly he waved and cried:"The 'Komp' is in. Hurry, Father, they're waiting for us." They spurred their horses and clattered on to the floating ferry, the Komp. It was attached to stout ropes on both sides. The ropes stretched across the river and were wound on large wooden pulleys. There were several wagons and riders on the wide platform of the Komp.

Kate, following the example of Father and Jancsi, got off her horse and tied him to a hitching post."How will we get across? Row?"she asked.

"Watch these men, Kate. They'll pull the Komp across by

the ropes. We can help, too," said Jancsi. A bell sounded. Another answered from across the river. Everybody walked to the ropes. "Here, Kate. Grab this rope! Pull when they say ' Hooo-ruck!' "

"Hooo-ruck!" Kate pulled for all she was worth. "Hooo-ruck!" they cried with every pull. The Komp began to move. "Hooo-ruck! Hooo-ruck!" chanted everybody, pulling and slacking. The far bank seemed to come nearer and nearer. They could see other wagons and riders waiting. There was a scraping sound when the Komp touched bottom and came to a stop. A man on the bank fastened it to a high post.

"Coming back tonight, Mister Nagy?" he asked Father when they rode past him.

"Yes, Géza, we'll bring about twenty horses. Wait for us."

The road led through a small forest of acacia trees. Their branches were heavy with clusters of white flowers. The air was drenched with their sweet, heady perfume. White petals drifted in the breeze, covering the ground like snow.

As soon as they left the forest, they saw the first corrals. They were huge grassy squares, surrounded by tall fences. Long, low stables and a few white cottages were scattered among them. Corrals and buildings formed an immense triangle. In the distance hundreds of horses were grazing placidly. Here and there a horse herder sat his horse, motionless as a statue against the blue sky. One of them saw Father and rode to him. He was an old man, but straight-shouldered and strong, with snow-white hair and a clearly modeled, sunburned face. Under bushy white eyebrows his black eyes were sharp as an eagle's.

"Welcome, Mister Nagy. We got your message. The boys are ready for the roundup." He looked at Kate and Jancsi. "The young ones could stay with my wife, out of harm's way.

Father shook his head. "Jancsi is working with us this year;

he is old enough to know what it's all about. But—Kate, I think you'd better stay with Árpád's wife."

"Oh, Uncle Márton, please let me go too. Please!" cried Kate.

Father looked at the old herder. Árpád shook his head. "If those horses stampede, Mister Nagy, you know what it means! A roundup is no place for a girl child."

'She isn't a girl child. She's almost as good as a boy,' said Jancsi stoutly. "Father, let Kate ride with me. I can take care of her."

Father hesitated for a second. Then he said: "Kate, you kept your word to me once. Will you promise me now to keep close to Jancsi and not to scream or yell no matter what happens?" He was very serious. "If these wild horses hear one of your famous screams, they'll run right off the face of the earth."

"I promise!" said Kate, looking straight into his eyes.

"Very well, you may go with Jancsi. Árpád! You take two men and start the drive from the north. Send four men to me. Two will go with Jancsi and Kate and drive from the east. I'll take two men to the west."

Even Árpád's straight back expressed his disapproval as he rode away. They saw him stop and speak to the men.

"Jancsi." Father's voice rang sharp—he was giving orders now. "You are one of the men today. Do you know what to do?"

"Yes, Father. I ride slowly to the east fields, about two miles from here. When I pass the last herds, I turn and start the drive back to the corrals. If they stampede, I ride with them and try to take the lead to turn the herd."

"If they stampede, you take Kate out of the way and let the herders turn them. Understand?"

Then Father gave his orders to the waiting herders, and they rode off.

Kate and Jancsi followed the two young herders in silence. They rode slowly, keeping well away from the grazing horses. Kate watched the men. She wondered if they ever got off their horses or were grown to them. Straight, yet supple, their bodies followed the swinging movement of the horses in perfect, smooth rhythm.

Jancsi touched her arm and whispered:"You won't scream, Kate? Promise?" He looked worried.

"I won't make a sound, no matter what happens. Thank you for sticking up for me."

A tall split rail fence showed in the distance. "Here's where we spread out," said one of the herders.

Kate was terribly excited. They were riding along the fence now, about fifty feet from each other."Stampede, stampede," kept ringing in her ears. What if they stampede? But everything went well. They turned back towards the corrals. At their approach there was a ripple of movement in the herd. They stopped grazing, neighed uneasily, but weren't frightened. Slowly they began to move in the direction of the corrals. Jancsi and Kate were behind them, the herders slightly to the sides.

Jancsi took off his hat and wiped his forehead. His first roundup was going off well and he felt very proud. The herd was moving peacefully—surely there wouldn't be any trouble. But—what was the sudden stir in front there? He stood up in the stirrups, saw a flock of partridges fly up, heard the sharp, frightened neighing of the leaders, saw the whole herd sway and swerve . . .

"They're turning! Get out of the way, Kate! Follow me!" he yelled. It was too late. The frightened herd was thundering down on them. He couldn't stop to help Kate. His own horse was caught in the panic and raced at breakneck speed. Looking around, he saw Milky go like a white flash in the other direction, with Kate bent close to his neck. He yelled:"To the left, Kate!"It was useless. He could hardly hear his own voice in the deafening tumult. His own words flashed in his memory:"If they stampede, I take the lead to turn the herd!"

With a desperate struggle he pulled at the reins, his horse swerved to the right. The herd followed! "Now back to the corrals, if I can only keep ahead of them! Come on, Barsony!" He dug his heels into the horse's sides. Almost flying over the pasture, he turned his head to look for Milky. Why, the herd must have split in half! There was Kate to his far right, racing ahead of more horses then he had behind him! She was leading them to the corrals!

"What a girl!"shouted Jancsi."Hurray!"

He was almost at the first corral gate. He checked his horse, pulling him sharply to one side. The wild horses thundered past him and raced around into the enclosure. He closed the gate quickly, just as the rest of the herd rushed into the adjoining corral. Milky, shivering and snorting, pressed close to Bársony. Kate grinned at Jancsi as she closed the gates. "Look at the herders,"she said with a wink;"we beat them to it."

The two men looked rather sheepish and bewildered. There was no time for conversation, though. Father's herd came in, closely followed by old Arpad from the north. When all the horses were safely closed behind the gates, a cottage door opened and Árpád's wife came out ringing a bell."Dinner ready," she cried.

Father turned to the silent herders."How did my youngsters behave?"

The herders grinned sheepishly. "Behave, Mister Nagy? Behave? Why, the two of them turned the worst stampede we ever saw and brought the herd in, before we knew what happened."

"What?" cried Árpád and Father together.

"I didn't scream, Uncle Márton; did I, Jancsi?" cried Kate.

"She didn't, Father. A flock of partridges started them off. But can she ride! She rides 'most as good as you!"

"That's saying a lot, Sonny," smiled old Árpád. "Your father is the best horseman in seven counties. But tell us all about it while we eat."

They dismounted and walked to the cottage. In the doorway Arpad took off his hat. "Welcome to my house and table," he said.

"Welcome, and thank the Lord you are all here," cried his wife. "When I saw this girl child ahead of the horses, I thought we'd be picking her up in little pieces instead of sitting down to dinner! My, my, what is this world coming to! When I was her age, and a stout, strong girl I was, I had to sit by the window and sew all day, and here she is, no bigger than a flea, racing with the best of you. Oh, oh, forgive my chatter, sit down and eat hearty, you must be starved!"

"Womenfolks talk more than magpies—sit down and welcome," said Árpád.

He said a prayer and a huge pot of steaming stew was set on the table.

"Now, let's hear the story," said Father when everybody was served. Jancsi laughed. "The story of a flea on horseback. She has a new name, Father. We can't call her screaming monkey any more!"

Little by little, the story was pieced together. "But how did you know what to do, Kate?" asked Father.

"There was nothing else to do," she said calmly. "I remembered what Jancsi said about taking the lead if they stampeded. I didn't have to take it—they chased me!" She grinned. "Then we came to the horse yards—"

"Corrals, Kate," interrupted Jancsi.

"Corrals, then. Anyway, I saw you pull Bársony to one side. So I did the same thing. It was easy!"

Old Árpád shook his head. "A guardian angel watched over you, child. You were in great danger."

"Maybe—maybe it was my mother," whispered Kate with sudden tears in her eyes.

There was a long silence. Father spoke then in a husky

voice:"I shouldn't have let you go, Kate, but now that everything is over, I am very proud of both of you."

From THE GOOD MASTER
Illustrated here by Imré Hofbauer

Rosina Copper had been a first-class polo pony and in the end she became a star show jumper, but in between her life was hard. In this extract Meg, who has stables of her own, and Angela, who tells the story, rescue this starved mare from a dirty outbuilding. The story is based on fact, and, like most of Kitty Barne's stories, it is really about a difficult job well done. Her own interests lay with music and drama, not with horses—except as they were part of the English countryside of Sussex she knew so well. Perhaps this is partly why "Rosina Copper, Mystery Mare" is such a good story. She describes the mare's bad time sympathetically but without any sentiment, and the piece given here, free from the clutter of technical detail you might expect to find, really gives the atmosphere of an old-fashioned stable yard.

KITTY BARNE

Rosina Copper

IT wasn't far. In no time, it seemed, Fred was saying'"Ere you are, Mum," and we were turning into a hundred yards or so of broad drive to find ourselves in front of most imposing stable gates thrown wide open, a clock tower with a clock (not going) in the arch over them.

They were, or had been, very grand and beautiful stables. The big house, empty for a long time, Meg said, stood back off the road, hidden away by trees, but if it lived up to its stables it must have been very grand and beautiful too; we never saw it. There was a big quadrangle full of doors, all of them tight shut; Meg drove into the stable yard and drew up, and I hopped out at once and took a run around it, looking into the windows and trying the doors. I couldn't see much because the glass was so dirty; however, here and there it was broken and I could look through and see the untidy mess they were all in after the auction. Then I came upon a door that opened and I found myself in a fine square harness room, quite empty, just one old very dusty saddle hanging up on the wall. They'd lit a fire in the open grate—for the auctioneer, I suppose—and the bonfire smell mixed with the leather-polish-horse smell and did its best to fill the room. But oh, *how*

337

empty it was! The emptiness of empty stables is the worst kind, I said to myself—nothing at all left but the smell. All the same, these stables weren't really empty. Where were the ponies we'd come to see?

A doorway led to a flight of steep stairs—I'm always inquisitive about doors and stairs and paths and I thought I must just have a look. I brushed past a rusty old stove—oh, they'd kept themselves warm enough no doubt when the coachman lived there, but, my goodness, it was cold now. I flew up the stairs; the coachman's bedroom; a room beyond with a pale brownish paper that had once been pink and satiny and was still peppered all over with bright pink squares and oblongs and ovals where the coachman's wife had hung her pictures. Nothing at all in it but a roll of cracked linoleum. Beyond it another room, chocolate-colored, and a small low door that led into a big hayloft, still with a small mound of hay in one corner. There a black cat, quite a young cat with a shining, carefully-groomed black satin coat, came walking towards me, his tail straight up in the air like the mast of a little boat, his best manners on show. He was a very smart, well-fed looking cat; no shortage of mice in an empty stable, one could see that. He opened his yawning mouth, salmon pink like the coachman's wife's wallpaper, and gave a very small mew. I picked him up, and he instantly settled down in my arms and started to purr. So down the stairs we went together.

"That all you've found?" said Meg, but she gave the cat's head an absent-minded stroke and scratched him a little under his chin. He purred louder, but she sighed. "Oh, dear, how full of horse ghosts it is—and humans. I wonder what's become of the owner, the Squire, as we used to call him."

"There don't seem to be any horses anywhere," I said.

"Well, there wouldn't be up those stairs, would there? We shall find ourselves bidding for the stable cat."

Rosina Copper

She looked around the once beautiful yard, weeds shooting up between the cobblestones, a mat of thick grass around the pump and trough, a broken half door banging in the wind, and gave a sigh.

"Quite derelict. Very sad."

"I did look into most of the loose boxes," I said, trying to excuse myself for having gone exploring. "They're empty."

It began to rain quite hard, a cold sleety rain.

"Where's Fred?" I asked.

'Gone hunting. Like you. He thinks there's a man about.'

There was, and Fred had found him. We heard the clattering of boots, those heavy ones they wear when they're cleaning carriages, and the jangle of an empty pail, and there was Fred and an old man, a real ancient this time. His braces hung down outside breeches even baggier and older than Fred's, his leggings hadn't had a polish-up for months. He gave a vague touch of his cap with the remains of the manners that went with the stables. Then he set down his pail and began to work the pump handle; Fred made his way over to us.

"Well, Fred," said Meg. "Anything doing?"

"Auctioneer'll be along soonish."

"But what's he going to auction?"

"Them two I told yer. They got to be sold without reserve— pay cost of stabling and food and that."

"Where are they? Can we see them?"

The old man drawing water heard that; he held out a large key and waggled it at us.

"Good afternoon," said Meg cheerfully, strolling over to him. "You're looking after those two horses, are you?"

"No, I ain't."

"Can we see them?"

The man nodded. "No one bin near 'em since afore Christmas," he said in a creaking, rusty voice, and clattered away with his pail, past a door that had once been blue and window sills that still held the remains of window boxes—a nice little house for a stableman, I thought, as we followed him out of the yard. There was an outhouse and that was where we were going. The door was tight shut and the old man set down his pail of water and fought with the lock, which his key refused to open.

There was a small window and Meg and I both tried to peer in while we waited, but we could see nothing through its spiders' webs and grime. The sleet was turning to snow and it was coming down with a wind like a knife behind it. "Do you hear them?" whispered Meg, and I nodded. I could hear restless hoofs on the stone floor inside; one, anyhow, of the poor prisoners knew there was someone about.

"She's stuck," grumbled the old man. "They ain't bin taken outer the stable for weeks an' weeks," and he looked at the key as if it was its fault.

"'Ere, lemme 'ave a go at it," wheezed Fred, and at last, muttering and quarreling, together they turned it. In we went, thankful to get into shelter.

It was very dark. I stood there blinking, and trying to distinguish what we were supposed to be looking at. I could just make out two loose boxes with a pony in each. As my eyes got used to the light I could see that one was a gray colt, a biggish pony, very dirty, rather frightened, and inclined to kick. No one had bothered to clean him out, no one had dreamed of giving him any grooming. The other one looked even worse. She was a mare, a small, very thin, very miserable creature, her head turned into the corner away from us. A shiver ran over her now and again, otherwise she never moved.

"What's their history? D'you know?" asked Meg.

The old man knew nothing. He'd watered them and given

them a bit of hay every day but no one had asked him to. He'd done it because, he said, someone had to.

"Couldn't let them die, could I?" he demanded angrily.

"But they must belong to someone," said Meg.

He said they didn't. Not to no one.

Fred chimed in.

"No good, either or which. Riding school don't own up to 'em. The colt ain't broken and the old mare's that wild no one can get on her."

Wild? I couldn't believe it. She stood drooping in her corner, head down, eyes half shut, her three white stockings nearly hidden in the filthy straw. Anything less wild you could hardly imagine; she looked like nothing but a poor old sheep. Meg went up to her to give her a pat and speak to her, but all she did was to tremble from head to foot.

"Very nervous," said Meg, and "No good to anyone," said the old man. And then we all trooped out again.

It began to snow quite hard and we as near as possible went home. However, we didn't quite because the auctioneer and his clerk arrived with a small boy in tow just as Meg was backing the car out. He was pretty annoyed at having to turn up again, and he grumbled away to us. Why these two animals weren't put on with the others he couldn't imagine. That riding school had hired these stables for the auction and then cleared out, taking the green parrot that belonged to them, and, he'd been told, the contents of the till which didn't. No one's business to see to anything. And *what* weather. Was the fire lit in the harness room?

"No," I said, "it's not."

He was cross and cold, but he was conscientious. We would have to wait a bit and see if anyone else turned up.

"Wait how long?" enquired Meg.

"An hour, say."

The wind howled and the snow whirled round the derelict, magnificent stable yard. Meg and I got into the car again— Fred had disappeared, probably to sit by the fire of his new friend—the black cat still in my arms and still purring like a little dynamo. "That's a very determined cat," said Meg, looking at him. "And he knows he's onto a good thing."

"He's like a happy hot water bottle, I said.

But we didn't talk. Meg sat perfectly still and I could do nothing but dream of the stables as they had once been, horses' heads looking out of the half doors, grooms grooming and hissing, stableboys washing carriage wheels, a tremendous clattering of hoofs when the carriage and pair went out with the coachman in white breeches on the box, a groom in a top hat beside him.

"*Lovely* stables," I murmured to myself. "They *could* be, I mean."

"They *were*," said Meg.

Presently the auctioneer put his head in at the car window and said to Meg:

"Nobody come. It's only you wants to buy 'em."

"And I don't want to much. In fact I'm not sure I want to buy them at all. I couldn't see them in that awful dark stable."

"I'll have them brought out for you," said the auctioneer, getting on with the business. Then he added to the small boy, "Cut along and find the old chap. He'll be about somewhere."

So Meg and I got out of the car and waited.

"The colt's a bit uncertain," said the auctioneer, trying to do his duty by the animals he had to sell. "Don't feel sure they'll get him out. He's a good strong pony though—when you get him into condition. Fifteen hands."

He was quite right. The colt wouldn't leave his box, he kicked at the very idea. He'd had no handling at all—anyone could see that.

"Will I bring out the mare?" asked the old man, fed up with the whole thing.

"May as well," said Meg.

So there she stood, the poor little mare, shivering and shivering. A chestnut mare, they said, though you'd never have known what color she was, her coat was so harsh and so dirty. The snow came down good and hard onto her and on us all. The auctioneer turned his collar up. "Let's see her move," he said perfunctorily. I could see he thought Meg quite mad to dream of buying either of these wretched creatures.

The old man walked the mare away—and a pair of very old down-and-outs they looked; she seemed almost too weak to stand, every rib showed through her miserable coat. However, he pulled himself together and trotted her back—and a good thing he did, for suddenly a miracle happened. She threw her head up, pricked up her ears, and broke into

the trot that one day was going to set the crowd cheering.

Rosina Copper's trot. Courage, spirit, pride, she still had them all, and something in her told her to show them, even if it was the last thing she did on earth.

I heard a gasp of surprise. And a grunt from Fred. The auctioneer was looking the other way, the old man was rubbing his legs; they had noticed nothing.

Meg bought them both for £12.

"I'll throw in the cat," said the auctioneer with a grin.

From ROSINA COPPER, MYSTERY MARE
Illustrated here by Imré Hofbauer

Field Gates

Among present-day writers of fairy tales, Alison Uttley is perhaps closest to the continuous tradition of fairy folklore, whether she is writing of primitive happenings or of history or about the woodland animals whom she humanizes as man has done for centuries. In the stories of Sam Pig and Tim Rabbit, country lore and custom are finely blended. Alison Uttley says when a writer "marries fantasy with familiarity, something is born which combines the two, if truth is also present." Her familiarity with the North Country of England is directed by imagination in these little stories as surely as it is in her longer works. Few children can stay outside the magic world of field and hedgerow where Tim Rabbit has his adventures.

ALISON UTTLEY

Slipper-Slopper

MRS. RABBIT went to market one fine day, and there she bought a pair of fine brown leather slippers for her son.

"He will be a gentleman, a real gentleman, in these splendid slippers," she said to herself as she hurried home along the lanes to the little house on the common.

"Here's a pair of slippers for you, Tim," said she, taking them out of her string bag, which bulged with peas and beans and lettuces. "You can wear them tomorrow. Always wear a new thing on a new day, my son."

Tim was delighted with their slipperiness and shininess. He gazed at them while he and his mother sat at tea, and he nursed them in his arms all evening. He took them to bed with him, and slept with them hanging on the bedpost.

The next morning he awoke early and put them on his little slim feet. Never had he seen such a slippery pair of shoes! His feet went sliding in and out as he walked carefully downstairs, holding on to the banister lest the slippers should slip downstairs without him. "Slipper-slopper" they went, as they flapped on each wooden step.

"Do fasten your slippers, Tim," cried Mrs. Rabbit, looking up from the frying pan in which she was cooking mushrooms and wild sorrel leaves—a tasty rabbit dish.

"They won't stay on, Mother. They are such slippery slippers," answered Tim, giving them a hitch as they dropped off at the heels.

All day he went slipper-slopper, up and down the fields and across the common. The grass was bruised as he stumbled along, and stones got between his toes. He tumbled down and scrambled to his feet again with a very pink face. The field mice stopped to look at him, and they laughed up their furry sleeves.

"Look at little Tim Rabbit!" they whispered. "He thinks he is a fine gentleman, wearing big slippers like that! They are too large for him. All he can do is to go slipper-slopper over the meadows, like Emily Duck."

Tim was much annoyed, but although he tied his fine slippers with twists of Hare Grass, and stuffed leaves in the toes, still they flipped and flopped as he walked.

So he sat down, and took them off, and hung them up in a gorse bush! Then he pattered home without them.

Mrs. Rabbit went to market again next week, and returned with another pair of slippers for her son. "He will be like a dainty maiden in these," she said to herself, as she tripped along the path. "There never has been such a pretty pair of slippers on our common within living memory."

"Try these, Tim," said she, taking them out of her little rush basket, along with apples and onions.

Tim looked with sparkling eyes at the little red slippers. He was sure they would not go slipper-slopper, they were so neat and trim.

He was happy at their brightness and redness, and he took them to bed with him, and slept with them under the pillow.

The next morning he came downstairs, wearing the pretty red slippers. "Squeak! Squeak! Squeak!" they went.

"Don't make such a noise, Tim. I can't hear myself fry,"

exclaimed Mrs. Rabbit, looking up from the pan where the
eggs sizzled.

"I can't help it, Mother. They won't be quiet," said Tim,
giving his slippers a tap of annoyance.

All day the little slippers squeaked, out of the burrow, into the wood, across the fields and spinney. "Squeak!" they went, like a couple of mice.

The ants ran out of his way when they heard Tim coming, and the beetles scurried up the ferns to watch him pass. The squirrels sat in the trees, laughing at him behind their furry paws.

"Oh! Look at Tim Rabbit! He thinks he is a niminy-piminy lady, wearing gay slippers like that, and all he can do is to go Squeak! Squeak! like a bat on a summer night!"

Tim was rather cross, and he wrapped cool dock leaves around his slippers, but still they wouldn't be silent. He soaked them in the stream and rubbed them with dandelion juice, but they squeaked even louder. So he took them off, and hung them in a blackberry bush. Then he ran pitter-patter home.

A week later, Mrs. Rabbit went to market again, and on a stall kept by an ancient dame, she found a pair of remarkable slippers. She packed them with her gooseberries and carrots, and carried them home in triumph. "A fairy might wear these slippers," she told herself, as she walked through the fields.

"Try these slippers, Tim," cried she gaily, and she took the tiny pair from her green leaf-parcel. "These won't squeak or slipper-slopper. I paid a mighty price for them!"

Tim looked at the little white slippers, soft and dainty, and he laughed with glee. They were wonderful! He was sure they wouldn't go "Squeak! Squeak!" or "Slipper-slopper".

He put them on the tablecloth and admired them all evening, and at night he carried them carefully upstairs, and slept with them cuddled to his heart.

The next day at cock-crow he was up, dancing round his room in the little slippers. Then he ran downstairs, and the little white slippers made no sound at all, not a breath or rustle.

"Oh! How you startled me!" cried Mrs. Rabbit, jumping up and dropping the toast in the fire. "How quiet you are, Tim!"

"They don't make any noise, Mother," answered Tim, stooping down to stroke his little slippers.

He padded out of the house, over the fields, and onto the moor. The bumblebees and the peacock butterflies didn't hear him coming till he frightened them with his shadow. The blackbird jumped out of his way with a fluttering heart, and the thrush cried out in terror as he drifted by.

"'Pon my word, Tim Rabbit! I thought you were a stoat," he exclaimed. "Why don't you walk properly? It isn't manners to startle your friends!"

The hedgehogs sat under the gorse, laughing at him from behind their prickles.

"Look at Tim Rabbit!" they cried. "He thinks he is a fairy, dancing away on those white slippers, and all the time he is only like a shadow, a nothing, a nothing-at-all. Ho! Ho!"

Tim was now very cross indeed, and he picked a peascod from the little wild pea, and popped it in his slippers to make a rattling noise, but the slippers were silent. He tried to sing, to shout, to whistle, but his voice was like the drifting leaves while he wore the magic slippers.

So he took them off, and hung them in a hawthorn tree, where they looked like a bunch of May.

When he got home, Mrs. Rabbit exclaimed, "Now Tim! Here you are without any slippers again! I shan't get any more for you. You must go out tomorrow and find all the lost pairs, and then I can take them back to the market."

So Tim sat quietly by the fire, and he wondered where his slippers were.

When he came down next morning, he skipped up to his mother on his little furry toes, and gave her a hug.

"Come along, Tim," she laughed, and she poured the porridge

into the little wooden bowls and put the honey on the table.

"It is nice to have no slippers. I don't want to be a fine gentleman, or a niminy-piminy lady, or even a fairy," said he, and he rubbed his feet together under the table, and screwed up his happy toes. But he had not forgotten that he had to find all those lost slippers.

He ran to the gorse bush, and the blackberry bush, and the hawthorn tree, but the slipper-slopper slippers, and the squeaking slippers, and the dainty fairy pair had all gone. He scampered up and down, in and out of burrows, in woods and fields and copses, seeking in hedges and ditches, in nooks and crannies. The other rabbits hunted with him, but no one could find the lost slippers.

Where had they gone? The brown pair had been taken from the gorse bush by little Jenny Wren. The red pair had been taken from the blackberry bramble by Cock Robin. The white pair had been taken from the hawthorn tree by Mr. Magpie.

So Tim played hide-and-seek with all the other rabbits, and nobody could run as fast as he. Then he ran home to his mother, hopping and skipping, on his own fleet furry toes, for he vowed that never again would he wear any slippers.

From THE ADVENTURES OF NO ORDINARY RABBIT
Illustrated by Alec Buckels

A mistake in the factory turned a road sprinkler into a fire engine, and the result was some odd adventures, some of which are described here. Perhaps the secret of Leila Berg's success in humanizing vehicles is that she sees them almost as small children—and the behavior of small children is something she understands very well, from her own family, from work in nursery schools and from tours with a children's theater. She sees, above all, the combination of toughness and delicacy which is a child's imagination. She writes attentively and carefully to achieve that spontaneous sound of stories that are told, and into them she puts her intense appreciation of everyday things.

LEILA BERG

The Fire Engine Runs Away

EARLY one morning the bells went down.

Number Eight Thousand and Eight waited till the driver slid into his seat and let in the clutch. *Fft!* they were off, and all the firemen slid down their poles just in time. Out of the gate in less than a minute, with the light flashing on and off, TINGALING TINGALING TINGTING.

Number Eight Thousand and Eight tore down the road. "We'll beat the record today, I'm sure of it," he was thinking. "We're the top brigade, we are, and we can beat everyone."

Way down the street, he saw clouds of smoke puffing into the sky. A flame, like a torn flag, flapped from the roof, and *roared*, as flags roar in the wind.

Number Eight Thousand and Eight was rather surprised. He had always thought smoke and flames were kept in a special cupboard in the practice yard. "It must be a new idea of Mr. Entwistle's," he said to himself, "just to give us a change."

His driver made him stop outside the smoking house, and all the firemen dashed out.

They unrolled the hoses.

They connected the pumps.

They hacked with their axes.

They began to wheel the escape ladder up to the walls.

Everything was just the same as usual. Number Eight Thousand and Eight was panting away with excitement and feeling fine.

Just then, someone leaned out of a window and shouted: "Help!"

At that very second, when Number Eight Thousand and Eight was still thinking what jolly fun it all was, he suddenly realized it was a real fire.

He had never been to a real fire before.

He had only pretended before.

"I don't like it," he said.

"I'm frightened," he said.

"I want to go home."

He was still a very young fire engine.

He panted. He gathered all his strength together. "I'm going," he cried.

The hand brake slipped . . . and suddenly—huh huh huh huh prrrrrrrrrrrrr Number Eight Thousand and Eight was off and away down the road. The escape ladder and the pumps were still aboard, the hoses were flying behind, and Jim Price, poor boy, was tumbling off the back, completely flabbergasted.

Down the road went Number Eight Thousand and Eight, roaring with fright.

Only one thought was in his mind—to get away from that horrible fire.

"I would never have gone if I'd known it was a *real* fire," he kept saying to himself between gasps. "They should have told me. It isn't fair. Mr. Entwistle's horrid, and I'll never play with him again. I won't be quick for him any more."

Down the road he went—over the traffic lights—crashing through the gates of the level crossing—over a bridge, swaying and clanging—and into a quiet country road . . .

Now he ran along steadily. Bees were working softly at the side of the road. Cows put their square heads over the hedge and gazed at him without surprise.

Through the soft, green countryside flashed this bright red, clanging fire engine.

First Farmer Brown heard him. TINGALING!

"My goodness," cried Farmer Brown, knocking his head against the fence he was mending. "Is my hayrick on fire?" And he dropped his pliers, and he dropped his wire, and he tore off down the road after the clanging fire engine.

Farmer Tom heard him next. TINGALINGALING!

"My barn!" he shouted. "Is my barn alight?" And he dropped his shears—for he was trimming a hawthorn hedge—and he picked up his jacket, and he tore off down the road after Number Eight Thousand and Eight.

Tim Jones heard him next. "My new hut!"

Then Jack Squire—"My hen house!"

Then Daniel King—"My shed!"

Loose shirts flapping, old jackets flying, they all tore after him, each of them sure as sure that the bells were ringing for *his* fire.

Number Eight Thousand and Eight was dead tired. He was running out of gas. He couldn't go much farther. With his last gasp, he crashed through a fence, and stopped dead in the middle of a field.

Farmer Brown reached him.

Farmer Tom reached him.

Tim Jones followed.

And Jack Squire.

And Daniel King.

They all came up puffing and snorting and holding their sides. They stared.

Then they wiped the sweat off their faces, mostly with the back of their arm, but Farmer Brown used a blue spotted handkerchief. And without a single word, without a single glance at Number Eight Thousand and Eight, they all tramped silently back to the work they had left at the clang of a fire engine. They said nothing to anyone. It wasn't *their* fire.

Farmer Brown picked up his shears and went on mending his fence. Farmer Tom took up his shears and went on cutting the hedge.

And Tim Jones and Jack Squire and Daniel King all went on doing the ordinary jobs that they were doing when Number Eight Thousand and Eight tore so wildly through that quiet countryside that never heard a fire engine in a month of Sundays, and frightened the life out of them.

Number Eight Thousand and Eight stood in the field, exhausted. The poppies swayed round him, fire engine red. A butterfly flew into his cabin, and flew out again.

"What shall I do, what will become of me?" cried Number Eight Thousand and Eight to himself. But he couldn't speak to anyone. He couldn't explain. He hadn't a drop of gas left.

Next morning, poppy petals were scattered over the Fire Engine.

A huge crow came and perched on him, flapping his ragged wings with hoarse surprise. "CAW!" he said "CAW!" And he examined the fire engine carefully with his sharp beak.

Number Eight Thousand and Eight didn't say a word.

A bright bird, a yellowhammer, flew like a sunbeam from a tree, and stood on the bell. "Let me ring it, PLEASE!" he begged.

Number Eight Thousand and Eight said nothing.

Dandelion heads floated slowly into his cabin. Fat furry bees bumbled by. Butterflies chased each other in and out of his windows. And swallows played swooping games over his roof.

The sun climbed higher and higher in the sky, then began to fall again. Soon it would be evening.

And still the tired fire engine stood in the middle of the field, and said nothing.

The crow seemed rather angry that he was still so silent. "What a bore!" he shouted. "What a bore!" And he flapped his big wings, and flew away slowly, flappily.

But a little robin came and sat on his bonnet. His front was the same red as the fire engine. He sang sweetly to the fire engine of sunshine and rain, dew on the soft green grass, and flowers. "Sweet spring, soft summer" he kept saying. And the bright little yellowhammer stood on the bell and said: "Sing it again, PLEASE! Sing it again, PLEASE."

So the fire engine rested in his field of poppies. And soon he forgot about the fire that really *was* a fire, the noise and the shouting, and the need to be brave.

Day followed day, week followed week. And still the fire engine stood in his field, quiet and peaceful.

Then the green leaves turned crimson, then brown. The swallows flew away to find warmer, bluer skies. Everyone left the fire engine; the butterflies, the bumblebees, the bright little yellowhammer, they all left him.

Only the robin came to see him, now and then. But most of the time the robin stayed near the farmhouses where people put crumbled bread for him on their window sills, and the hens let him share their grain.

The fire engine was lonely . . . cold, sad and lonely.

One early morning, while the frost was still thick on the ground, a man came tramping down the lane. He was tired, dog-tired, and his heavy shoes scraped the stones as he went, *ssscrunch, ssscrunch.*

But when he saw the fire engine, he stood stock-still and stared, and the breath came out of his mouth like a singing kettle, and his spiky eyebrows went up and down.

"Well, I'm jiggered!" he said out loud. And in a minute he

was over the fence, tired, heavy boots and all.

Now the fire engine could see him, and he could see the fire engine.

He had a stick over his shoulder with a kettle on it, and an old cracked cup, and a spare pair of socks that he had washed in a stream. They were still wet. As a matter of fact, they weren't drying at all. They were turning into ice. "Iced socks!" he had been saying angrily to himself as he walked along. "Iced socks!"

Seeing the fire engine seemed to cheer him up. He looked at him for a long time, then, suddenly, he put out his cold, blue hand and stroked him.

The fire engine felt very odd when he did that. It seemed to the fire engine that someone had once done that before . . . someone . . . somewhere. . . . But his engine was cold and silent. He was all frozen up, and it was impossible for him to remember.

Then the man took his kettle and his cup off the stick, and he put them in the cupboard where the firemen used to keep their breathing masks. Then he took lots of little packages, of tea, and sugar, and such things, and put them in the small cupboard next to the water tank.

Then he did something that really surprised the fire engine. He took his wet socks off the stick, and he began to clean the fire engine.

He wiped and he polished, till Number Eight Thousand and Eight was red and shining again, and the socks were muddier than they had ever been.

The fire engine was rather troubled. "He must like me a lot to do that with his nice clean socks," he thought to himself. "And yet he has only just met me."

Then the tramp gave a long, happy sigh. He climbed inside the engine, he switched on the light, and he sat down on the long wooden bench that the firemen sit on when they ride to fires. And with his hands under his head and his knees up, he sang a song very softly. And it *did* seem to the fire engine that he used to know that song. But his engine was cold, and he couldn't remember.

Then the man laughed softly to himself, and went to sleep. The fire engine could hear him breathing, steadily and deeply. And somehow his eyebrows seemed quite a bit flatter and softer.

That afternoon, when the old tramp had wakened up from his sleep, he began to poke about in the fire engine.

Number Eight Thousand and Eight was not at all sure that he liked that. He felt very stiff, and the thought of having to move horrified him. But he could see that the old tramp had something at the back of his mind.

He began to be more and more nervous. He wanted to say to the tramp, "Leave me alone. I'm all right where I am. I'm all frozen up. I haven't any more strength left in me."

But he couldn't say a word, because his engine wasn't running. And the old tramp went on prodding about, poking about, and humming to himself.

At last the tramp suddenly pulled out a large tin of gas. "I knew it!" he shouted at the top of his voice. "I knew it!" And he unscrewed the cap of the fire engine's gas tank and poured in the gas. *Bup bup bup bup* . . . Then he dashed around to the front and swung the starting handle.

The fire engine felt sick. He felt ill. He started to cry.

"Why, oh why, won't this beastly old man go away and leave me alone?" he sobbed quietly to himself. "I don't want to work again. I don't. I don't. I don't."

He sobbed so hard that he shook all over. And his engine began to run. And now he was sobbing out loud.

And as he stood there, shaking and sobbing, a new wonder-

ful warmth began to creep through him, and the stiffness and the rustiness began to smooth themselves away, and his engine began to purr softly and gently and powerfully, as it always used to do in the days that he thought he had forgotten. And the fire engine began to remember.

He remembered how he had been made in the workshop.

He remembered how he had been painted.

He remembered Mr. Middleton with his snow-white handkerchief, and Mr. Billings who stroked him so lovingly and pulled his fire bell, and the man from London who had tested him and said he was "a lovely job," and Mr. Entwistle at the fire station with all his medals, and Jim Price who had climbed his escape ladder even though he was frightened and had won the Cup in the end.

And he remembered the fire that was a *real* fire and how he had run away from it.

"Jiminy!" shouted the old tramp. "Jiminy Jaminy Jix!" And stepping into the cabin, the old tramp pulled the fire bell. "TINGALINGALINGALING!"

And the fire engine *was* a fire engine again.

From FIRE ENGINE BY MISTAKE
Illustrated by Biro

Eleanor Farjeon died on June 5th, 1965, at the age of 84. With a passionately literary father and a musical mother, with a family background of books, theatricals and, always, talk, it is not surprising that she was one of the most prolific and varied writers of our time. Her stories, full of quirks of humor and magic, have an eager immediate feel about them; they seem to be told personally to each reader. To her the smallest incident was full of promise, and she could find enchantment in a London street just as well as in her favorite county of Sussex. Country lore and country rhymes lie behind many of her stories—among them, this one of Little Boy Pie, which is told to a small boy by old sailor Jim, who likes to recall his fantastic past.

ELEANOR FARJEON

Little Boy Pie

ONE summer, when I was a small boy, I had to keep the birds out of the peas. The peas were wanted as food for the cattle, and if the birds had their way the cattle would go short in winter.

From break of day till dusk, I sat in the field, and when the birds came near me to steal the peas I shook my rattle at them and sang:

> *Fly, rascals, fly,*
> *Or I'll make you into pie!*

Maybe they knew what the words meant, and maybe they did not; but whether they did or not, they flew away at once. Then I felt like a hero who had won a battle. The rooks and the starlings were the foe I had put to flight.

But as often as they flew away, back they came again. It seemed as though they would not learn their lesson. I could not think why they kept coming back. It must be for some very strong reason, indeed, a reason more strong than their fear of me. It made me angry to see them defy me, and again I shook my rattle at them, and sang my song. So all that summer the birds and I did not love each other.

There was one rook, a bold black chap, the biggest of the lot, who did not mind my rattle or my song. He stayed among the peas, eating his fill, till I came so near that I could all but touch him. If ever I did catch him, I said to myself, I would surely take him home to my mother to be made into a pie. Rook Pie would be a tasty dish, and no mistake!

I crept like a mouse up to the big black bird, and put out my hand to grab his tail. And at once, as though he could hear my very shadow moving, off he flew with a loud "Caw-Caw!" for all the world as though he had the laugh of me. But, "You wait, old chap!" I called after him. "I'll have you yet!" And I shook my rattle again, and sang:

> *Fly, rascal, fly,*
> *Or I'll make you into pie!*

One hot day, in the noon, when the sun stood at the top of the sky, I took my dinner out of a bag I had with me, and began to eat. It was the sort of food I liked: two big bits of bread, with a slice of cold bacon inside them. I had to open my mouth wide to bite right through them, and the taste of bacon in the middle of the bite seemed to me as nice as any food could be.

Each bite filled my mouth quite full, and I had to chew and chew before I was ready for the next one. This was hard work on a hot day, and maybe that was why in the middle of a bite my jaws fell idle, my head began to nod, and my eyes to close. Before I had half done with my bread and bacon, I was asleep.

When I woke up I was not in the same place at all. I was lying at the edge of a field that was full of as queer a crop as I ever hope to see. It wasn't beans, and it wasn't peas, and it wasn't grass, or corn, or roots of any sort. No, what grew in that field, if you'll take my word for it, was slices of bread and bacon blowing in the wind.

Dear me, how good they did smell to a hungry boy like

me! As quick as quick, I ran into the field and took a bite out of a slice as it grew. But I had hardly begun to chew it up before I heard a loud flutter of wings, and a harsh voice sang:

Fly, rascal, fly,
Or I'll make you into pie!

There, in the middle of the field, was a great black rook, as big as a giant, it seemed to me, and I was but a little tot who did not stand as high as his tail. The rook was rattling his wings, and singing my own song at me, and when I saw how big he was, I took to my heels and ran for dear life.

"I'll never go near *that* place again!" said I to myself.

But in a little while I began to feel my hunger anew, and in spite of the rook I just had to creep back, to try to steal another slice. This time I managed to snatch two bites before he came at me with his wings and his song, and I only got away just in time.

You might think that cured me for good and all from trying to go into the bread-and-bacon field; but when a boy wants his dinner as badly as I did, he forgets to be afraid; and so, for a third time, I stole around the field, slipped in at a new place, and began to eat.

This time I got three bites down, and just as I was feeling that all was going well, down came the rook on me, quicker than rain in April, and before I could run he had the tail of my little coat in his beak.

Up he flew, up, up, up, till I thought he was going to bump into the sun; but no, he only flew as high as the top of an elm tree, where his nest was swaying in the wind. Such a great nest it was, as round and as black as a pot. Inside sat his big black wife and his little black family, and when they saw what he'd got in his beak, they all began to caw so loud that I could not hear myself think.

"Why, Daddy," said the Mammy Rook, "you never mean to say you've caught that fat little rogue who is always coming after the bread and bacon?"

"That I have!" said Daddy Rook, "and if you want to please us all, you'll make him into pie."

"Little Boy Pie is a tasty dish, and no mistake!" said Mammy Rook; and all the baby rooks cawed with joy:

"Little Boy Pie! Little Boy Pie! Give me a slice of Little Boy Pie!"

"Hand him over, Daddy," said Mammy Rook, "and I'll turn him into pie in a jiffy."

"Catch him, then!" said Daddy Rook, and tossed me across the nest from his strong beak. But he tossed just a little too strongly; instead of falling into the nest, I landed on the other side of it, and before Mammy Rook could seize me in her claws, I jumped! Yes, I jumped from the very top of that tall elm, and fell down, down between the leaves and branches, until at last I came to the ground with a bump.

Little Boy Pie

When I opened my eyes, I was sitting in my own field, with my own bread and bacon in my hand, and the rooks all busy at it among the peas. I jumped up and swung my rattle, and sang my song at the top of my voice:

> *Fly, rascals, fly,*
> *Or I'll make you into pie!*

Off they flew as quick as comets, and when they had gone I ate up my bread and bacon.

But now I knew why the birds came back again and again, in spite of me and my rattle. They came back because birds, like boys, are hungry. I must not let them eat the peas, for then the cattle would go short, but when I got home that day I went into my own bit of garden and made a place for the birds to come and eat. I got my mother to give me a bit of bread to crumble there every day, and I begged my father to bring me a coconut to hang up for the tits. I even saved bits of bacon out of my sandwich, and threaded them on strings, and hung the strings of fat between two twigs.

So, if I had to keep the birds off with one hand, I fed them with the other; if I frightened them out of the field, I invited them into the garden. After that it seemed to me that the birds and I were not quite such enemies as we had been. Even though the rooks and starlings scolded me, the robins and the tits became my friends.

From JIM AT THE CORNER
Illustrated by Edward Ardizzone

I end this book with one of those fine, honest, civilized stories about happy family life which are the glory of books for children in the last century. Juliana Ewing and Randolph Caldecott (who made illustrations for two of her books) present a picture of English rural life that is robust as well as beautiful. Juliana Horatia Gatty, born in 1841, spent her childhood in an English vicarage, enjoying the company of brothers and sisters, writing with the encouragement of her mother, a tireless author herself, who realized that her daughter's gift surpassed her own. When Julie married Rex Ewing, she embarked on a lifetime of journeys, following her army husband to Canada and later back to England. The scenes of her stories reflect the places she lived in; the people she met may be used as models; and the lively, thoughtful children in her books show how well she understood the young. Above all things, she loved a garden, and the story from which this extract comes is built around an old book about herbs given to a family of children. From this book, they get the idea of planting flowers along the roadsides and in the fields to please travelers, hence Mary's nickname, Traveler's Joy. Until the Old Squire and Mary's father have settled their dispute about a footpath, the children are told to keep out of the field, but one day Mary is given some rare double cowslips, or hose-in-hose, as country people call them, which she cannot resist planting.

JULIANA EWING

Mary
Plants the Hose-in-Hose

SINCE I became Traveler's Joy, I had chiefly been busy in the hedgerows by the high roads, and in waste places, like the old quarry, and very bare and trampled bits, where there seemed to be no flowers at all.

You cannot say that of Mary's Meadow. Not to be a garden, it is one of the most flowery places I know. I did once begin a list of all that grows in it, but it was in one of Arthur's old exercise books, which he had "thrown in," in a bargain we had, and there were very few blank pages left. I had thought a couple of pages would be more than enough, so I began with rather full accounts of the flowers, but I used up the book long before I had written out one half of what blossoms in Mary's Meadow.

Wild roses, and white bramble, and hawthorn, and dogwood, with its curious red flowers; and nuts, and maple, and privet, and all sorts of bushes in the hedge, far more than one would think; and ferns, and the iris which has such splendid berries, in the ditch—the ditch on the lower side where it is damp, and where I meant to sow forget-me-nots, like Alphonse Karr, for there are none there as it happens. On the other side, at the top of the field, it is dry, and blue

373

succory grows, and grows out on the road beyond. The most beautiful blue possible, but so hard to pick. And there are Lent lilies, and lords and ladies, and ground ivy, which smells herby when you find it, trailing about and turning the color of Mother's "aurora" wool in green winters; and sweet white violets, and blue dog violets, and primroses, of course, and two or three kinds of orchis, and all over the field cowslips, cowslips, cowslips—to please the nightingale.

And I wondered if the nightingale would find out the hose-in-hose, when I had planted six of them in the sunniest, coziest corner of Mary's Meadow.

For this was what I resolved to do, though I kept my resolve to myself, for which I was afterwards very glad. I did not tell the others because I thought that Arthur might want some of the plants for our Earthly Paradise, and I wanted to put them all in Mary's Meadow. I said to myself, like Bessy's great-aunt, that "if I was spared" I would go next year and divide the roots of the six, and bring some off-sets to our gardens, but I would keep none back now. The nightingale should have them all.

We had been busy in our gardens, and in the roads and byelanes, and I had not been in Mary's Meadow for a long time before the afternoon when I put my little trowel, and a bottle of water, and the six hose-in-hose into a basket, and was glad to get off quietly and alone to plant them. The highways and hedges were very dusty, but there it was very green. The nightingale had long been silent, I do not know where he was, but the rooks were not at all silent; they had been holding a parliament at the upper end of the field this morning, and were now all talking at once, and flapping about the tops of the big elms which were turning bright yellow, while down below a flight of starlings had taken their place, and sat in the prettiest circles; and groups of hedge sparrows flew and mimicked them. And in the fields round about the sheep baaed, and the air, which was very sweet, was so quiet that these country noises were the only sounds to be heard, and they could be heard from very far away.

I had found the exact spot I wanted, and had planted four of the hose-in-hose, and watered them from the bottle, and had the fifth in my hand, and the sixth still in the basket, when all these nice noises were drowned by a loud harsh shout which made me start, and sent the flight of starlings into the next field, and made the hedge sparrows jump into the hedge.

And when I looked up I saw the Old Squire coming towards me, and storming and shaking his fist at me as he came. But with the other hand he held Saxon by the collar, who was struggling to get away from him and to go to me.

I had so entirely forgotten about Father's quarrel with the Squire, that when the sight of the old gentleman in a rage suddenly reminded me, I was greatly stupefied and confused, and really did not at first hear what he said. But when I understood that he was accusing me of digging cowslips out of his field, I said at once (and pretty loudly, for he was deaf) that I was not digging up anything, but was planting double cowslips to grow up and spread amongst the common ones.

I suppose it did sound rather unlikely, as the Old Squire knew nothing about our game, but a thing being unlikely is no reason for calling truthful people liars, and that was what the Old Squire called me.

It choked me, and when he said I was shameless, and that he had caught me with the plants upon me, and yelled to me to empty my basket, I threw away the fifth and sixth hose-in-hose as if they had been adders, but I could not speak again. He must have been beside himself with rage, for he called me all sorts of names, and said I was my father's own child, a liar and a thief. While he was talking about sending me to prison (and I thought of Harry's dream, and turned cold with fear), Saxon was tugging to get to me, and at last he got away and came rushing up.

Now I knew that the Old Squire was holding Saxon back because he thought Saxon wanted to worry me as a trespasser, but I don't know whether he let Saxon go at last, because he thought I deserved to be worried, or whether Saxon got away of himself. When his paws were almost on me the Old Squire left off abusing me, and yelled to the dog, who at last, very unwillingly, went back to him, but when he just got to the Squire's feet he stopped, and pawed the ground in the funny way he sometimes does, and looked up at his master as much as to say, "You see it's only play,"and then turned around and raced back to me as hard as he could lay legs to ground. This time he reached me, and jumped to lick my face, and I threw my arms round his neck and burst into tears.

When you are crying and kissing at the same time, you cannot hear anything else, so what more the Old Squire said I do not know.

I picked up my basket and trowel at once, and fled homewards as fast as I could go, which was not very fast, so breathless was I with tears and shame and fright.

When I was safe in our grounds, I paused and looked back. The Old Squire was still there, shouting and gesticulating, and Saxon was at his heels, and over the hedge two cows were looking at him; but the rooks and the starlings were far off in distant trees and fields.

And I sobbed afresh when I remembered that I had been called a liar and a thief, and had lost every one of my hose-in-hose; and this was all that had come of trying to make an Earthly Paradise of Mary's Meadow, and of taking upon myself the name of Traveler's Joy.

(*Here follows an interval of five months.*)

. . . Next morning I was sitting, drawing, in the schoolroom window, when I saw the Old Squire coming up the
drive. There is no mistaking him when you can see him at all.
He is a big, handsome old man, with white whiskers, and a
white hat, and white gaiters, and he generally wears a light
coat, and a flower in his buttonhole. The flower he wore this
morning looked like—, but I was angry with myself for
thinking of it, and went on drawing again, as well as I could,
for I could not help wondering why he was coming to our
house . . .

Twenty minutes later James came to tell me that Father
wished to see me in the library, and when I got there, Father
was just settling his eyeglass in his eye, and the Old Squire
was standing on the hearth rug, with a big piece of paper in
his hand. And then I saw that I was right, and that the flowers
in his buttonhole were hose-in-hose.

As I came in he laid down the paper, took the hose-in-hose
out of his buttonhole in his left hand, and held out his right
hand to me, saying:"I'm more accustomed to public speaking
than to private speaking, Miss Mary. But—will you be
friends with me?"

In Mary's Meadow my head had got all confused, because I
was frightened. I was not frightened today, and I saw the
whole matter in a moment. He had found the double cowslips,
and he knew now that I was neither a liar nor a thief. I was
glad, but I could not feel very friendly to him. I said,"You can
speak when you are angry."

Though he was behind me, I could feel Father coming
nearer, and I knew somehow that he had taken out his glass
to rub it and put it back, as he does when he is rather surprised
or amused. I was afraid he meant to laugh at me afterwards,
and he can tease terribly, but I could not have helped saying
what came into my head that morning if I had tried. When

you have suffered a great deal about anything, you cannot sham, not even politeness.

The Old Squire got rather red. Then he said, "I am afraid I am very hasty, my dear, and say very unjustifiable things. But I am very sorry, and I beg your pardon. Will you forgive me?"

I said, "Of course, if you're sorry, I forgive you, but you have been a very long time in repenting."

Which was true. If I had been cross with one of the others, and had borne malice for five months, I should have thought myself very wicked. But when I had said it, I felt sorry, for the old gentleman made no answer. Father did not speak either, and I began to feel very miserable. I touched the flowers, and the Old Squire gave them to me in silence. I thanked him very much, and then I said—

"I am very glad you know about it now . . . I'm very glad they lived . . . I hope you like them? . . . I hope, if you do like them, that they'll grow and spread all over your field."

The Old Squire spoke at last. He said, "It is not my field any longer."

I said, "Oh, why?"

"I have given it away; I have been a long time in repenting, but when I did repent I punished myself. I have given it away."

It overwhelmed me, and when he took up the big paper again, I thought he was going, and I tried to stop him, for I was sorry I had spoken unkindly to him, and I wanted to be friends.

"Please don't go," I said. "Please stop and be friends. And oh, please, please don't give Mary's Meadow away. You mustn't punish yourself. There's nothing to punish yourself for. I forgive you with all my heart, and I'm sorry I spoke crossly. I have been so very miserable, and I was so vexed at wasting the hose-in-hose, because Bessy's great-aunt gave them to me, and I've none left. Oh, the unkindest thing you could do to me now would be to give away Mary's Meadow."

The Old Squire had taken both my hands in his, and now he asked very kindly—"Why, my dear, why don't you want me to give away Mary's Meadow?"

"Because we are so fond of it. And because I was beginning to hope that now we're friends, and you know we don't want to steal your things, or to hurt your field, perhaps you would let us play in it sometimes, and perhaps have Saxon to play with us there. We are so very fond of him, too."

"You are fond of Mary's Meadow?" said the Old Squire.

"Yes, yes! We have been fond of it all our lives. We don't think there is any field like it, and I don't believe there can be. Don't give it away. You'll never get one with such flowers in it again. And now there are hose-in-hose, and they are not at all common. Bessy's aunt's aunt has only got one left, and she's taking care of it with a shovel. And if you'll let us in we'll plant a lot of things, and do no harm, we will indeed. And the nightingale will be here soon. Oh, don't give it away!"

My head was whirling now with the difficulty of persuading him, and I did not hear what he said across me to my father. But I heard Father's reply—"Tell her yourself, sir."

On which the Old Squire stuffed the big paper into my arms, and put his hand on my head and patted it.

"I told you I was a bad hand at talking, my dear," he said, "but Mary's Meadow is given away, and that's the deed of gift which you've got in your arms, drawn up as tight as any rascal of a lawyer can do it, and that's not so tight, I believe, but what some other rascal of a lawyer could undo it. However, they may let you alone. For I've given it to you, my dear, and it is yours. So you can plant, and play, and do what you please there. 'You, and your heirs and assigns, forever,' as the rascals say."

It was my turn now to be speechless. But as I stared blankly in front of me, I saw that Father had come around, and was looking at me through his eyeglass. He nodded to me, and said, "Yes, Mary, the Squire has given Mary's Meadow to you, and it is yours."

From MARY'S MEADOW *and
other tales of Fields and Flowers
Illustrated here by Robin Jacques*

Guide
to Further Reading

The Cottage Door

THE THREE LITTLE CATS AND THE THREE BAD TOMS

by Diana Ross
THE LITTLE RED ENGINE AND THE ROCKET
THE LITTLE RED ENGINE GETS A NAME *1945*
THE LITTLE RED ENGINE GOES HOME *1959*
THE LITTLE RED ENGINE GOES TO MARKET
THE LITTLE RED ENGINE GOES TO TOWN
THE LITTLE RED ENGINE GOES TRAVELLING
THE STORY OF THE LITTLE RED ENGINE *all New York: Transatlantic Arts, Inc.*

THE CHRISTMAS CUCKOO

by Frances Browne
GRANNY'S WONDERFUL CHAIR *New York: E. P. Dutton & Co., Inc., 1963*

PUSS AND PUP

by Josef Čapek
HARUM-SCARUM *New York: W. W. Norton & Company, Inc., 1936*

The Door of the Great House

THE GREAT CRUMBLING HOUSE

by *Bruce Carter*
THE CHILDREN WHO STAYED BEHIND *Baltimore: Penguin Books, Inc., 1964*

A PICNIC AT THE MANSION

by *Elizabeth Coatsworth*
ALICE-ALL-BY-HERSELF *1937*
AWAY GOES SALLY *1934*
THIEF ISLAND *1943 all New York: The Macmillan Company*

TOM TIT TOT

by *Eleanor Farjeon*
THE SILVER CURLEW *New York: The Viking Press, Inc., 1954*
by *Amabel Williams-Ellis*
FAIRY TALES FROM THE BRITISH ISLES *New York: Frederick Warne & Co., Inc., 1964*
ROUND THE WORLD FAIRY TALES *New York: Frederick Warne & Co., Inc., 1966*

THE SLAYING OF THE WOOERS

by *Andrew Lang*
TALES OF TROY AND GREECE *New York: Roy Publishers, Inc., 1963*
PRINCE PRIGIO AND PRINCE RICARDO *New York: E. P. Dutton & Co., Inc., 1961*

The Door of the Shop

MRS. CUMFITT'S SUGAR MICE

by *Eva-Lis Wuorio*
THE ISLAND OF FISH IN THE TREES *Cleveland and New York: The World Publishing Company, 1962*
THE LAND OF RIGHT UP AND DOWN *Cleveland and New York: The World Publishing Company, 1964*

THE SADDLER'S HORSE

by *Sidonie M. Gruenberg* (*ed.*)
MORE FAVORITE STORIES OLD AND NEW (rev. ed.) *New York: Doubleday & Company, Inc., 1960*

TUMBLE-DOWN SHOP

by *Rachel Field*
THE RACHEL FIELD STORY BOOK *New York: Doubleday & Company, Inc., 1958*

MRS. PEPPERPOT BUYS MACARONI

by *Alf Prøysen*
LITTLE OLD MRS. PEPPERPOT *New York: Ivan Obolensky, Inc., 1960*
MRS. PEPPERPOT AGAIN *New York: Ivan Obolensky, Inc., 1961*
MRS. PEPPERPOT TO THE RESCUE *New York: Pantheon Books, Inc., 1964*

The Garden Gate

A MYSTERIOUS DOG

by *Louisa May Alcott*
UNDER THE LILACS *Boston: Little, Brown and Company,* 1877
UNDER THE LILACS *New York: Collier Books (pap.),* 1962
LITTLE WOMEN *Cleveland and New York: The World Publishing
    Company,* 1946
LITTLE WOMEN *New York: Collier Books (pap.),* 1962
GOOD WIVES *New York: E. P. Dutton & Co.,* 1953
LITTLE MEN *Cleveland and New York: The World Publishing
    Company,* 1950
LITTLE MEN *New York: Collier Books (pap.),* 1962
JO'S BOYS *Cleveland and New York: The World Publishing
    Company,* 1957
JO'S BOYS *New York: Collier Books (pap.),* 1962

TEDDY ROBINSON'S NIGHT OUT

by *Margery Williams Bianco*
THE LITTLE WOODEN DOLL *New York: The Macmillan
    Company,* 1923

by *James Flora*
KANGAROO FOR CHRISTMAS *New York: Harcourt, Brace &
    World, Inc.,* 1966

by *Wanda Gág*
MILLIONS OF CATS *New York: Coward-McCann, Inc.,* 1938

by *Joan G. Robinson*
DEAR TEDDY ROBINSON *Baltimore: Penguin Books, Inc.,* 1966

by *Margery Williams*
THE VELVETEEN RABBIT *New York: Doubleday & Company,
    Inc.,* 1958

386

MISS LARK'S ANDREW

by P. L. Travers
MARY POPPINS 1934
MARY POPPINS COMES BACK 1935
MARY POPPINS FROM A TO Z 1962
MARY POPPINS IN THE PARK 1952
MARY POPPINS OPENS THE DOOR 1943 *all New York:*
  Harcourt, Brace & World, Inc.

The Door of the Train

A TRIP BY TRAIN

by Helen Clare
FIVE DOLLS IN A HOUSE *New Jersey: Prentice-Hall, Inc.,*
  1965
FIVE DOLLS IN THE SNOW *New Jersey: Prentice-Hall, Inc.,*
  1967
by Pauline Clarke
THE RETURN OF THE TWELVES *New York: Coward-McCann,*
  Inc., 1963

RIDING IN THE CARS

by Laura Ingalls Wilder
BY THE SHORES OF SILVER LAKE (rev. ed.)
FARMER BOY (rev. ed.)
LITTLE HOUSE IN THE BIG WOODS (rev. ed.)
LITTLE HOUSE ON THE PRAIRIE (rev. ed.)
LITTLE TOWN ON THE PRAIRIE (rev. ed.)
ON THE BANKS OF PLUM CREEK (rev. ed.)
THE LONG WINTER (rev. ed.)
THESE HAPPY GOLDEN YEARS (rev. ed.) *all New York:*
  Harper & Row, Publishers, 1953

The Kitchen Door

DICK AND THE BEANSTALK

by *Walter de la Mare*

ANIMAL STORIES *New York: Charles Scribner's Sons, 1940*
MAGIC JACKET *New York: Alfred A. Knopf, Inc., 1962*
PENNY A DAY *New York: Alfred A. Knopf, Inc., 1960*
TALES TOLD AGAIN *New York: Alfred A. Knopf, Inc., 1959*

BUNCHY AND THE PASTRY DOUGH

by *Miriam Clark Potter*

MRS. GOOSE AND HER FUNNY FRIENDS *Philadelphia: J. B. Lippincott Co., 1964*
THE MOUSE WHO LIKED TO READ IN BED *Philadelphia: J. B. Lippincott Co., 1958*

BETSY GOES TO SCHOOL

by *Dorothy Canfield*

UNDERSTOOD BETSY *New York: Holt, Rinehart & Winston, Inc., 1946*

THE SCARECROW OF SCATTERBROOK

by *Louisa May Alcott*

A ROUND DOZEN ed. by A. T. Eaton. *New York: The Viking Press, Inc., 1963*

GALLDORA AND THE LITTLE CAT

by Michael Bond

A BEAR CALLED PADDINGTON *Boston: Houghton Mifflin
    Company, 1960*
MORE ABOUT PADDINGTON *Boston: Houghton Mifflin
    Company, 1962*
PADDINGTON HELPS OUT *Boston: Houghton Mifflin Company,
    1961*
PADDINGTON MARCHES ON *Boston: Houghton Mifflin
    Company, 1965*

by Carl Sandburg

THE WEDDING PROCESSION OF THE RAG DOLL AND
THE BROOM HANDLE, from Rootabaga Stories. *New York:
    Harcourt, Brace & World, Inc., 1922*

THE WHEEL ON THE SCHOOL

by Meindert DeJong

FAR OUT THE LONG CANAL *1964*
SHADRACH *1953*
TOWER BY THE SEA *1950*
THE WHEEL ON THE SCHOOL *1954 all New York:
    Harper & Row, Publishers*

THE STORY OF THE ELEPHANT WHO PRETENDED
TO BE A MOSQUITO

by Rudyard Kipling

JUST SO STORIES *New York: Doubleday & Company, Inc., 1952*
JUST SO STORIES *New York: Avon Books (pap.), 1966*

by Philip M. Sherlock

ANANSI, THE SPIDER MAN *New York: Thomas Y. Crowell
    Company, 1954*

The Door of the School

THE CHINA SPANIEL

by Richard Hughes
THE SPIDER'S PALACE *New York: Random House, Inc., 1960*

COUNTING THE CLASS

by William Mayne
DAY WITHOUT WIND *New York: E. P. Dutton & Co., Inc.,*
  1964
WHISTLING RUFUS *New York: E. P. Dutton & Co., Inc., 1965*

GINGER ON THE FIRE ESCAPE

by Eleanor Estes
GINGER PYE 1951
PINKY PYE 1958
RUFUS M 1943
THE MIDDLE MOFFAT 1942
THE MOFFATS 1941 *all New York: Harcourt, Brace & World,*
  Inc.

The Bedroom Door

MY FIRST FROCK AND TROUSERS

by David Fletcher
CONFETTI FOR CORTORELLI *New York: Pantheon Books, Inc., 1957*
THE KING'S GOBLET *New York: Pantheon Books, Inc., 1962*

by Rumer Godden
CANDY FLOSS *1960*
HOME IS THE SAILOR *1964*
IMPUNITY JANE *1954*
THE DOLL'S HOUSE *1962*
THE FAIRY DOLL *1956*
THE STORY OF HOLLY AND IVY *1958 all New York: The Viking Press, Inc.*

by Richard Hengist Horne ("Mrs. Fairstar")
MEMOIRS OF A LONDON DOLL *New York: The Macmillan Company, 1923*

by Thelma Hsiung
THE ADVENTURES OF LITTLE BROTHER *New York: Abelard-Schuman, Ltd., 1964*

by Moyra McGavin
THE HOUSE IN THE ATTIC *New York: Coward-McCann, Inc. 1966*

THE LITTLE SWEEP

by Charles Kingsley
THE WATER BABIES *New York: E. P. Dutton & Co., 1957*
THE WATER BABIES ed. by Kathleen Lines. *New York: Franklin Watts, Inc., 1961*

391

The Gate of the Sports' Field

FOOTBALL BOOTS
MARMADUKE AT THE RACES
JENNINGS ARRIVES LATE

by *Alberta Armer*
SCREWBALL *Cleveland and New York: The World Publishing Company, 1963*

by *B. J. Chute*
SHIFT TO THE RIGHT *New York: The Macmillan Company (pap.), 1944*

by *Beman Lord*
BATS AND BALLS 1962
MYSTERY GUEST AT LEFT END 1964
PERFECT PITCH 1965
QUARTERBACK'S AIM 1960 *all New York: Henry Z. Walck, Inc.*

Miniature Doors

MARIA MAKES FRIENDS

by *Mary Norton*
THE BORROWERS 1953
THE BORROWERS AFIELD 1955
THE BORROWERS AFLOAT 1959
THE BORROWERS ALOFT 1961 *all New York: Harcourt, Brace & World, Inc.*

by *T. H. White*
MISTRESS MASHAM'S REPOSE *New York: G. P. Putnam's Sons (pap.) 1960*

CONVERSATION WITH A SALMON

by *Andre Norton*
STEEL MAGIC *Cleveland and New York: The World Publishing Company, 1965*

The Stable Door

BROWNIE'S RIDE

by Kathleen Green
PHILIP AND THE POOKA AND OTHER IRISH FAIRY
TALES *Philadelphia: J. B. Lippincott Co., 1966*

by Ruth Manning-Sanders
PETER AND THE PISKIES *New York: Roy Publishers, Inc.,
1958*

THE ROUNDUP

by Kate Seredy
THE CHESTRY OAK *New York: The Viking Press, Inc., 1948*
THE GOOD MASTER *New York: The Viking Press, Inc., 1935*

ROSINA COPPER

by Kitty Barne
ROSINA COPPER, MYSTERY MARE *New York: E. P. Dutton
& Co., Inc., 1956*

by Ursula Bruns
PONIES *New Jersey: D. Van Nostrand Co., Inc., 1960*

by Monica Edwards
MIDNIGHT HORSE *New York: Vanguard Press, Inc., 1950*

by Mary Elwyn Patchett
BRUMBY COME HOME *Indianapolis: The Bobbs-Merrill Co.,
Inc., 1962*
BRUMBY, THE WILD, WHITE STALLION *Indianapolis: The
Bobbs-Merrill Co., Inc., 1959*

Field Gates

SLIPPER-SLOPPER

by Alison Uttley

LITTLE RED FOX AND THE WICKED UNCLE *Indianapolis: The Bobbs-Merrill Co., Inc., 1963*

SNUG AND SERENA GO TO TOWN *Indianapolis: The Bobbs-Merrill Co., Inc., 1963*

TIM RABBIT'S DOZEN *New York: Transatlantic Arts, Inc.*

WASHERWOMAN'S CHILD *New York: Transatlantic Arts, Inc.*

THE FIRE ENGINE RUNS AWAY

by Leila Berg

FOLK TALES FOR READING AND TELLING *Cleveland and New York: The World Publishing Company, 1966*

LITTLE BOY PIE

by Eleanor Farjeon

JIM AT THE CORNER *New York: Henry Z. Walck, Inc., 1958*

MARTIN PIPPIN IN THE DAISY FIELD *Philadelphia: J. B. Lippincott Co., 1963*

THE LITTLE BOOKROOM *New York: Henry Z. Walck, Inc., 1956*

MARY PLANTS THE HOSE-IN-HOSE

by Juliana Ewing

LOB LIE-BY-THE-FIRE AND THE STORY OF A SHORT LIFE *New York: E. P. Dutton & Co., Inc., 1964*

THE BROWNIES AND OTHER STORIES *New York: E. P. Dutton & Co., Inc., 1954*

394

INDEX

to authors, *artists* and ORIGINAL BOOKS

Adamson, George, 25, 33, 38, 73, 195, 200–201
ADVENTURES OF A BROWNIE, THE, 325
ADVENTURES OF GALLDORA, 215
ADVENTURES OF NO ORDINARY RABBIT, THE, 353
Alcott, Louisa May, 115
ALICE-ALL-BY-HERSELF, 67
Ardizzone, Edward, 87, 369
Aveline, Claude, 223

Barne, Kitty, 337
Bawden, Edward, 78
Berg, Bjorn, 108, 110
Berg, Leila, 355
Bianco, Margery Williams, 91
BIRD THAT FLEW INTO THE SEA AND OTHER STORIES, 226

Biro, 357, 358, 361, 364
BOBBY BREWSTER'S SHADOW, 273
Brisley, Joyce Lankester, 179
Brisley, Joyce Lankester, 183, 184
Brooker, Christopher, 234
Browne, Frances, 23
Buchanan, Lilian, 268, 270, 272
Buckels, Alec, 349, 352
Buckeridge, Anthony, 281
BUNCHY, 185
BY THE SHORES OF SILVER LAKE, 166

Canfield, Dorothy, 187
Čapek, Josef, 45
Čapek, Josef, 46, 48, 49, 51
Carter, Bruce, 55
Chapman, Elizabeth, 275
Clare, Helen, 149
Coatsworth, Elizabeth, 61
Cockett, Mary, 99

Copley, Heather, 191
Craik, Dinah, 311

DeJong, Meindert, 217
de la Mare, Walter, 169
Dinsdale, Mary, 287
DOCTOR BOOMER, 308

Estes, Eleanor, 237
Ewing, Juliana, 373

FAIRIES AND
ENCHANTERS, 75
Farjeon, Eleanor, 367
FIRE ENGINE BY
MISTAKE, 365
FISHING PARTY, THE,
235
FIVE DOLLS IN THE
SNOW, 157

Gill, Margery, 243
GINGER PYE, 245
GOLDEN HEN, THE, 21
GOOD MASTER, THE, 335
GRANNY'S WONDERFUL
CHAIR, 43
Gri, 19

HARUM-SCARUM, 52
Hofbauer, Imré, 332–333,
343

Horne, Richard Hengist, 249
Hourihane, Ursula, 85
Hughes, Richard, 229

Ionicus, 63, 65

Jacques, Robin, 117, 123, 298,
307, 377
JENNINGS GOES TO
SCHOOL, 290
JIM AT THE CORNER,
371
John, Diana, 207, 214
Jones, Harold, 261

Keeping, Charles, 170, 174
Kingsley, Charles, 257

Lang, Andrew, 77
Ledésert, Margaret, 226
Leslie, Cecil, 155
LITTLE OLD MRS.
PEPPERPOT, 112

MARMADUKE AT THE
RACES, 279
Marshall, Leslie, 253
MARY POPPINS, 146
MARY'S MEADOW, 381
Mayne, William, 233

Index

MEMOIRS OF A
 LONDON DOLL, 255
Miller, Margaret J., 301
MISTRESS MASHAM'S
 REPOSE, 299
"Mrs. Fairstar," 249

OUT WITH FELICITY
 AND JONATHAN, 105

Paterson, H., 314, 322
Paull, Grace, 95
PENNY A DAY, 177
Prøysen, Alf, 107

Robinson, Joan G., 127
Robinson, Joan G., 128, 131,
 133, 134
Robinson, Richard G., 103
ROSINA COPPER,
 MYSTERY MARE, 344
Ross, Diana, 13

Sedgwick, Modwena, 205
Sendak, Maurice, 221
Seredy, Kate, 327
Seward, Prudence, 56, 58
Shepard, Mary, 143
SPIDER'S PALACE,
 THE, 231

STREET OF LITTLE
 SHOPS, A, 97
SUGAR AND SPICE, 89

TALES OF TROY AND
 GREECE, 82
TEDDY ROBINSON, 135
Todd, Barbara Euphan, 193
Todd, H. E., 267
Travers, P. L., 137
TRICYCLE TIM, 59

UNDER THE LILACS,
 125
UNDERSTOOD BETSY,
 190
Uttley, Alison, 347

WATER BABIES, THE,
 264
WHEEL ON THE
 SCHOOL, THE, 221
White, T. H., 293
Wilder, Laura Ingalls, 159
Williams, Ferelith Eccles,
 278, 279
Williams, Garth, 162
Williams-Ellis, Amabel, 69
WORZEL GUMMIDGE,
 202